CW00669454

THE BLACK MASS OF
BROTHER SPRINGER

Also by Charles Willeford

Proletarian Laughter (poetry)
High Priest of California
Pick-Up
Wild Wives
Lust is a Woman
The Woman Chaser
Deliver Me From Dallas
Understudy For Love
No Experience Necessary
Cockfighter
The Machine in Ward Eleven (coll.)
Poontang and Other Poems (poetry)
The Burnt Orange Heresy
The Difference
A Guide For the Undehemmorrhoided (autobiography)
Off the Wall
Miami Blues
New Hope for the Dead
Something About a Soldier (autobiography)
Sideswipe
New Forms of Ugly (non-fiction)
Kiss Your Ass Goodbye
The Way We Die Now
Everybody's Metamorphosis (coll.)
I Was Looking for a Street (autobiography)
Cockfighter Journal (non-fiction)
The Shark-Infested Custard
Writing and Other Blood Sports (essays)
The Second Half of the Double Feature (coll.)

THE BLACK MASS OF
BROTHER SPRINGER
CHARLES WILLEFORD

INTRODUCTION BY JAMES SALLIS

a WitSend book

wit's end
publishing
New Albany, Indiana

{December 2003}

Copyright © 1958 by Universal Publishing and Distributing Corp.
Copyright renewed 1986 by Charles Willeford. This edition
copyright © 2003 by Betsy Willeford
Introduction copyright © 2003 James Sallis

All rights reserved. No part of this publication may be reproduced or transmitted in any form or by any means, electronic or mechanical, including photocopy, recording, or any information storage and retrieval system now known or invented, without permission in writing from the publisher, except by a reviewer who wishes to quote brief passages in connection with a review written for inclusion in a magazine, newspaper, broadcast, etc.

Set in Sabon

Published by Wit's End Publishing (www.sendwit.com)
book designed by oiva design group (www.oivas.com)

ISBN: 1-930997-35-3

All WitSend titles are edited by Juha Lindroos and Kathleen Martin.

Contents

INTRODUCTION BY JAMES SALLIS   7

THE BLACK MASS OF BROTHER SPRINGER   13

THE ORDAINMENT OF BROTHER SPRINGER   181

THE WORLD AS WILLEFORD AND IDEA

BY JAMES SALLIS

GREAT WRITING, MY old friend Gene Wolfe says, lies not in doing something better than someone else, but in doing something that no one else can do at all.

Nailed in place for some weeks now while recovering from surgery, I've had the rare blessing of unbridled reading and, with this introduction promised, spent those weeks reading and rereading, with nary an excuse in sight, the works of Charles Willeford, who seems to me the very exemplar of what Gene meant.

No one writes like Willeford. In much the same way as Jim Thompson and David Goodis, he was able to take advantage of a window of opportunity that existed in the Fifties and hitch a ride on the mile-long train of original paperback novels. Turning in product that seemed to conform, these writers in fact produced books largely sui generis, books deeply stained with the personalities of their authors, like the indelible grime beneath a mechanic's fingernails. "I had a hunch that madness was the predominant theme and normal condition for Americans in the second half of the century," Willeford once said, a madness that spilled into every word he wrote, from the sinister car salesman of *High Priest of California* to *Miami Blues'* Freddy Frenger and *Sideswipe's* Troy Louden. The normal condition. Reading Willeford's work in bulk, as I have done these past weeks, can be like attending a family reunion of Lou Fords, walking into a roomful of Ripleys.

It's with Chester Himes, I think, that Willeford best compares; they seem at times two sides of a single coin. Both were literary writers whose tales of obsessed individuals fascinate as much as they repulse. Both, willfully, wrote from society's narrowest outside edge, each phrase and scene saturated with a sense of the absurd, of suffering, of the many ways in which society twists its people into monsters and the many ways in which they visit violence back upon that society. In Himes and Willeford, savagery and comedy are forever bedmates. They do not subvert the genre so much as they defy it: Don't hold back, baby, show me what you can do, show me what you have.

As I wrote in my book *Difficult Lives*, I believe that popular fiction at its best offers a unique portrait of its time. It sends tendrils down to the very baserock of what we are as a nation and who we are as individuals, shines a light into corners where crouch our deepest fears, unvoiced assumptions, basest aspirations. *The Invasion of the Body Snatchers* tells us far more about cold-war paranoia and the American dream as lived in the Fifties than any shelf full of sociology texts.

The Black Mass of Brother Springer appeared in 1958, Willeford's fourth published novel. *High Priest of California*, 1953, had seen print as half of a Royal Giant, bound with Talbot Mundy's adventure novel *Full Moon*. Willeford wrote it while stationed at Hamilton Air Force Base; weekends, he'd drive down to San Francisco, check into the Powell Hotel, and spend both days writing. Its tale of used car salesman Russell Haxby introduced the kind of amoral protagonist that was to become a Willeford trademark. In 1955 Beacon Books, like Royal a wing of Universal Publishing and Distributing, brought out *Pick-Up*, with its tale of a failed painter and the woman who, walking into the diner where he works as short-order cook, changes his life. A year later Beacon issued Willeford's third novel, *Wild Wives*, double-bound with a reprint of *High Priest*.

When *Black Mass* came out, Willeford was thirty-nine years old, two years retired after twenty years' service in the Army and Air Force. If *Cockfighter*, as many believe, is Willeford's purest existentialist novel, one to be taken at the level of Horace McCoy's *They Shoot Horses Don't They* and Albert Camus' *L'Etranger*—and this is arguably the case—then *Black Mass* is a close second, its double: another *monstre délicat*, its *semblable*, its *frère*. For the existentialist, consciousness, the very core of our being, is an emptiness waiting to be filled by arbitrary choices. We must practice faith in the absence of belief. We become ourselves through our actions.

The Black Mass of Brother Springer was Willeford's original title, one which Universal, more comfortable with titles on the order of *Hitch-Hike Hussy*, quickly rejected. The publisher also rejected Willeford's tongue-in-cheek suggestion for an alternative title, *Nigger Lover*, bringing the book out as *Honey Gal*. An entry in the author's diary for September 1957 states that Bob Abramson of Universal Publishing bought the novel for $250 on acceptance and $250 on publication, "a hell of a low price for six weeks of hard work."

Briefly, the novel tells the story of a stalled writer who, desperately trolling for a story, meets a retired Army sergeant who has taken over the Church of God's Flock in a kind of preemptive strike and now is about to jump ship. First, though, he ordains Sam Springer and sends him off to Jax to serve as pastor of an all-black church. There, Brother Springer becomes entangled in the civil rights movement, including a proposed boycott of city services.

> On my part, I had no personal motives, nothing to gain one way or another. I didn't believe in what I was doing, and I didn't disbelieve in it either. I was indifferent. But the plan was interesting, almost exciting, and I wanted to see how it would work out.

The novel is replete with typically marvelous bits of description ("The outside of the chicken was a beautiful color—the shade of a two-day bruise on the tender side of a woman's thigh") and typically Willefordian slyness (during Brother Springer's initial sermon, on Kafka, he muses: "And I was trying to make them think! How unfair of me, how unlike a minister of the gospel!").

Beware enterprises that require new clothes, Emerson warned. Willeford is seldom funnier than when writing about clothes (Hoke Moseley's yellow jumpsuits come to mind), and each of Springer's transmogrifications is heralded by new clothing. When, after selling his novel, he goes to his workplace to resign, he dresses in

> a pair of leather sandals, a pair of red linen slacks, a pale yellow sport shirt imprinted with tiny red rickshaws, and a white linen jacket. I placed dark sunglasses over my nose, and a straw hat with a solid yellow band upon my head. These clothes had been purchased several weeks before and had been put aside for the occasion.

On the bus to Jax, now become Brother Sam Deuteronomy Springer, he muses on the puissance of his ill-fitting dark twill suit.

> As the Abbot had implied, clerical garb made the minister; I had not been given any other instructions to go with the uniform. The mere donning of my black suit changed me, not only in the eyes of the world, but in my own eyes.

And near book's end, following his apostasy:

> We looked through racks until I found a suit that I wanted. The material was thin, a mixture of dacron, nylon and polished Egyptian cotton. The color was a glistening tint of powder blue, matching my eyes exactly. The jacket, without shoulder padding, hugged my round shoulders perfectly. . .
> In less than an hour I was a new man, if clothes do make the man. To go with my blue suit I had purchased a Hathaway button-down shirt with tiny blue-and-red checks. A knitted maroon tie looked well with the shirt, and to match the tie I had chosen a pair of all-wool maroon socks. Broad-winged cordovan shoes and a chestnut Tyrolean hat with a gay yellow feather in the band completed my outfit.

As Marshall Jon Fisher pointed out in a piece for the Atlantic a few years back, Sam Springer is "a characteristically Willefordian amalgam of selfish mercenary and well-meaning drifter," careening through life with little thought for the future, borne from one moment's need, one moment's chance opportunity, to the next. He became a writer as capriciously as he becomes a reverend, he leaves his wife with hardly a moment's regret or serious consideration, he sheds the old skin and slithers away.

In some regards, of course, America is a land with no past or future, only an eternal present, and Willeford's work is filled with characters looking to start over, as though continual reinvention were the very juice and squeezed pulp of the American experience: Hoke Moseley in his return to Singer Island, Troy Louden with his one big score before retiring to Haiti, Frank Mansfield whose life will end (and begin again?) once he wins Cockfighter of the Year.

It's a wonderful, defining moment when late in the novel ex-sergeant Abbot Dover returns to tell Brother Springer that he made a mistake in ordaining him, to admit that he's read Springer's novel, and to thank Springer for making it possible for him to find love. Of the boycott he asks:

"But do you care? Does it make any difference to you, Springer, one way or the other?"

"No. Not really." I didn't lie to Dover. His flat blue eyes with their frank and piercing stare demanded the truth and nothing else.

"I found that out when I read your novel. A clever little book. Why not? You're a well-read man, and the characters said brittle and clever things, the surface brilliance of a thousand books you've read, and not an original idea of your own on a single page. Cute situations, complications in the right places, and the inevitable straight romantic plot with the obvious ending. You don't know a damned thing about people, and even less about yourself."

That the novel bears indelibly the mark of its creator, all of that creator's bright and dark, was something Willeford believed deeply; it is also something that, reading him, we come to believe. If popular fiction is the secret and true history of its time, so can the novel at its best become the inmost record of self. In an essay from 1953, published thirty-five years later in Mystery Scene and reprinted in *Writing & Other Blood Sports* (Dennis McMillan Publications), Charles Willeford addresses the creative process:

The novel is a case history of the writer. It is the story of his life written as well as he can write it. It never ends; it goes on day after day, year after year. He is his own hero, his own heroine, his villain, his minor characters —the thoughts of each of these are his own thoughts twisting and churning and wrenched alive and crawling from his conscious and unconscious mind. He writes because he must, because to fail as a writer means to fail as a man. . .

When I first began to write it was an act of desperation. It was a blind search, and at first every trail I followed led to the inside of a deep cave. I was searching with my conscious mind instead of my heart. . .

I lost all hope; I reached the point where I no longer cared what people thought about my writing. And that is when I began to write. . .

I scrapped all of my early efforts and started over again. I put my feelings, my heart, my life, my innermost thoughts on paper.

That, my friends, whether that art comes wrapped in lurid, waxy covers or swaddled in the imprimatur of prestigious publishers, is high art.

Following the Civil War, pawn shops were filled with brass instruments left over from military bands. Dirt cheap, they were taken up by black musicians, many of them ex-slaves, who on these instruments searched for and created a new music, a specifically American music, jazz. So too with writers such as Chester Himes, Jim Thompson and Charles Willeford. They took up a form poorly suited perhaps to the measure of their vision and by sheer force of personality, by will and brute creativity, bent the form to their end, bringing into the world a music never heard before, a new and enduring art.

SOFTLY—I DIDN'T want to waken Merita—I eased the window up as high as it would go and inhaled the aroma of ammonia, stale food, discarded socks and some air that wafted lazily up the air shaft. Less than three feet away I could see into another hotel room, almost the same as mine, and observe the heavy breathing of an old geezer sleeping like the only man left in the world without a conscience.

Far below, three or four stories at least, a harsh feminine voice berated someone very cleverly indeed, without pause.

"How," I wondered, "did I, the Right Reverend Deuteronomy Springer, wind up in a place like the Anderson Hotel on the edge of Harlem in New York City?"

To think was difficult. I was very tired, and there was a feeling of unreality, almost impossible to pinpoint, that made me feel like an observer watching someone else do very foolish things, amusing things, that were somehow unimportant to the real me. But the real me was beginning to merge with this strange energetic creature who was also me. I ran my fingers through my thick black hair— long hair, and I had always favored the crew cut—and I liked the heavy feel of the long straight hair. It helped my impersonation.

"Dear God," I prayed, sticking my head out the window and peering up at the small square of blue sky at the top of the air shaft, "deliver this poor lost sinner from temptation and show him the Glory Road, for Yours is the power and the glory, forever. Amen!"

This short prayer revived me somewhat. I grinned wryly, and pulled in my head. I now prayed naturally, systematically, automatically, painlessly, somewhat like the bond-a-month savings plan where you work, or the bond-a-month savings plan where you bank. I picked up the bottle of gin on the dresser and took a snort. The bottle was less than half full and I lowered it a full inch before I took it away from my lips. My stomach was flushed with sudden warmth, and I was now fully awake. I caught a glimpse of myself in the mottled full-length mirror on the bathroom door, and smiled grimly at my reflection.

Some minister of the gospel! Standing in the center of a sleazy hotel room, naked except for a pair of dirty boxer-type shorts, with long, pale skinny legs, long hairy arms, and hunched shoulders, I resembled a bank clerk rather than a minister. Except for my eyes; they were too large for my thin face and contained inner lights glowing like hot, blue flames. "Lit and nourished by gin at $4.15 per fifth," I thought ruefully. I turned away from the mirror and counted my money again in the canvas money belt. Counting money belonging to yourself, and not to a bank or a firm or someone else, gives a man uncommon pleasure, I had discovered. I riffled through the bills quickly. I had counted the money so many times, and it was all there, $4,053. A lot of money. . .

Merita turned over in bed and I turned to see if she was awake. She wasn't; she slept peacefully, beautifully, like a contented cat. She was the wonderful color of real coffee, not instant coffee, but expensive, exotic coffee, diluted with pure, thick, yellow cream. The fairest of them all. And she was this beautiful color all over. Quite unlike the expensive women at Miami Beach who sought the same golden brown for their bodies but were cheated by vacant strips of dead white across breasts and hips. Convention, convention. I shook my head. It was all so very sad. These women on the beach were paying, perhaps, as much as thirty-seven dollars a day, and were only rewarded with a semi-tan. It didn't seem fair. Merita now; she didn't have to expose her wonderful body to the sun to maintain her golden color.

Merita lay on her right side, her legs like opened scissors. Her legs were long and shapely, and the straight toes were close together, the nails painted blood-red, matching her fingernails. I marveled at the extreme height of her hip, and the sharp downward slope to the narrow waist. Her hips were wide and deep, without fat, and her waist was almost narrow enough for me to span with my hands. But she was filled out marvelously above her narrow waist, above her flat, tender belly. A perfect thirty-eight, and most of the thirty-eight was in the long evenly matched breasts, not in a thick, meat-padded back. Merita's back arched, and when she stood erect, she carried herself like a queen.

A golden queen from some forgotten race in time—a high priestess of love. Where in the world had those desk clerks found the presumption to turn us away? The Anderson was the third hotel we had tried before getting a room the afternoon before. Prejudice is more subtle in New York, but unmistakable. No Room at the Inn. But perhaps the hotel clerks were suspicious of my cloth? Perhaps it was strange to these clerks that a man wearing black and a white, backward collar should be registering at all with a beautiful dark-skinned girl at his elbow, and using the name of Mr.. William Johnson. Of course. I laughed softly. That was it! They were merely playing it safe, afraid for their jobs, and prejudice or the knowledge that Merita was a Negro did not enter into the situation at all. Even the clerk at the Anderson had smiled—and what had he called me? "Padre!" Again I laughed softly. He had mistaken me for a Catholic priest on an illicit holiday instead of a minister of the Church of God's Flock. How stupid of me! I had been so anxious to get Merita into bed I hadn't used my head. I should have discarded the clerical garb and purchased a plain suit of some kind.

I was not Mr. William Johnson anyway, was I? No, I was the Right Reverend Deuteronomy Springer of the Church of God's Flock, Jax, Florida. However, that wasn't true either. I was actually Sam Springer, Novelist, from Miami, Florida, playing at being the Right Reverend Deuteronomy Springer. . .

But was I really playing? I did not know. Somewhere along the way, my personality had been transferred to the role of minister, and the novelist had disappeared. Yet had I not now regained my identity because of the lovely girl in the bed, and the things we had done together during the night? These had not been the things, maybe, a real minister would sanction. Still, they had not been the actions of a novelist, either . . . Not this novelist, at least, who had been a quiet, faithful husband, somewhat dull, and a man who had never failed to mow the lawn every other Saturday morning.

It was all very confusing, but there was the money . . . and the time for decision was now, and it had to be the *right* decision.

Again I reached for the gin bottle, but I stayed my hand. No more. Not now. A prayer, perhaps? I sank to my knees. The nubby, well-worn nap of the carpet hurt my bare knees, and I quickly got to my feet. The hell with prayers! Who did I think I was kidding?

Shaking my head to dislodge the cobwebs of confusion, I returned to the open window and stared morosely into the deep well of the air shaft.

MONEY IS THE root of all goodness. To talk disparagingly about money is the privilege of those who have money. There are also those people who state matter-of-factly that "money isn't everything." This statement is also true, but only so long as one has money.

If I was overly preoccupied with thoughts about money that morning, I had plenty of reasons, too many of them. I did not have any money. I knew it, and the Thrifty Way Finance Company of Miami knew it, or suspected it, but my wife did not know it and she did not suspect it. Oh, I had a few dollars. Eighty-seven dollars and forty-two cents to be exact. That wasn't very much money. I'll explain:

I was living in a year-old project house in an area of Greater Miami known as Ocean Pine Terraces. My house was four miles away from the ocean; there were no pines in the area because they had been bulldozed away to make room for the new homes, and there were no terraces. The section of Southern Florida known as Ocean Pine Terraces was as flat as Florida can be for as far as the eye could see.

My monthly payment of $78.60 on my house was five days overdue.

My car payment on my three-year-old Pontiac was one month overdue. A small payment, only $42.50 per month, to be sure, but there were seven more such payments to go before the Pontiac, purchased second-hand anyway, would be mine.

The furniture in my two-bedroom-Florida-room project house was not lavish or expensive; it had been chosen with care, and had only amounted to $2,800 in all, including the large metal desk that I considered mandatory for my work, and the portable television set.

On my furniture, however, I still owed $2,030, in monthly payments of $105.50. Two months had elapsed since I had made a payment on this "set of sticks." The Thrifty Way Finance

Company Manager had loaned me $150 two weeks before, and "set of sticks" had been his term for my furniture, not mine. (An interesting point of law: Who owned the furniture? The furniture company, the finance company, or me?)

I owed the milkman $5.40 for the current month, the grocer for groceries delivered during the month, the telephone bill, the television repair bill for a new booster for the picture tube, and several other sundry bills, including an unfulfilled pledge at the Unitarian Fellowship Society.

As an ex-accountant, the figures interested me, but I did not really worry about the bills; I worried about the cash and/or credit to keep going, to continue my way of life. It was a wonderful way to live.

I was a writer, a novelist to be exact. There may be some who will say that the publication of one novel does not make a man a novelist. I disagree. The publication of my novel, *No Bed Too High*, had provided me with an escape from a fate worse than death, and that fate was a dead-end position as an accountant with the Tanfair Milk Company, Columbus, Ohio.

No matter how old you are, you still need milk! That was Tanfair's slogan. As the company accountant, I had made out the check for $25 to the milkman in the southwest area of the city who had submitted the winning slogan in the company-wide contest.

Ten years hunched over a desk clutching a No. 2 pencil in my fingers, adding and subtracting, multiplying and dividing, and writing reports had driven me to the brink of madness. I so detested my job I was willing to do anything to escape from it. The idea for the novel had flashed into my mind during a coffee break, and for eight months I had worked over my novel at night, sitting at the kitchen table in our small apartment. Adding and subtracting words, multiplying and dividing situations and characters, I had completed a handwritten novel containing approximately 70,000 words. After I had the manuscript typed, I mailed it to a publisher in New York. It was returned. I mailed the ms. to another publisher, and two weeks later I received an advance royalty payment and a contract from the Zenith Press. But I didn't quit my job immediately. I waited. Fearfully.

Six months passed before my book appeared in print, and I received the six free copies promised in the contract. The novel was printed on fairly good paper and was bound in a material closely resembling cloth. And the book was dressed up in a gaily colored dust jacket. Artists today have forgotten how to draw pictures of things, but the large splotch of red on a solid yellow background, and the meaningless spidery lines dripping away from the red splotch gave the jacket a modern look. The title and my name were both correctly spelled, and altogether it was an impressive little book. Set in 10 pt. type the book was easy to read, and it read ten times better than it had in typescript. I read it through in one sitting and was amazed at how interesting it had become in print.

I was a novelist.

The contract and the check for $250 had not really convinced me, but the physical handling of the bound volume sold me at last.

The next morning following the arrival of my six books, I donned a pair of leather sandals, a pair of red linen slacks, a pale yellow sport shirt imprinted with tiny red rickshaws, and a white linen jacket. I placed dark sunglasses over my nose and a straw hat with a solid yellow band upon my head. These clothes had been purchased several weeks before and had been put aside for the occasion.

"You look beautiful!" my wife told me admiringly, and I agreed with her.

I dawdled over my breakfast, discussing future plans with my wife, and presented myself at the office exactly one hour late for work. I did not go to my desk, however, because I had cleaned it out the evening before. I went instead to Mr. Louis Carlisle's antechambers (the manager of Tanfair Milk Company) and asked his secretary, Mrs. Burns, for an appointment.

"My, don't we look gay this morning!" she exclaimed.

"In Columbus, yes," I said, "but in Florida, this attire is quite the thing. Now if you will inform Mr. Carlisle that I am waiting. . ."

Mrs. Burns disappeared into the inner office of the manager, and within two minutes she reappeared, smiling, and held the door open for me. "Mr. Carlisle will see you now, Mr. Springer."

"Thank you, Mrs. Burns."

Although Mrs. Burns had evidently briefed the manager on my attire, Mr. Carlisle couldn't hide the surprise in his eyes, nor the anger in his voice.

"What in the hell is that get-up supposed to mean?" he asked rudely.

"I am leaving for Florida today, Mr. Carlisle," I stated calmly, "and I came to say goodbye and submit my resignation."

"Your resignation is not accepted!" he snapped. "The semi-annual audit is due; the quarterly reports and the end of the month billings must be finished by tomorrow morning, and you can get back to your desk right now!"

For ten years I had lived in fear of Mr. Carlisle, but I didn't hate him. It was his position I feared. Like all salaried Americans, I had the deeply instilled fear of being fired and the very real knowledge that I could be fired at any moment. This fear is not ever-present, but it lurks in the subconscious, leaping out when a mistake of some kind is made in your work, or when you realize how long you have been working at the same place without any advancement. The longer a man works for one firm, and the older he gets, the greater the fear. But as I looked down at Mr. Carlisle, taking in his bald head, his mottled red face and his clipped white mustache, I marveled that I had ever had any fear of this little man and his little position. The publication of my novel had made me superior to him, to the company and to any and all types of employment. I was now a man of letters, a free agent, a man who could live by his pen and by his brain!

"My new book is out," I said quietly, ignoring Carlisle's mad outburst, "and I have brought you an autographed copy." I placed the novel in the manager's in-basket. "The novel retails for $2.75, but the autograph increases the value by approximately one dollar, and since it is a first edition, you would be wise to hang onto it for a few years if you wish to sell it at an even greater profit."

"You wrote this book?" Mr. Carlisle asked, suspiciously, picking up the novel and peering at the title.

"Yes."

"*No Bed Too High*. Hmm. Is it a sex novel?"

"You will find out when you read it." I reached out my hand. "And now, goodbye, Mr. Carlisle. I'm off for Florida."

Without thinking Mr. Carlisle shook my hand for a second and then withdrew his limp paw quickly and glared at me.

"You mean you're quitting? Just like that?"

"Yes." I looked at my fingernails. "Unless you want to match the salary Hollywood has offered me for doing the scenario . . . fifteen hundred a week."

This was a bald lie, of course, but Mr. Carlisle didn't know the difference, and at that very early stage of being a novelist I thought this offer very likely myself.

"All right!" Mr. Carlisle set his lips in a tight line. "Go ahead and quit! Give up a good job without notice. Leave me in a hole. But you'll get no severance pay without giving two weeks notice!"

I smiled, turned casually and sauntered out of the office. At $25 a year, my severance pay would have been $260, more than the advance on my novel, but it was worth that amount and more to leave the building without a backward glance. I did not say goodbye to any of my associates nor to any of the employees at the company. There would have been many false congratulations, but every one of the remarks would have been tinged with envy and bitterness. I knew this, and my abrupt leave-taking gave my departure an air of mystery I rather enjoyed.

I withdrew my savings, a small nest egg of $2400, telephoned the Beacon Storage Company to pack our belongings, and Virginia and I left for Miami on the midnight coach flight after a tearful farewell scene with my mother-in-law.

SITTING IN MY study in my project house in Ocean Pine Terraces, I had relived this scene many times in my memory, and it never failed to put me into a good mood.

I looked out the window and observed my wife hanging up wet sheets on the line in the backyard. A new washing machine, a new refrigerator, and a new electric stove had been included in the new house and had only added a few dollars a month to the house payments. My wife found great pleasure in these appliances after the inconvenience of the small apartment in Columbus. But except for the appliances and the television set, the woman had few pleasures in life. She hated Florida, although she never said so, and her memories were concentrated on Columbus, Ohio. After a year in Florida, her conversation was almost entirely about her former friends and bygone days in Columbus. Lately, she even talked about the good times she had had at John Adams Junior High School.

At first she had been elated by the published novel and then excited by the magic of Florida. She had written too many glowing letters about our house in Ocean Pine Terraces, the fabulous beach, the night clubs we had gone to upon our arrival, the wonderful climate and so on and, as a consequence, she no longer had any friends in Columbus. Except for her mother, no one answered her letters anymore, and she had not made any new friends in Miami. I was unconcerned about my wife's happiness.

This way of life suited me fine. I slept well, I ate well, and each morning after a hearty breakfast I retired to my study, sharpened a dozen pencils and sat at my desk all day. Although I had never managed to think of a new idea for a novel, I had written several stories and an extremely brilliant essay on D. H. Lawrence's novel, *The Plumed Serpent*. The fact that the essay and none of the stories had been purchased by any of the magazines I had sent them to did not bother me in the least. I was a writer, and I expected a few setbacks. And besides, the short stuff was merely fill-in work until I could get embarked upon another novel.

After the $250 advance from the Zenith Press, I had received no more royalties. The book had not sold very well in hard covers. But six months after moving to Florida, the Zenith Press had sold the reprint rights to a paperback house, and I had received a check for $1100 as my share. I considered this a handsome share, and I had sorely needed the money when I received it. The $1100 was now gone, however, and to continue my way of life I needed money. Something would turn up. . .

"Hey!" I shouted through the open window, "how about putting on some coffee?"

"As a matter of fact," my wife shouted in reply, "I intend to in a minute, as soon as I have finished hanging up the laundry."

Virginia had this habit of adding "as a matter of fact" before, or in the center, or at the end of each sentence. For a while I had been rather irked by it, but I had become accustomed to the little trick and was no longer bothered by the term. She had picked up this phrase from watching television interview programs, I supposed, and at least it padded her small talk.

Deep down in my heart I knew that there was a very simple solution to my money difficulties. I was an excellent accountant; Miami had a need for accountants as well as Columbus, and all I had to do was take a job and get out of debt, slowly but surely.

Now that I was down to $87.42 I turned the pages of the *Miami Herald* to the want ads for the first time since moving to Florida. I did this reluctantly, but I also made up my mind to work only as long as it was necessary to get out of debt. While I waited for the coffee, and as I idly flipped the pages, a short news item at the bottom of page twelve caught my eye and saved me from another fate worse than death.

CGF MONASTERY ON THE BLOCK

Orangeville, Fla.—The Church of God's Flock Monastery, established in 1936, is being sold, according to the Rt. Rev. Jack Dover, Abbot of the Protestant order since 1954.

All monks have been reassigned, and only Abbot Dover has remained at the monastery to oversee the sale of the property. No reason was given for the closing of the monastery.

Long a part of the Orangeville scene, monks of The Church of God's Flock order were self-supporting, raising goats, Key limes and oranges, and selling CGF Orange Wine on the premises.

It took a writer to see the possibilities in that news item! I carefully tore the piece from the paper and went into the kitchen where Virginia was pouring hot water into two cups for instant coffee.

"Read this," I told my wife, handing her the news item.

"Is it a sale?" she asked.

"In a way. Read it."

While Virginia squinted at the newsprint, I spooned the coffee dust into our cups and stirred. She sat down at the table and returned the clipping. "Do you want to buy the monastery, dear?"

"No, Virginia. I plan to do an article on the monastery. Today, people all over the United States are vitally interested in things religious; self-help, homilies that will help them get through their days. How to live a day at a time, how to keep warm, a prayer a day keeps boogers away. You see this stuff all of the time in the papers, in books, in magazines. Are you following me?"

"Oh, yes."

"Well, I'm going up there to Orangeville and see this Abbot Dover and find out what's going on. I've been reading Thomas Merton paperbacks ever since they started coming out, and according to him there's a big boom in this monk business. Of course, he's a Trappist and a Roman Catholic instead of a Protestant monk, but I can't understand why any monastery would close. It's too good a set-up. No financial worries, no responsibilities, no children, no friends; just wholesome work, a few prayers and a little meditation."

"That sounds like the way we live," my wife said, with a touch of melancholy in her voice. "Back in Columbus, as a matter of fact—"

"Now listen," I cut her off. "We are getting a bit low on funds, and if I can get an inspirational article out of this trip we will be back in the money. *This Week* magazine pays fifteen hundred dollars for a good lead article. If *This Week* turns the article down, I can sell it to the *Miami Herald* for fifty dollars. If the *Miami Herald* turns it down, I'll expand the article into another inspirational book, condense it, and sell it to the *Reader's Digest*. Can you see the possibilities?"

"What are you going to write about, Sam?"

"I'm going to write the truth. That's all. Evidently, the monastic way of life is crumbling, and there has to be a reason. I don't know what that reason is, of course, but what if there is a secret moral discouragement throughout the country that we don't suspect? It says in the news item that the monks have all been reassigned. Where have they been sent? Why were they reassigned? This is news, my dear, and people today want to find out everything pertaining to religion—and especially about monks. In a valueless society, half-Republican and half-Socialist, monks and hermits are the only people left with any individuality. If they go, where does that leave the rest of us? Don't you see?"

"As a matter of fact, I don't. Your coffee is getting cold."

"You're right. The coffee is getting cold. And I really don't know what I'll find up there. It may be a dead trail, but on the other hand, I may run into a swarm of *Life* reporters and photographers beating me to the story. But I have to see for myself. I haven't been able to think of anything to write about for a long time, and this story has potential. When you finish your coffee, pack a bag for me."

"How long will you be gone?"

"A couple of days, maybe three. No more."

That evening Virginia drove me to the Greyhound Bus station and I purchased my ticket for Orangeville. I decided that the trip would be cheaper by bus than it would be with the car, and besides she needed the car to get to the supermarket. While we waited for the bus to leave, I reassured Virginia that I would only be gone for three days at the most.

"Have you got any money?" I asked.

"As a matter of fact," she replied, "I only have about three dollars."

"Here." I gave her a five dollar bill. "This should be enough until I get back."

I boarded the bus, took a seat by the window, and waved good-bye through the blue-tinted window to Virginia as the bus pulled away from the station.

It was not until the Greyhound stopped at Melbourne, Florida, about a hundred miles up the coast, that I realized I had only purchased a one-way ticket to Orangeville. Why did I do that, I wondered, when a roundtrip ticket would have been substantially cheaper?

I knew all right. My conscious mind knew, and my subconscious mind also knew. . .

Every year in these United States, thirty per cent of the husbands leave their wives and go elsewhere. A large percentage of these deserting husbands return, mostly those with children; they miss the children. Others are brought back reluctantly by court order when they are caught. Many return because they miss their wives, and when they realize that taking care of their own laundry, meals, sex, and so on is quite a chore when alone in a room somewhere. Some of the errant husbands are persuaded to return by relatives, ministers, and by repentant wives.

Many, however, get away. For the determined man, it is a relatively simple matter to disappear in the United States. The first step is to leave and go to another state, preferably a fairly large city in another state. The second step is to change the name, and then get the name certified as legally correct. The easiest way to do this is to register at any Social Security office and obtain a number to go with the new name. No questions are asked at the Social Security office, and within a few days you will find yourself with a new Social Security card. Next, obtain a state driver's license. Although it plainly states at the bottom of the Social Security card that it is *not for identification*, the driver's license bureau usually will accept the card for identification anyway, that is, if they ask for any identification.

With new identity established, the husband can now find a job and go to work. Within a few months his identity is firmly established in the new city, and he can have a pocket full of cards; engraved calling cards, membership cards to the YMCA, the local Toastmaster's Club, Kiwanis, Boosters, Athletic Club, and with a saving's account at any bank, a membership card for the Diner's Club.

The key to successful escape is "determination." The deserting husband must be willing to forsake forever his wife, his children, his relatives, his friends, his old Army buddies, and his former way of life. This isn't easy, and although statistics reveal that thirty percent try to get away every year, only five percent make it. But when one considers that we have about fifty million married men in the United States, five percent is a lot of loose husbands.

I was not concerned with the others, I was only concerned with myself. And as I rode through the dark Florida night, I examined my motives. When I purchased a one-way ticket to Orangeville, I certainly did not intend to desert my wife. I bought the ticket unconsciously. "Give me a ticket to Orangeville," I said. That was all. But my sensitive conscious mind knew that my way of life was in danger. By becoming a writer I had escaped a dull, unrewarding, life-sapping job as an accountant in Columbus. My thoughts that morning while sitting peacefully in my study—surrounded by books from the library, magazines, writing tablets and carefully sharpened pencils—had been forced into examining ways to obtain money, and the only way I really knew how to make money was as an accountant.

What was I doing on this bus, riding to a tiny Florida village, and what could I possibly find at a dying monastery that would be worthwhile to write about? What indeed? I could fool my wife, but how could I fool myself? I was merely exhausting the few dollars I had left in a foolish expenditure, which brought, in turn, the necessity for fulltime employment that much closer. . .

For a full year I had enjoyed the fruits of a published novel. In the peaceful quiet of Ocean Pine Terraces, I had watched the husbands of the neighborhood leave for work in the morning, and I had watched them return in the evening. A pitiful crew. While watering my lawn in the early evening I had watched them drive into their open carports, and I had waved to them kindly. I felt sorry for them, and although I knew I was hated and envied by most of the husbands on my quiet block, I could understand their feelings. As a writer I was above any outward show of emotion, and gradually, as the days lengthened into weeks, into months, I was incapable of feeling any kind of emotion.

That year had taught me how to live, how to see, how to enjoy and to fully realize what I had missed in life by working for more than ten years hunched over ledgers at the Tanfair Milk Company. At first my heart was filled with compassion for the others. I felt sorry for everyone. I loved everyone. How could I have felt otherwise? But there was no way to show my feelings, so I did not let myself betray them.

How could I tell my next door neighbor, a trust officer at the Citizen's Bank, that I felt sorry for him? When I saw him drive into his carport and dismount from his new car with a bulging briefcase under his arm, my heart flooded with pity for this poor fellow. His light would be on far into the night as he worked over papers from the bank. Could I have told him about the bright red cardinal that perched on my window ledge every morning, and how beautiful the little bird was, and how I missed the little thing when it failed to put in an appearance?

Of course not. The only things I had in common with my banker neighbor were the chinch bugs in the lawn!

I knew these working men. I had been one myself before becoming a writer, and I knew how they kidded themselves into believing that what they were doing mattered.

Gradually, as the weeks passed, I shut all thoughts of my neighbors out and lived entirely within myself. I wrote down my vagrant thoughts, snatches of imaginary dialogue, and a few short stories—the article on D. H. Lawrence. I read three and five books a week from the public library, books I had always wanted to read and had not read, and I reread many of my favorites. Once or twice a week I would drive to the beach and sun myself, lying quietly on the hot sands and basking in the subtropical rays of a bright and kindly sun. By myself I would swim out past the pounding surf, float on my back, and open my eyes to the changing colors of the sky. I was fully, vitally alive, and aware of the beauty of the world; the world that had been denied to me in the changing climate of Columbus, confined in the thick woolen clothing I had been forced to wear; the tight collars and the damned neckties.

And to the dismay of my wife, I had gradually become celibate. How many months had it been? I counted on my fingers—five months—a long time to do without sex. But I was above it, and the thought of sex left me indifferent, uncaring—it was all so boring anyway, and messy on top of that.

As a writer I lived in my mind. That was enough. I sighed deeply, an anguished sound brought up from deep within my chest. The sound awakened my companion, an elderly gentleman in a gray wash-and-wear Dacron suit, and he glared at me.

"What's the matter, buddy? You sick?" He asked.

"No," I replied angrily. "Are you?"

"I ain't making no noises like I was dying." The old man turned his head away from me and went back to sleep.

Orangeville, population 603, was not a regular stop on the run from Miami to Jax, and the driver had his big bus in gear and on the highway again before I realized that I was on the ground. My Timex wristwatch indicated that it was four a.m., and there wasn't a single light shining in the little town. With my small overnight bag between my knees, I blinked sleepily in the darkness and wondered where the monastery was and how I could find it in the blackness.

I didn't feel like standing in a dark filling station waiting for daylight, and I was in need of a cup of coffee. A mile or so back we had passed a SAVE! chain gas station, well-lighted by neon tubing, and I started back down the highway toward this oasis. There would be a Coke machine, anyway, and light, and an attendant to shoot the breeze with, at least.

Facing the light traffic, I walked on the edge of the highway until I reached the all-night filling station. After a session in the men's room, I talked to the station attendant, a young man in his late twenties who taught American history at the Clewiston High School to supplement his income.

He was glad to have company and talked animatedly about a current project his students were working on: a class skit depicting the balances of government, which a friend of his at Florida State University had set to music.

Waiting politely for a break in the monologue, I asked the teacher-attendant where the famous Church of God's Flock Monastery was and how I could get there.

"It's closed," he said.

"I know, but the Abbot is still there, and I have an appointment with him."

"Did you ride the bus all the way into town?"

"Yes, and then I walked back down here."

"You shouldn't have done that. You should have asked the driver to put you off at the monastery. It's five miles back." He jerked his thumb in a southerly direction.

I cursed and looked at my watch again. Four forty-five.

"I'd better start walking," I told the attendant.

"If you want to wait until six-thirty, I'll drop you off when my relief comes," he offered eagerly, reluctant to see me leave.

"No," I shook my head. "The exercise will wake me up."

We shook hands formally and I departed, carrying my light bag. The night was pitch black, and there was a smell of smoke in the air that came in strongly and then drifted away again from a muck fire several miles away. I could make out a faint red glow on the horizon, and I recalled that there always seemed to be untended fires in central Florida. Cars on the highway were few and far between, and the highway was a straight gray line through the empty countryside. The night was noisy with crickets and insects of all kinds, and every five minutes on the dog, a bull alligator roared from the depths of the swamp oozing back from the right side of the highway.

I walked with an infantry pace, ninety steps a minute, which would give me a rate of two and one-half miles an hour if I stopped for a break of ten minutes after the first hour. I was in no hurry, and I found the walk very pleasant, especially the sunrise part. A Florida sunrise is different from other sunrises. First the sky, which has been completely black, turns pearly gray, all at once, as though a dimmer switch had been thrown; a few moments later, the dimmer is turned up full to bright, and the sun is up. The sunrise doesn't sneak in, like mood music; it comes on full, and the state is flushed with a white heat; the sweat begins to flow, and you don't think you will be able to stand it. But somehow, high noon is no hotter than daybreak. So long as the sun is shining there is a maddening sameness to the heat, which most Northerners never seem to get used to.

An archway constructed of concrete brick and stucco, painted orange, fronted the entrance to the monastery, and a yellow gravel road led to a small line-up of one-room structures that resembled an abandoned motel. There were seven of the one-story cabins, and each of them was painted a different tint or shade of orange. At the far end of the short stretch of cabins, a fair-sized Butler building—also painted orange—gleamed in the sun, with a wooden, orange cross nailed to the slanting roof. This building, I supposed, was the chapel. Multicolored croton grew thickly about each building; interspersed with the croton were blue century and castor-bean plants, gallberry bushes, Florida cherry hedges, scrub palmettos and red, triple-blooming hibiscus. All of the untended foliage was well-choked by gama grass and assorted weeds. Over the first cabin, marked OFFICE and ABBOT in old English script, lettered in black paint beside the screen door, a galloping flame vine had been trained across the roof, and the spreading plant completely covered one entire side of the building.

Twenty feet behind the row of cabins, an orange grove, of perhaps twenty or twenty-five acres, stretched up and over a rise of ground and reappeared in the distance, halting atop a small hill that held a crudely constructed, slowly revolving windmill. Downwind, which did not help, a waist-high corral, dotted with seven packing boxes, had once held goats; I could tell by the smell.

In front of the Abbot's cabin or "cell," a man in a black, ground-length cassock performed calisthenics, counting "One, two, three, four" in a loud practiced voice of command. I lit a cigarette and watched him as he bobbed to "burpies," an exercise so tiring it made me weary to watch him. The Abbot was a thickset man, at least six feet tall; with a round, hard paunch and a closely shaven head well-tanned by the sun. His face was red and wet from the vigorous exercising, and his nose was a misshapen potato grafted sloppily onto a flat, freshly-scraped face. Flat blue eyes, set well apart, looked me over appraisingly, but he did not stop the exercising or the counting. There was something odd about the man I could not fathom for a moment, and then I noticed that his eyebrows were also shaved away, and there was a silver medal (a pair of crossed rifles and a cross-bar labeled Expert Rifleman) pinned to the cassock above his left breast. Shaved eyebrows are unusual, and not every man of God wears a shooting medal, and this combination, I decided, accounted for the strangeness.

"Good morning," I said. "Are you Abbot Dover?"

"One—!" he screamed with a rising inflection. "Two, three, four!" And he stopped at the position of a soldier at Attention, breathing heavily. "These burpies are rough, boy! Ever try any?"

"Not since I got out of the Army," I laughed.

"I am a soldier of the Lord," he said easily. "Had your breakfast yet?"

"No, sir," I replied. "Just a Coca-Cola down the road."

"Come on in then, and we'll whomp up something."

I followed the Abbot into his cabin, sat down at the table, and slid the overnight bag under my chair. Before I had a chance to look around the room, the Abbot questioned me as he broke eggs into a large frying pan on the electric stove.

"Are you a pilgrim, boy? Or are you interested in a little real estate? Or are you just a bum looking for a handout?"

"I'm a little of each, I suppose," I answered warily. "I'm a writer, and I read in the Miami paper about your monastery closing and thought there might be an article in it."

"There might be at that, but I don't want any publicity. There's been too much already, and a dead dog knows enough to lie down. Do you want some grits with your eggs?"

"Yes, sir."

The room was much larger inside than one would suspect from looking at the outside, and the arrangement of the furniture had been planned to give as much space as possible to the center of the cell. An apartment-sized refrigerator sat in one corner; next to it was a four-unit electric stove, and there was a doorway leading to a separate bathroom. A studio couch, covered with rumpled sheets, was alongside one wall, and the table where we ate breakfast was beneath the window. In a sort of an alcove by the bathroom door there was a disordered desk piled high with books and papers, and on a narrow shelf above the desk there were more books, most of them Bibles. The terrazzo floor was bare and the furniture, including an easy chair and its flanking end table and lamp, was Sears-modern.

I sat down to breakfast and ate hungrily. The Abbot set a good early morning table. We ate four fried eggs apiece, a pile of grits, a heaping plateful of hoe cake dripping with melted margarine and orange marmalade, and then we talked over coffee, taking turns on the filling of pottery cups from a huge gray enamel pot on the stove.

"I'll tell you about the Church of God's Flock monastery, Brother Springer, and then you'll know for yourself why it isn't worth an article in a newspaper or magazine." Abbot Dover took a large bite out of a plug of Brown Mule, chewed contemplatively for a moment, and then spat into a pot containing a giant philodendron.

"You'll let me be the judge, then?"

"No. I won't okay anything you write, and if you do write anything I'll issue a denial."

"That doesn't sound fair—"

"Of course it isn't fair! Who said it was? Now," he pointed to a framed eight-by-ten-inch photograph of a Negro thumb-tacked to the wall, "take a good look at that nigger's face."

I got up from my chair and examined the photograph. The Negro in the photograph was very old, and his eyes seemed to return my inquisitive stare. The photo had been taken full face, and beneath a square chin the Negro wore an old-fashioned Herbert Hoover collar and a black string tie. His hair was a thick, white skull cap resembling an English barrister's wig with the curls clipped off. The face wore a solemn, dignified expression, and there was a quiet beauty to the sharp, well-defined bone structure, especially the high cheek bones. Except for the tell-tale flattened nose and the shiny blackness, the face could have belonged to a Justice of the Supreme Court. In his youth, this had been a very handsome man indeed. I was surprised that I thought so. This was the first Negro countenance I had ever studied at close range, and it was somewhat of a surprise to see character so deeply etched in a black face. Up to that moment, I had thought that all Negroes looked pretty much alike.

"That is the Right Reverend Cosmo Bird of Birmingham, Alabama," the Abbot said, "founder of the Church of God's Flock, and the man who started the monastery."

"I don't believe I've ever seen such beauty in bone structure before," I said admiringly. "He could have been a movie star with a face like that."

"Well, he started the church in Birmingham. He made a pile of dough in nigger property in Pratt City, and he put most of the geedus into the establishing of more churches. There are three in Birmingham, two in Mobile, one in Atlanta, one in Nashville, one in Tuscaloosa, and one in Jax. All of them are as poor as hell.

"When he kicked off in 1936 he left the rest of his money to a fund to establish a monastery here in Orangeville. He already owned the property here through some real estate deal, and in 'thirty-six, this location was really isolated. An ideal spot for a monastery. That was before they put the main highway through, and long before anybody ever thought of a freeway seven miles away.

"He was an idealist, you might say, and way ahead of his time so to speak. He believed that white men and Negroes could learn to love one another, and the balance of the monastery was to be one white man to every Negro. In 1936 that was easy. There was a depression, and a monastery was a good place to sit it out. There were six monks in the beginning, three white men and three Negroes. They pitched tents, cleared out the palmettos and the jungle, built the cabins, planted the orange grove and set the place up. It worked fine for the first two years. The first abbot, a white man by the name of Terence Norton, kept a diary, and I read it when I took over in 1954. They had quite a struggle.

"In 1939 the trust money began to run out, and along with the lack of money, the trustees up in Birmingham began to lose control. First there would be all niggers here and then there would be all white men. This kind of trouble flared up off and on until the war started. The monastery also got some national publicity during the war when all of the monks refused to be drafted. They were willing to go into the Army as chaplains, with a commissioned status, but they wouldn't go in as privates. Too bad. They all went to jail except for the one white man and one nigger who were both too old to be drafted anyway. Do you begin to see the picture?"

"It doesn't sound much like a religious order."

"The Church of God's Flock has never been formally recognized as a real religion by any of the organized Protestant combines, but still, when you count the chips, it's religious enough. All of our churches preach the Bible, and what do any other churches preach? The teachings of the Bible. And the churches old Cosmo Bird established are all still going, even if they are poor. The big foul-up was the monastery. Orangeville, Florida, is too far away from Birmingham to be controlled. Correspondence takes time, and there was never any regular inspection visit from the trustees or representatives. As a consequence, the abbot in charge, whoever he happened to be, had a nice control of the dough on hand. Some of these earlier Abbots absconded with the dough, others kept the monks on short rations, and they'd quit, and so on. Being the abbot was like—did you ever read *The Golden Bough*?"

"I've heard of it."

"There's a legend in *The Golden Bough* that really fits this place. Some small Greek island had a king, and the only way you could be the king of this island was to kill the current monarch and take his sword. So no matter who was king, he had to sweat blood all of the time because at any moment some son-of-a-bitch might be sneaking up on him with a knife. Well, that's about the size of it here."

"You seem to have avoided being killed," I remarked.

"That's because I got down to fundamentals." The Abbot smiled broadly, opened the screen door and spat a stream of tobacco juice into a withered sparkleberry bush. "You're looking at a man who only made one mistake in his life. I've never mentioned this mistake to anybody, but maybe you can learn something from my mistake. I'm originally from Lincoln, Nebraska, and when I was a boy we didn't have many niggers up there. I went to a movie one Saturday afternoon, and I took a seat high in the balcony where you were allowed to smoke. Pretty soon a nigger girl came along and sat down beside me and gave me a proposition. She only wanted two-bits, and I was only eighteen at the time and, in Lincoln, Nebraska, nookie was hard to come by. So I gave the girl a quarter; she popped it into her mouth and we climbed to the very last row in the balcony. I dropped my pants, the girl dropped hers, and bent over the seat—can you picture this?"

"Very well, sir," I said politely, holding my breath.

"Well, this was the exact moment that the damned projector broke down. The film stopped, the screen went white, the houselights were turned on while they fixed the projector, and every son-of-a-bitch and his brother turned around and looked up at the little square hole in the projection room. Here I was, right under it, with my pants around my ankles, and this nigger girl with her dress all hiked up and bent over the seat, you see—what are you laughing at?"

"I think it's funny." I wiped my streaming eyes.

Abbot Dover scowled darkly, which made me break into fresh peals of laughter. He nodded soberly.

"I suppose it is funny at that. Anyway, I spotted a former school teacher in the audience, two women friends of my mother's, a dentist and several boys that I knew around town. Nobody laughed at me; they were horrified, I supposed, because I had a pretty good reputation. I pulled up my pants and scooted down the stairs, and I've never been back to Lincoln since. I joined the Army in Saint Louis, and I stayed in the Army until I retired in 1954. The moral of that story is never look at the projector when it breaks down."

"It sure is a good story," I said weakly, holding my sides.

"I didn't mean to get off the track, but one mistake can change the course of your entire life. I vowed never to make another, and I haven't. I came out of the Army a retired first sergeant, with a nice bank account and a yen to settle in Florida. I still don't think it's safe to go back to Nebraska. This was in 1954. I'm wheeling down the highway out there in my new Ford convertible, and I spot this place. It was after dark, and I thought it was a motel, so I pulled on in. There were only three monks here then, two niggers and one white man. They put me up for the night, and the next day I saw what the situation was and took over. The place was going to rack and ruin."

"How did you get control so easily?"

"I told them I'd put the monastery on a paying basis. The orange grove was ready for picking, but the three monks were too lazy to get their butts out there, and they were living on goat milk and grits. The original fund was long gone; there were two years of back taxes due on the property, and the Abbot, a tall, lean ornery son-of-a-bitch named Hank Childers, didn't have enough sense to pound shit in a rathole. All he knew was how to keep the two niggers in their place. Childers was a fruit tramp and didn't even know how to read and write his own name. The two niggers were decent enough men, but they just sat around reading the Bible. They were real monk types who needed the right kind of leadership. And I provided it.

"I hired some pickers and made a few dollars out of a crop that would have rotted on the trees in two more weeks. I got rid of the goats, and I chased Hank Childers away with a plank across his rear end after I found out the lay of the land. I sat in here and read through all of the accumulated papers, paid the taxes, had the property titles searched up in Orlando, and then bought myself a monastery for a one dollar bill. I'm the sole owner, much to the dismay and chagrin of the nigger trustees up in Birmingham. Have a chew?"

"No, thanks," I waved away the plug of Brown Mule, "I don't know how you did it. What are some of the details?"

"Uh, uh," Abbot Dover shook his head and grinned. "I've told you enough already."

I pulled the news clipping out of my shirt pocket, unfolded it, and handed it to Abbot Dover. "This is the news item that was in the Miami paper. What happened to the monks? Where were they reassigned?"

Abbot Dover glanced incuriously at the news item, crumpled it into a small ball, and flipped the wad of paper in the general direction of a wastebasket.

The late Cosmo Bird, Brother Springer, was a man of vision. He worked out a method of perpetuating the Church of God's Flock forever. But he died, and forever is a long time. His plan was fairly sound, however, and the church is still going, as I told you before. If the monastery had been established near Birmingham, for instance, the church would be at least twice as large. The original idea was to have two types of monks here. One, the contemplative type who stay until they die. The other type was to take seminary training here and, when it was completed, they were supposed to go out as ministers to either an established Church of God's Flock church or to start a new one. The monastery was not only to be self-supporting, it was to make money, and also, each church was to kick in so much money each month. The abbot was to be the titular head of the church, like the Pope in the Roman Catholic church. Have you ever studied religious history?"

"No, sir. Well some, I guess. I saw the movie about Martin Luther."

"In other words you don't know a damn thing about religious movements. Anyway, all churches have a rough row to hoe at first go round. Some of the earlier popes were worse bastards than I am, believe me, and I am only looking out for Number One. The provisions were all spelled out, and I followed them. Everything I've done is legal and by the book. I reassigned the two Negro monks to the churches needing ministers in Mobile and Atlanta, and I ran Hank Childers off the property."

Abbot Dover rubbed perspiration off his bald head with a dish towel, carried the dirty breakfast dishes into the bathroom, placed them gently into the washbowl, and turned on the tap.

"So now, each of the Church of God's Flock churches has a minister—except one. That's the little church in Jax. When I sell this place, and I've got several deals cooking, I plan to stop by Jax on my way to Washington, D.C., and ordain one of the lay church members there and give him the church. My work will then be done, with God's help, of course."

"Do you have the power to ordain a minister, just like that?" I asked, unable to hide the surprise in my voice.

"I told you I was titular head of the church didn't I? Who else could do it except me?"

"There's so much; it hasn't all sunk in, I guess. But how, as a sergeant in the Army, did you pick up so much knowledge about religion?"

After scattering a cupful of Tide onto the dishes in the washbowl, Abbot Dover returned to the table and sat down.

"Look, Brother Springer," the Abbot said softly, his flat, blue eyes shining with merriment. "Don't get the idea that just because a man is in the Army that he's a stupid son-of-a-bitch. In the Army I was what you might call a fair-weather first sergeant. In peace-time it was very pleasant to be a first sergeant, but when the bugles blow for war—and they blew them twice on me—I looked around for a softer assignment, out of danger. The safest spot of all is that of Chaplain's assistant, and this was the duty that saw me through World War II and the Korean fracas. This is very pleasant work. You assist three or four chaplains, usually a Catholic priest and a couple of Protestant ministers. Once in a while you see a Hebe, but not often. And you keep the administration, what little there is, going along, writing letters to mamas, telling them their boys are getting spiritual advice and so on, keeping little card files on the soldiers concerning their religious preferences, getting a detail to sweep the chapel, and answering the telephone. I used to listen in on those chaplains—Brother, they never had it so good. They all had commissions, and they were raking in from three to ten times as much money as they did on the outside. I never met a chaplain who wasn't a phony—"

"Come now, Abbot," I protested. "That's a pretty strong statement!"

"It's true, nevertheless. I've been watching you as I've talked. Your mouth has been hanging half open half the time. Tell me, Brother, did you ever meet a minister like me before?"

"No, sir, I sure didn't!"

"Well I'm the only honest minister you'll ever meet! I've got the Bible down pat. I've read the Bible again and again. I didn't have much to do, and I wasn't averse to writing a sermon now and then when one of the chaplains was stuck. But you'll never see me put on any mealy-mouthed act about saving your soul or any crap like that. Because I can tell you right now, you don't have a soul and neither do I. When we die, and we will if we stick it out, a black curtain will drop before our eyes, and the hunger pains will disappear from our bellies. You're an educated man and a writer so you must know something about people. Do you honestly believe that there is such a place as Heaven, milk and honey, two-bit cigars, and that there's a golden throne waiting someplace for you to put your lazy ass on?"

"I don't believe that. No. But ministers do, I'm sure they do."

"Nope. You're as full of crap as a Christmas turkey if you believe that. I'm a minister, and I've got the papers to prove it. You could be a minister too. It is merely another occupation, that's all, no different from any other soft job. Most ministers are smarter than ordinary people, and the only real difference is, they are a lot lazier. The stuff they put out in the pulpit is entirely different from what they believe. I know how they work. If they are really good, they get into the big pay brackets like the revival circuits. In fact, the less a minister believes, the more effective he is when he talks about religion."

I didn't know what to think. It was very strange to hear such talk from a man wearing a cassock, and Abbot Dover looked holy, even with the shiny rifleman badge dangling from his chest. The shaven head, the absence of any eyebrows, and the direct, frank stare of his alert blue eyes were disconcerting. Not that I have ever been a religious man, although I have fooled around with Unitarianism a little; it was the conviction in his voice that got to me. And along with being convinced, I could picture thousands of ministers in their Sunday pulpits, preaching to more thousands like myself who believed in nothing—and both of them, ministers and congregations, dead serious, and yet, no one believing in anything! Why did they do it?

"Why does a man become a minister then, Abbot Dover? Why would any man deliberately choose to lead a false life?"

"That's easy," the Abbot shrugged. "Why did you become a writer?"

"I wanted to escape from a miserable job. I was an accountant."

"There's your answer. A man becomes a minister to escape honest employment, and two, he wants to make money. The latter category is in the minority, of course. The majority of the men who wear the cloth are looking for simple security with the minimum of effort. Others want power. If I wanted power, I would become a priest in the Roman Catholic Church. I am one of the minority. I don't care about power; I am interested in money. The strange thing is that when you go after money through the church, you usually get power along with it. Power and money go hand and hand."

"It doesn't seem like an easy life to me. A minister with even a small church has got weddings to perform, christening, baptizing, sermons to prepare, sick people to visit, fundraising—"

"Do you call that work?"

"His time isn't his own! The minister is on call twenty-four hours a day."

"Jesus Christ, Brother Springer!" the Abbot said sharply, "a man has to do something!" Going to his desk, the Abbot picked up a Bible and brought it to the table. "It's all in here. Every verse in this Bible can be turned into a sermon by any man who knows how to talk on his feet. You can preach a lifetime and never get through this book. Right?"

"I suppose so," I said wearily.

"You're broke, aren't you?"

The tone of his voice dropped several levels and was so compassionate I looked up from the table and let his eyes catch mine. I couldn't meet his level, inquisitive stare and I dropped my gaze to the shooting medal on his chest.

"I'm almost flat, Abbot Dover," I admitted.

"I suspected as much. And you aren't much of a writer either, are you?"

"I've got a published novel to my credit," I said, half-defiantly.

"What have you written since, and how long ago did you write your novel?"

"I haven't written anything since. But I will. All I need is an idea."

"Why don't you give writing up and get a job? Do you want a job? I'll get you an accounting job in Clewiston. A few people over there owe me some favors."

"No." I shook my head. "I'm a writer, and even if I starve to death, I'll never go back to that kind of work. If I have to, I'll wash dishes for a meal, but I'll never put my head in the trap again."

"Good. You're a gambler, and I had you sized up right. When I leave here I'm going to Washington and I'm entering the Soldier's Home. A man with twenty years service is entitled to domiciliary care there for the rest of his life. I'll get a room, free board, and I also get to keep all my retired pay. With what I've saved, and at no cost for the essentials in life, I should be able to live a long time. I can ride up to New York for a play once in a while, spend a few months going through the Smithsonian, and gently fritter away my life. As you may have noticed, I like to talk, and I like to talk to soldiers. We speak the same language. I am getting out of life . . . all there is to get.

"I'm in a position now to do you a favor, and I like you. I'm going to give you the opportunity to write. Whether you ever write another line or not doesn't make a damn to me, but this is your chance. How much money do you have?"

"Not quite sixty bucks."

"Give me twenty."

"I've only got sixty between me and nothing."

"I heard you the first time. Give me twenty of it, and I'll ordain you as a minister of the Church of God's Hock and send you up to Jax to take over the Jax church."

"I can't do that—"

"You can have the Bible. It's all in there, Brother Springer. The trustees in Jax will give you a few dollars a month and a small house to live in next to the church. You can write six days a week and preach a couple of sermons on Sunday. If you're too lazy to do that, you're too lazy to live."

"Oh, I wouldn't mind doing it," I said protesting, "but I don't know how!"

"Are you prejudiced against niggers?" Abbot Dover asked sternly.

"Of course not."

"The church in Jax is an all-Negro church. If you can't fool a bunch of niggers, you're in pretty bad shape. Besides, you'll like it."

"Ordain me then," I said, in sudden decision. I took a twenty-dollar bill out of my wallet and placed it on the table.

Abbot Dover raised his skirts and shoved the bill into the hip pocket of the pair of plaid walking shorts he was wearing beneath the cassock. Opening the door to his closet he looked through a thickly packed rack of dark clothing, pulled down a black covert cloth suit and tossed it to me.

"Try that on for size."

The length of the trousers was okay, but the waistband was much too large, four or five inches too big. The coat was a size 44, and I feel better with a 42.

"That's fine," Abbot Dover nodded approvingly. "A little large, but you can have the pants taken in when you get to Jax. If they ask you why the suit's too big—and I don't think they will—tell them you've been fasting. I've got two shirts that'll fit. What's your neck size?"

"Fifteen-thirty four."

I put on one of the shirts with the backward collars, and after a little difficulty, I managed to loop the collar button in back. The bib front of the shirt was black and the rest of it was white, including the stiff, narrow collar. I transferred my belt, and after tightening it, and shoving the excess waistband of the trousers in the rear, and putting on the coat, the suit fit fairly well. The shoulders were too wide, but the sleeve length was perfect. As long as I didn't button the jacket, nobody would notice how loose it was, I decided.

"All right, let's go," the Abbot ordered, opening the screen door.

"Go where?" I asked.

"To the chapel."

We walked down the gravel path to the chapel, and Abbot Dover threw open the corrugated iron double doors, exposing his convertible Ford. We squeezed by the car, climbed over a pile of stacked benches, and I dropped back hesitantly when Abbot Dover knelt at the small altar. He bowed his head silently for a moment, got heavily to his feet, and lighted a candle in a pewter holder on the altar with a Zippo lighter. A crudely-carved wooden cross nailed to the wall, a light blue bath towel over the altar, and the flickering candle were the only adornments. And yet I was awed, impressed even, when Abbot Dover raised his arms level with his shoulders and lifted his face to the ceiling.

"God," he said somberly, "I've got a writer here, and he needs a place to be. He's a good man and a gambler. In Your name, take him into Your heart and blood and give him Your love. He really needs a break. He'll make a good minister and will spread Your teachings to Your flock in Jax, and they need a man like him in Jax. But give him something besides a cotton string for a backbone. Amen."

The Abbot let his arms fall limply, dropped his head on his chest, and then crossed himself. Turning around quickly, he placed his right hand on my shoulder.

"Kneel, boy," he ordered. I knelt at his feet, and he steepled his fingers and closed his eyes. "I ordain you—what's your first and middle name?"

"Sam is my first name," I whispered, "but I dropped my middle name when I became a writer."

"I'll give you one then. I ordain you Sam Deuteronomy Springer, Pastor of the First Church of God's Flock in Jax, Florida." He bent down over me and stage-whispered, "Do you want to say a prayer?"

"I can't think of one," I whispered back.

"Okay." After helping me to my feet, the Abbot shook hands with me and patted me on the back "That wasn't so tough, was it?"

"No," I lied. The perspiration had soaked through my thick coat, and I removed it and carried it over my arm as we left the chapel. Back in his office, the Abbot printed my name neatly on a mimeographed form, and dated the paper, which officially made me a preacher. I folded the completed form and put it into my wallet.

"Now you use that middle name up in Jax," the Abbot told me seriously. "Deuteronomy is a good middle name for a minister, and the niggers will like it. When you get to Jax report to Dr. Fred Jensen's office. He's a nigger dentist, and he heads up the board of trustees for the Jax church. You'll get *a* warm welcome, I can assure you. He's written me several letters asking for a minister, and you'll fit in fine."

"I'm a little nervous about it, but I'm a writer and I should be able to write a sermon as good as anybody else."

I packed my sport clothing into my small bag, shook hands again with the Abbot and walked up the highway. As soon as I reached the highway I had a terrible thought, and I rushed back to his office and burst through the screen door.

"How many people have you ordained and sent to the church in Jax?" I asked angrily. "For all I know you've sent a dozen men up there, and there may not even be a Church of God's Flock in Jax!"

"Good for you!" The Abbot laughed joyously, throwing his bald head back and bellowing. "Healthy skepticism makes a good minister. But don't worry, boy, everything's on the up and up. Go with God."

"Okay," I said sullenly. "But if this is a con game, I'll come back down here and beat the hell out of you!"

"You were a godsend, Reverend Springer. I'm closing the books on the last church. I wouldn't snow a man under about anything like this. I may be crooked, but I'm an honest man. Go on up to Jax, and put your faith in the Lord!"

I grinned. "Thanks, Abbot. I'll drop you a line one of these days."

"Do that. Soldier's Home, Washington 25, D.C. I'll be glad to hear from you. Any time."

For the third time that morning we shook hands. When I reached the highway I turned and waved. A grin on his red face, the Abbot waved back.

"Go with God!" he shouted. I walked along the edge of the highway toward Orangeville where the bus would pick me up and take me to Jax . . . and my new vocation.

I WAS VERY uncomfortable in my new role. The thick convert-cloth suit was not the right apparel for Florida, and yet I was reluctant to remove the coat in the bus like the other male passengers. Somehow I felt that as a minister of the Gospel I should set an example. But an example for whom? Did I, as a minister of the Church of God's Flock, Jax, have to set an example for everybody or just for my parishioners?

As the Abbot had implied, clerical garb made the minister; I had not been given any other instructions to go with the uniform. The mere donning of my black suit changed me, not only in the eyes of the world, but in my own eyes.

As a draftee I remembered how the entire group of us had acted when we first got our uniforms and were put on a train for Fort Ord. Before boarding the train, several of us had procured bottles, and on the train we had been under minimum control of the sergeant who was in charge of the packet. At each station we had screamed at the girls; we had gotten as drunk as possible, and several of the draftees had carved their initials into the paneled walls of the smoker. The mere act of putting on a soldier's uniform had transformed us into irresponsible persons, or so we thought. As a group, all decked out in tight, unfamiliar uniforms, the clothes made us men, and we performed our new parts as we imagined a group of soldiers would do if they were turned loose on a holiday. Not one of us would have done any of the scandalous things we did on that train if we had been dressed in our regular civilian clothing.

Later, during basic military training, we had the opportunity to learn how real soldiers were supposed to behave on passes and leaves, but in that early stage of soldiering, in brand new uniforms, we did not know. At least we were later given training as soldiers. As a new minister, I was on my own, and I had to act like a minister at all times . . . and I didn't know how.

The bus ride from Orangeville to Jax was the only opportunity

I would have to set my role, and I put my mind to the problem. One night in Miami I had taken my wife to the Green Lobster for dinner, and it had been an expensive evening. The cheapest dinner—which we ordered—on the menu was $4.65. At the next table, two Roman Catholic priests, both of them bloated and red-faced, were consuming the specialty of the house, Maine lobster. I was resentful. As they dipped great chunks of white, delicious meat into bowls of melted butter and washed the food down with individual bottles of iced Sauterne, my resentment grew to unreasonable proportions and spoiled the taste of my mixed-seafood platter.

"How did these bastards get off?" I thought. I examined the menu, and with an accountant's accuracy I checked the items on their table with the prices on the right side of the card. Dinner for the pair, including the wine, came to $28.32, including tax. A tip of five dollars would bring the cost up to $33.32! "Fantastic!" I had thought, "How could two priests, who were supposed to be under the strictest vows of poverty, pay such a sum for an evening meal?"

I didn't resent the food they ate—everybody is entitled to eat—but why eat in such an expensive restaurant? The money they were spending on this rich food was being paid for by poor, low-wage earners who could ill-afford to give money to the Roman Catholic church! What right did they have to spend so much money on food?

At the time, I was looking at the situation with the eyes of a non-Roman Catholic, and I was highly prejudiced against those two bloated characters in black suits. It wasn't right. Now that I was wearing a black suit and a backward collar, how was I supposed to feel? My attitude had not changed: I still didn't believe it was right for a minister to gorge at the expense of others. I would eat simply, I decided, and with refined restraint. I had that responsibility to the world as well as to my yet unknown parishioners. Within a few minutes I had an opportunity to test my resolution.

The Greyhound stopped at a filling station in the middle of nowhere, and a large perspiring woman of forty or so mounted the steps with some difficulty. She wore a billowing housedress and carried a large hamper under her arm. There were several empty seats but she chose to sit beside me.

"Do you mind if I sit here, Father?" she asked pleasantly in a sweet high voice.

"Of course not, Madame," I replied, "please do."

Although I did not want anybody to sit next to me while I was planning my future actions, I couldn't very well tell her so—not in my new black uniform. After she was settled—and the driver hadn't even changed to high gear—she opened the hamper and unwrapped a whole baked chicken. As she unpeeled the Reynolds Wrap from the chicken, a maddening aroma filled my nostrils. The outside of the chicken was a beautiful color—the shade of a two-day bruise on the tender side of a woman's thigh—and I was forced to look away and fix my eyes on the plains. There was a gentle tug at my sleeve. I turned. With a smile on her round face, the woman held out a paper plate piled high with three pieces of chicken and a giant mound of potato salad, moist with mayonnaise. And next to a gleaming piece of chicken breast there were three white puffed biscuits.

"Could you eat something, Father," the woman said kindly, "I have plenty."

"I'll take a biscuit," I half-whispered.

"Oh, no!" She shook her head. "Take the plate. I'll fix another for myself. I have plenty!"

"No," I said hoarsely. "Just a biscuit."

She did not press me, and I nibbled on a fluffy tender biscuit, chewing slowly and pondering the wisdom of my refusal to take an ample share of the proffered bounty. My throat was dry, but I came to the conclusion that my decision was sound. Somehow, without even trying, I had made up for the two greedy priests and their feast in Miami's Green Lobster. I examined my traveling companion. She was too fat, at least fifty or sixty pounds too fat. Her short brown hair was tightly curled from a new permanent. Her buttocks and legs were so fat that a goodly portion of her rear end flowed beneath the arm rest and reached well onto my seat. She gobbled away at the potato salad with a small red plastic spoon, stripped long chunks of meat away from various chicken portions with sharp white teeth, and popped whole biscuits into her mouth.

"You are too fat," I said unpleasantly.

Her pale blue eyes popped slightly, and she stopped chewing and stared at me.

"I said you are too fat," I repeated. "What are you doing about it?"

"I'm trying to cut down, Father," she managed to get out.

"It doesn't look that way to me."

"I know I eat too much, Father, but I'm hungry all of the time. The doctor gave me a prescription for Dexedrine, but they made me nervous and I couldn't sleep." She looked at the remainder of the food on her paper plate for a moment, and then covered the plate with a napkin and returned the uneaten food to the wicker hamper.

"Have you ever tried prayer?" I asked, looking boldly into her eyes. "Are you unhappy? Does your husband admire your obesity? Do you like the way you look?"

"No, I'm not unhappy, Father, I don't think. My husband kids me about being fat, but he's very kind otherwise. I wish I could lose weight; I really do."

"Then let us pray," I said, steepling my fingers. The woman was more than a little embarrassed and she looked about to see if any of the other passengers had overheard me. I said it louder. "Let us pray!"

The woman quickly bent her head and crossed herself. She closed her eyes tightly, and her face turned rose-color.

"Dear God!" I began. "Help this poor helpless woman in Your infinite wisdom and mercy to get rid of all of that excess flesh she is carrying around. Fat that is destroying her beauty in Your eyes, in the eyes of her husband, and in the eyes of the world. I don't believe, O Lord, I've ever seen such a fat woman before in all my born days, and she needs help to dissipate her greed. Greed is the deadliest of all sins, dear, sweet Jesus, and although this woman knows that she is greedy, she has found that Dexedrine does not help. Feed her instead, O Lord, on Your blood and bone and flesh so that she can enter the kingdom of Heaven a thinner and more beautiful woman. In Jesus' name, I implore you, O Lord!"

I finished my prayer and looked at the woman. Tears were streaming down her face, and her eyes were tightly closed. Her breathing was labored, and her chest heaved convulsively.

"Trent!" the bus driver announced as he braked in front of a small cafe on the edge of the tiny village.

The fat woman opened her eyes, picked up her hamper, and got to her feet heavily. She turned and looked at me for a long moment, and I stared her down. After dropping her eyes she whispered, "God bless you, Father," picked up the hamper and left the bus.

I shrugged. Evidently the woman had mistaken me for a Roman Catholic priest. However, I was well pleased with my first forage into the land of the true believers, and with new confidence I slept the rest of the way from Trent to Jax.

Jax, Florida, had a population of approximately 200,000 people. Half of these were Negroes, and the remainder was fairly divided between white people from Georgia and white carpetbaggers from the north and elsewhere. There were also a great many sailors; Jax was one of the main Atlantic stopovers for naval stores and the refueling of Navy ships. The city was considered an excellent port; it was well-sheltered from the sea some twelve miles away; there was a wide well-dredged channel in the Saint John's River, and ninety or more bustling piers to take care of oceangoing vessels. In addition to shipping, Jax did a fine business in lumber, concrete blocks, cigars, boat building and the fashioning of orange crates for the rest of Florida.

It was a busy, growing city, and although the pace of its inhabitants was a lot slower than those of an eastern city of comparable size, there was great interest in the making of money. Steel towers shot high in to the humid air, pneumatic jackhammers rattled away, and new motels and insurance companies appeared on the skyline almost daily. The influence of Georgia, however, was everywhere—in the snuff-laden drugstore windows, in the faded straw hats, in seersucker trousers and blue work shirts, and in the selection of music on the jukeboxes. This Florida city was the last stronghold of the white traditional southerner—a city where a northern lawyer in an office building would call a Negro client Mister, and where the same Negro would be arrested if he tried to drink out of a drinking fountain labeled *White*.

I couldn't have cared less. The social conditions and the making of money were none of my concern. All I had to do was to preach an honest sermon for my congregation once a week, and in return, the congregation would provide me with a house, some pin money, and the opportunity to write. This thought was uppermost in my mind as I threaded my way through the crowded bus station to the street.

I reluctantly parted with $2.98 for a straw hat, but I considered the hat a necessary purchase. A minister of the gospel doesn't go around bareheaded, and I settled for a straw floater instead of a heavy dark fedora. Bing Crosby always wore a straw hat when he played the part of a priest in the movies, and a straw hat with a gaily colored band added a dash of necessary worldliness to my black, ministerial garb. I returned to the bus station and took my small bag out of the locker, then looked up Dr. Fred Jensen's address in the telephone book. Another problem confronted me. As a minister, was I supposed to take a taxicab, or was I supposed to take a bus? I didn't know where Dr. Jensen's office was physically located even though I had the address, and a taxicab offered an easy solution to getting there with the minimum of effort. I didn't know the city transportation system either, and in my black suit I hesitated to ask anyone. Mine was an all-Negro parish, and at that stage of the game, I was apprehensive about letting any white man in on my new job. There was no reason to be embarrassed, but I didn't like the idea of saying to a stranger, "Pardon me, I am a minister looking for a church."

After consulting a street map at a nearby filling station, I walked. And I walked for two hours before I found Dr. Jensen's office. His office address was 717¼ N. Tremaine Street, and the other three-quarters of the building was a grocery store. The time was 4:42 p.m., and I asked a Negro boy polishing squash if Dr. Jensen was upstairs.

"I didn't see him leave, Reverend," the boy said, and I climbed the narrow stairway to the dentist's office.

I have always been more than a little leery of dentists. There is something peculiar about any man who deliberately plans to spend eight hours a day with his fingers in somebody else's mouth. I concede that dentists are necessary, but all the same, there is an area of suspicion about dentists that cannot be ignored. Dr. Fred Jensen, although he was as black as a modern picture frame, resembled other dentists I had known. He maintained an anonymous dignity, a serious countenance, and he had strong, capable hands. As I entered his office—or workshop—he was seated in his dentist's chair, smoking a filter tip cigarette and gazing pensively out the window.

"Dr. Jensen?" I inquired.

The dentist wheeled the chair about with a practiced whipping motion and smiled as he got up to greet me.

"You caught me napping, Reverend. Yes sir, you sure did!" He laughed pleasantly, deep in his throat, and extended a hand for me to shake.

"I am the Right Reverend Deuteronomy Springer," I said calmly, surprising myself with the ease of my claim, "and I'm the new pastor of the First Church of God's Flock here in Jax. Abbot Dover told me to contact you upon my arrival, and here I am."

"That's wonderful!" Jensen said. "Wonderful! We have needed a pastor sorely for many months, ever since the Reverend Wannop passed on to meet his maker, God rest his soul." Jensen rolled his eyes upward.

"And I am happy to be here," I replied. "Abbot Dover said that I had lived too long in my hermitage, and it was time to preach God's word to those who need it. Is Jax a wicked city, Dr. Jensen?"

"Yes, sir, it sure is, Reverend. It is just about as wicked a city as anyone could find in a month of Sundays, and you are sorely needed. Now, have you had your supper?"

"No, I just arrived on the bus from Orangeville, and I walked from the bus station directly to your office."

"You walked all the way over here?"

"Of course."

"I wish you hadn't done that, Reverend. If you had called me on the telephone I would have come over and picked you up in my Buick automobile. But now you're here, and I know you're hungry. Do you like ribs?"

"I am quite fond of ribs." I admitted.

"Then we'll go right now over to Jackie's Bar-B-Cue and have some. Jackie Linsey is one of our trustees, and I know he'll want to meet you right away, and I'll call on Mr. Clyde Caldwell to join us. He's the third trustee of our church, and a fine Christian and an excellent barber he is, too."

Dr. Jensen made his telephone call, and twenty minutes later I was sitting in a back booth inside Jackie's Bar-B-Cue Palace with a pile of hickory-smoked spareribs in front of me, and a huge plateful of french fries on the side. Accompanying the meal was a deep dish of cole slaw, well soaked in mayonnaise, a pitcher of iced tea, and the friendly rumble of Dr. Jensen's voice as he plied me with polite questions. Jackie Linsey, a short bald man with a thick middle and narrow shoulders, had pulled a chair up to the table instead of sitting in the booth, and he nursed a cup of black coffee while Jensen and I stripped greasy meat away from the ribs with our teeth.

Slightly nervous, I was grateful to be eating during the questioning. If I wanted time to answer, I had the perfect excuse of a full mouth to allow an adequate pause to think of a reply.

My replies to the polite, interested queries were cautious because everything I said was an out-and-out falsehood. It is very easy to lie, but the liar who cannot remember his lies is a liar who gets caught. Dr. Jensen was not an ignorant Negro; I had spotted his degree of dental surgery on the wall in his office. Jackie Linsey had a thriving business in his Bar-B-Cue Palace. In addition to a lively drive-in trade, the inside section of the cafe contained seven booths and a dozen tables, most of the seats filled with hungry rib and chicken eaters. Although I was the only white man eating inside, many of the drive-in customers I could see in automobiles through the windows were white men ordering ribs and barbecued chickens to go.

"Yes," I said to Dr. Jensen, wiping my greasy mouth with a paper napkin, "The Church of God's Flock offers the true Christian an opportunity to return to the basic truths of the Gospel. My early theological training in California at the California Bible Institute convinced me of the necessity of true meditation. That was my primary reason for entering the monastery at Orangeville. Have you been there, Dr. Jensen?"

"No, sir, I haven't, although I have always intended to visit it some day."

"Have you been there, brother Linsey?"

"I can't say that I have, Reverend. The Palace keeps me pretty busy, and although some may consider it a sin, I have been forced to stay open on Sunday. Oh, I go to church regular," he added hastily, "but many people have told me how nice it is to be able to get ribs on Sunday. I figured that by staying open on Sunday, many churchgoers are able to get out of their kitchens and go to church. By buying ribs here, you see, Reverend, they are free to worship in God's house without worrying about something at home on the stove."

"I see what you mean," I nodded, "but you must never lose sight of the fact that Sunday belongs to the Lord. Do you allow your help time off to attend church?"

"Yes, sir. Some I let off in the morning, and the rest for the evening service, but they all get a chance to go."

"Then I suppose it is all right. Who has been conducting the services while you have been without a regular pastor?"

"I have conducted some of the services," Dr. Jensen admitted modestly, "and Jackie has conducted a few, but most of them have been ably handled by Brother Caldwell, our other trustee, who should be along any minute. We have also had guest ministers from the Abyssinian Church of Lambs, the Truth Baptists of the Infant Jesus, and the Afro-Cuban Missionary Society. Reverend Ruiz from the Afro-Cuban Mission didn't speak English, and we trustees voted not to have him back after his sermon in Spanish. Although we feel he is a very fine minister, of course."

"It is all very well to listen skeptically to the faith and beliefs of others," I said solemnly, "as long as you are not influenced away from the basic truths in the Holy Bible."

"Amen!" Dr. Jensen and Brother Linsey said together.

At this moment we were joined at the table by Clyde Caldwell, a thin, narrow-faced Negro with a high sloping forehead and a closely cropped head. His lips were thin, and the corners of his mouth curved sharply downward. His dark eyes were alert and never still as he looked about the cafe. This was a man to watch, I thought. If Caldwell had conducted the majority of the services he had a working knowledge of religion, and he was not a man to get into a theological argument with until I had my feet on the ground. Introductions were made, and Caldwell sat down in the booth next to Jensen, facing me.

"I say it is about time, Reverend Springer," Caldwell said sharply. "I've written no less than seven letters to Abbot Dover requesting a new pastor, and I believe Dr. Jensen has written several letters himself."

"Three." Jensen nodded.

"Have you ever visited the monastery of the Church of God?" I countered.

"No. I work hard six days a week, and on Sunday I worship the Lord."

"Worship is not enough," I said sternly, "you must work for the Lord. Our monastery, gentlemen, is without funds and without monks. At the present time there are no laymen in training for the Church of God's Flock, and the monastery may close, leaving us to our own resources in Florida. To depend on Birmingham, except for the wisdom of their experience, is not feasible. They have their own churches to consider, and there are three in Birmingham, as you know. Where are our new ministers to come from unless we work and work hard? Why isn't there at least one Church of God's Flock in every city and village and hamlet in Florida? Why, indeed? It is because we are not working for God, gentlemen. Abbot Dover, a saintly man, prays daily for the strength to carry on his work, and he is at the end of his tether. Let us pray for the rejuvenation of our church and the increased entry of holy devoted men to our monastery at Orangeville."

I bowed my head and the others followed suit. I steepled my fingers, moved my lips silently for the time it took me to count to one hundred, and then I said, "Amen!"

"Amen!" repeated the three trustees in unison. "And now, gentlemen," I said. "Let's get down to business. Where is my church? Where is my residence, and how much do I get paid?"

We haggled, and we dickered.

Down to practicalities and away from nebulous discussion of religious topics, these were fine, realistic men I was dealing with, and I admired their business sense. There is more to administering a church than meets the eye, and these trustees had been through the mill. The church was a labor of love to these businessmen, but it was also a way to prestige in the Negro community. As the money talk began, with the inevitable haggling, they began to talk to me as a person as well as a minister. Some of the oily veneer of politeness dropped away, and I realized that much of the respect I had enjoyed earlier in our conversation was due to my being a white man in addition to being their new pastor.

After a pleasant hour with figures and the discussion of practicalities, e.g., rent, taxes, upkeep, amortization, etc., I was well pleased with the final settlement we had all agreed upon. My residence, next to the church, was rent free. A combination cook-maid named Ralphine—who was very old, they said, but capable—would clean the house, cook my meals and do my laundry. The trustees would pay her twenty dollars a month, and I was to give her free meals on the days she worked.

My salary, based on church attendance records of the past three years, was to be eighty dollars a month, payable in cash at twenty dollars a week on Sunday night after the evening sermon. Brother

Caldwell asked me if I would rather have the money all at once at the end of each month and I refused, pointing out to him that in a period of three months there are thirteen weeks, not twelve.

In services I was to receive a free haircut from Brother Caldwell once a week if I would agree to have it cut on Thursday. Saturday was his busiest day, and I agreed to Thursday providing I could get a free shave as well. After a brief argument I won my point.

Dr. Jensen generously offered to clean my teeth and give me a free examination of my mouth twice a year. I was grateful for his offer, and I promptly accepted. I never would have thought of that concession.

Jackie, no doubt to salve his conscience about staying open on Sunday, stated that I was welcome to have a free rib or chicken dinner at any time I so desired, and he hoped that I would visit him often. My agreeing with his policy to serve Sunday dinners earlier in our conversation had been a wise move on my part.

In return for my house, my salary and the free services from the board of trustees, I was to preach a two-hour sermon from 9 a.m. to 11 a.m. and an evening service from 7 p.m. to 9 p.m. every Sunday. Also, in the event enough interested students could be found, I was to teach a two-hour Bible class on Friday evenings. Funerals and weddings were left to my own discretion, but the previous fees charged for these important services, Dr. Jensen reminded me, had been ten dollars for weddings and five dollars for funerals. I could plan the elaboration of my services accordingly.

To relieve me from money worries, Brother Caldwell explained, the board of trustees always took charge of the morning and evening offerings and administered all funds collected. They also paid the bills of the church and the utilities on my house. Any expenditures I desired to make had to be cleared first by the trustees, and I was assured that no restrictions were meant or implied by this ruling, but that the rule had proved to be sound in the past, and at the present time there was no reason to change it that any of them could see.

I agreed wholeheartedly, thanked the board for the consideration of my time, and told them that I appreciated their kindness in refusing to load me with time-consuming administrative details. Such time was much better spent in visiting the sick and in the preparation of sermons, I informed them.

We parted amicably, and Dr. Jensen drove me to the Church of God's Flock. The building was a square clapboard box on a small lot next to a Do-It-Yourself laundry. A false-front steeple had been added to the church in front, but there was no bell because there was no belfry. Inside, the church contained benches enough to seat two hundred people, and there was an ancient upright piano next to a choir-box large enough for a choir of ten. A rough cross fashioned from undressed pine logs was nailed to the wall behind the altar, and on the altar itself there was a pewter loving cup and two pewter candelabra holding six candles apiece. The pulpit was a crude affair put together with unpainted knotty pine boards, and there was a large Bible chained to the slanting lectern inside the pulpit. There were six windows on each side of the church, badly in need of cleaning, and overhead light was furnished by a dozen exposed 100-watt bulbs dangling at the ends of cords from the low (for a church) fourteen-foot ceiling.

"At one time, our church was a garage," Dr. Jensen offered, lighting a cigarette.

"No smoking!" I said sternly. "Not in God's house!"

Dr. Jensen left the church immediately, and I followed him out switching off the lights before I closed the double doors behind us. I accepted a cigarette from him, and we took the short well-trodden path across the unkempt lot to the residence provided for the minister. It was quite dark by this time, and Dr. Jensen cautioned me before I climbed the steps to the porch.

"There's a hole in the gallery, Reverend, so watch your step till I get the lights turned on."

After Dr. Jensen opened the door with his key and switched on the lights, I followed him into the house. The light streaming through the front window revealed where several boards had been stripped off the porch leaving a space large enough for a rocking chair to fall through. But I was pleasantly surprised by the size and the appearance of the inside of the little house. There were four rooms, all of equal size; a bathroom-dressing room, a kitchen, a bedroom and a study, all of them furnished with well-worn bargain furniture. The kitchen contained a small refrigerator as well as an electric stove. I examined the bedroom, tested the single Hollywood bed and found it comfortable, and then returned to the study where Dr. Jensen waited for me.

"Well, sir?" he asked apprehensively.

"I am amazed at such opulence," I reassured the president of the board of trustees, "after the severity of my simple monastery cell."

"Good!" Dr. Jensen expelled his breath. "I would like to say something to you, Reverend." The dentist pursed his lips in an enormous pout and frowned. "For myself, I want to say that I am glad you are here. For the others—" he shrugged, "I cannot speak. You will have to prove yourself to them. I am in the throes of a deep personal problem."

He hesitated and I opened my mouth to say something, but he held up his hand. "No, Reverend, I won't burden you at this time, but after you are settled, and when I get to know you better, I will seek your counsel. Although you are undoubtedly a bona fide minister of our church, and I am speaking frankly, you are a white man, and there is an element of distrust deep within me of all white men. Our church has as one of its basic premises to love one another, white or black, but I will have difficulty in overcoming—" Dr. Jensen's face was twisted and distorted and he could not look me in the yes. "I hope I have not offended you, Reverend. I try to be a good man and a true Christian, and I feel that I can speak frankly to you."

"You can, Dr. Jensen," I said. "I am willing to serve the members of my parish twenty-four hours a day. I will be here tonight and every night. When you feel ready to unburden yourself, I will help you with the strength that has been given me by the Lord. And I will pray for you."

"Thank you, Reverend Springer. Again, I am glad that you are here to help lead us out of the wilderness."

We shook hands. I followed the dentist to the door, and as he cautiously dismounted from the porch, I called after him, "Go with God."

Alone in the house I opened all of the windows to let the humid air infiltrate the house. There was a gentle breeze, and the draft between the open window in the bedroom and the open window in the study was cool on my face. I undressed hurriedly, anxious to be rid of the stifling covert suit and, in my underwear, I explored my new quarters thoroughly. There was a slight slope to the floor; the frame building was set on brick columns three feet above the ground, but it was a gentle slant, and I felt that I could learn to live with it. A huge roll-top desk in the study with a swivel chair would be excellent for my work as a writer, and there was a leatherette couch along the wall for horizontal contemplation.

A small bookcase contained two yards of back number *National Geographic* magazines, several Bibles, a *Webster's Collegiate Dictionary*, and seven songbooks containing hymns. There was no thesaurus, and I would have to buy one when I received my first twenty dollars Sunday night. Every professional writer needs a thesaurus.

The barbecue sauce that had been so thickly soaked through the ribs I had eaten for dinner had been very hot, and I kept tasting the sauce in my throat and nose. I fixed a pitcher of ice water, turned out all of the lights, and returned to the desk to study.

As I slowly drank the ice water, a swallow at a time out of the pitcher's spout, I thought vaguely about my wife and wondered how she was making out. Perhaps I could send her ten dollars Sunday? No, she could hardly be helped by such a small amount. Maybe, after a few days, or weeks, she would telephone her mother for bus fare back to Columbus. I hoped so; I felt sorry for her all alone in Miami. But I could hardly bring Virginia to Jax, not after the nice home I had provided for her at Ocean Pine Terraces. . .

I sighed, and took another long swallow of the ice water. There were more important matters to think about than Virginia.

*No. 37. "I wait for the Lord . . . and in His words I do hope."
Psalm 130:5. Good for 1 hour, sometimes 2. Follow with "What
hast thou done?" Genesis 4:10 to fill in till time.*

The above was Sermon No. 37 in a small black notebook I
found in the roll-top desk the next morning after a night of fitful sleep. There were fifty similarly worded sermons in the little
book, and on the last page of the sermon listings there was the
cryptic note, *"Start at the beginning."* I assumed that after fifty
Sundays and fifty sermons, the late Reverend Wannop, my pre-
decessor, started all over again in the notebook, not in the Holy
Bible. Evidently these numbered sermons were all tried and true,
but they didn't help me any. How could I talk for an hour, perhaps two, on "I wait for the Lord . . . and in his words I do hope"
when this great black Bible was as mysterious to me as the original hieroglyphics of the Dead Sea Scrolls?

Oh, it was all very interesting, but this was Friday, and in two
days I had four hours to preach—two in the morning and two
more in the evening. My confidence in the simpleness of being a
preacher was waning fast.

The back screen door slammed, and I turned my head toward
the kitchen. An ancient black crone in a shapeless, dirty red dress
reaching to her ankles, was framed in the doorway. Bent nearly
double, she had to raise her head to look at me, and her gummy
smile revealed a single, yellow upper tooth in the near-center of
an obscenely pink mouth. She cackled thinly, removed a soiled
bandanna from her head. Her head was almost bald, but here
and there a tuft of white, kinky hair stood up crazily.

"Put the bandanna back on your head, woman," I said, closing
my eyes.

"I'm Ralphine, Captain," she stated in an impossibly high
voice, "and I wondered if you was ready for your breakfast or if
you's had it yet."

"Did Dr. Jensen send you?" I asked.

"Yes, sir. And it sure is wonderful to have a man of God in the house again."

"Okay. Fix me something, if there is anything to fix, and if there isn't get something at the grocery store and charge it to me."

Again the cackle, but the bandanna was back in place, and my eyes followed her thin pointing arm to the paper sack on the kitchen table.

"I has done stopped at the store," she said, and then after another meaningless cackle, she backed into the kitchen and began to busy herself with pots, pans and other assorted noises.

I lighted a cigarette and sat back in the swivel chair. Although Ralphine was only being paid five dollars a week by the trustees, I thought they could do better for me than that, but on the other hand, I was a single man in a small house, and a younger, more capable woman might cause talk. I must remember I was a minister at all times!

I returned to my contemplation of the preparation of my sermon and ignored Ralphine and the noises from the kitchen. The more I thought about the sermon, the more complicated my thinking got. How far could I go? The basis of any and all kinds of religion, as I knew them, had as a premise blind and unquestioning belief! First of all you have to believe, whether you were a Christian, a Shintoist, or worshipped a runty tree in the middle of a vast forest. But I was mixed up because I didn't believe in anything, not even in the figures I had added, subtracted, and multiplied so many years as an accountant in Columbus. I knew that figures could be made to lie, and only a clever man could detect the falsehood in the way figures were presented.

But theology, religion, was so complicated and obscure; where could I start? Where could I begin my sermon, where could I lead my parishioners, and how much would they believe of what I told them? Except for a few halfhearted appearances at Unitarian Fellowship meetings, I had never been to church in my life. I believed in nothing, and without believing I had to deliver two two-hour long sermons within two days. That is a lot of talk. As the holy abbot at Orangeville had said, "It is all in the Bible," but I could hardly read from the Bible for four hours straight.

I tried to remember the gist of the few Unitarian sermons I had heard and what the minister had said, but I could not remember any one thought with any clarity. There was a sermon concerning art in our lives that I recalled, all about the influence of modern art on our current civilization. But a sermon on art hardly seemed appropriate for a group of Negroes, and I didn't know any of the individuals I had met so far well enough to feel them out on the subject.

What *did* I believe in? By speaking on my own beliefs, thinly disguised as something else along the Bible party line, perhaps I could inject enough sincerity into my voice to put over a sermon.

Breakfast. A plateful of hot grits, fried white meat, and store-purchased white bread. By mixing some of the grease with my grits and using plenty of salt, the breakfast was excellent. I drank two cups of instant coffee and then hollered for Ralphine to clear away the dishes from my desk. Cackling, she carried the dishes, one at a time, into the kitchen.

"Did you enjoy your breakfast, Captain?" she asked me in her high rickety voice.

"It was fine, Ralphine, but tomorrow, toast the bread and get a stick of margarine at the store."

"Yes, sir." Ralphine wandered into the bedroom with a broom, bent in half, like a miniature bear shambling forward with a load of buck shot in its belly.

Working slowly on a yellow ruled tablet with a soft pencil, I began to write my sermon. The deeper I got into the text, the more I enjoyed it. I was writing again, at any rate, and the stuff was damned interesting. There was the bit from Sartre's *Being and Nothingness* that I remembered, and I elaborated on this theme for a few pages, and then I recalled K's conversation with the priest in Kafka's *The Trial,* and I had a few things to write about that wonderful conversation. For a few minutes my mind blanked out, and then I remembered a fragment of a scene from Henry Miller's *Tropic of Capricorn,* and I wrote down some of my thoughts on Miller's philosophy about money. This was a capital sport, and I enjoyed myself thoroughly, but what was I doing? In my neat, legible handwriting, I had covered two dozen sheets of paper. I reread what I had written and discovered a veritable mishmash; a confused and groping mind, lost indeed insofar as belief in God was concerned. Some of the writing was well done, but there were no references to the Bible. This was the touch my sermon lacked. Laboriously, I rewrote my sermon, and on every other page I inserted into the text a selected passage from the Bible. As a result of these additions, my sermon underwent a miraculous transformation. Such is the power of words, and words in themselves mean nothing. But then, actions meant nothing either, and inasmuch as the people who would attend church and listen to my sermon on Sunday were already believers who were afraid not to believe, my words could not influence them either for harm or for good.

Or so I thought when I reread my doctored sermon. Lunch. String beans, boiled potatoes, cornbread and iced tea. After eating heartily, I took a nap and slept until six that evening.

When I awoke I was in a kind of stupor, and my right arm was numb; I had been sleeping on it all afternoon. I walked about the rooms of the little house shaking my arm to get some feeling back into it. Ralphine was gone, but she had left a potful of mustard greens simmering on the Warm burner of the electric stove, and there was a plateful of cold cornbread on the kitchen table covered with a paper napkin. I nibbled on a piece of cornbread, then took a chair out onto the porch and sat down in the dark. Across the empty lot, black men and women ambled by the church along the sidewalk. Smoking cigarettes and watching the traffic, I noted that not a single white man passed by. There was a streetlight on the corner, and I could see the traffic plainly although nobody could see me in the darkness. I was an alien in this black corner of the world; dark laughter and loud, exuberant conversations floated across the lot from the passersby.

The mosquitoes drove me inside after an hour or so. Turning on the light above the desk, I picked up the Bible and read Revelations over and over again until I got sleepy enough to go to bed.

The sloshing of water awakened me the next morning and, in my underwear I followed the sound into the kitchen and discovered Ralphine washing my two minister shirts in the kitchen sink. Water was boiling on the stove, and I made a cup of instant coffee and silently watched the slow movements of the woman as she scrubbed away at the shirts.

"I'll need one of those shirts for tomorrow," I reminded her, "to preach in."

"They'll be ready, Captain. Do you want your breakfast now?"

"No," I said. "I'll be at the church."

I pulled on my black pants and slipped into my shoes. Having decided not to wear a sport shirt, I left the house in my undershirt and walked across the lot to the church, taking my sermon with me. In the pulpit I faced the empty benches, tried to imagine them full of people, and began to read my sermon aloud. My voice is not strong—it doesn't have much resonance, and it is too high for oratory—but I spoke as loud as I could in order to reach the back wall. The words sounded strange and meaningless to me as they reverberated in the empty building, but I was satisfied that I could at least be heard. With a pencil I underscored various words for emphasis and read straight through my sermon without pause. The moment I finished, I glanced at my watch. Forty minutes. Too short, much too short. I sighed and lit a cigarette. The front door rattled, and I quickly snuffed out the cigarette and put the butt into my pocket as a heavily built Negro woman, dressed in a pair of green slacks and a pink blouse, entered the church followed by six young girls.

"Good morning, Madame," I said, going down the side aisle to meet her, "I am the Right Reverend Deuteronomy Springer. What can I do for you?"

"I'm pleased to meet you, Reverend," the woman boomed, shaking my hand like a man, "I'm Rosie Durrand, Choirmistress." She then introduced me to the six young girls, giving only their first names. The girls were extremely shy and kept their eyes on the floor, and they moved their feet about nervously.

"We have come to practice, Reverend," Miss Durrand said. "But if you is busy and needing the church we can come back later."

"I'm glad you are here," I said hastily. "Very glad. We can go over the program together. In fact, I am overjoyed to know that we have a choir, and I am anxious to hear you sing."

This was indeed a break for me. I needed all of the padding I could get to fill in a two-hour service. With only a short forty-minute sermon prepared, the rest of my service now fell into place. I would begin with a long prayer. I would then call on two or three members in the congregation to lead the rest of us in a prayer. I would have the choir do a few numbers. Then, and only then, would I preach my sermon—and as slowly as possible. The rest of the time remaining I could always alternate with prayers, more songs from the choir, singing by the congregation and announcements. An announcement about the Bible Class, for instance, could take up ten or fifteen minutes. I could extol the virtues of learning the Bible, read and interpret a couple of passages here and there to show what I meant. Two hours would be easy—and for the evening service, I could merely repeat the morning session. . .

I was very happy to see Miss Durrand.

"Do you happen, by chance, Miss Durrand, to have a soloist? A soloist always helps to inspire a congregation to lift up their hearts to God."

Miss Durrand modestly lowered her eyes. "I forgot that you was new, Reverend," she said in rumbling tones, "but I am Rosie Durrand, and I do three sets a night at the Golden Chevel Club. I am also a Deep South Label recording star, and I have appeared on radio in Biloxi and Huntsville and on television, West Palm Beach. By those who are supposed to know, I am on my way up in the field of the blues."

"I'm sorry I haven't heard of you, but as you know Miss Durrand, I am recently arrived from the monastery at Orangeville."

"Yes, sir. That is quite all right." She generously waved her plump hand up and down.

"You don't happen to know, *I Got It Bad*—do you?"

"Of course I knows it! That's an old *Jump For Joy* number."

"Wonderful! How about playing it for me?"

Rosie Durrand sat down at the upright, and after a few flowing bars to flex her wrists, she sang the song hard and slow, bringing her voice up from below the belt. Her deep voice was feminine all right, but it was so thick and powerful it reminded me of Paul Robeson trying to sing falsetto and failing. As soon as she finished the song, I applauded, and so did the young choir girls. The clapping of small hands snapped me to a bit.

"Ahem," I said, "perhaps we'd better get on with the choir practice. But I did enjoy your song. When you finish, will you please leave a list of the songs you're going to do, and in the correct order, on the pulpit stand."

"I sure will, Reverend," Rosie said. "Do you have any favorites?"

"No, Miss Durrand. The selection of music is in your hands. And may God bless you."

I hustled back to my house with the sermon clutched to my

chest, and ate breakfast. After making a few notes to use on my Bible Class selling spiel, I shaved and donned my black suit and straw floater. At the door I informed Ralphine that she could go home as soon as she finished my laundry, and that I was dining out that evening. The closeness of the little house was beginning to stifle me, and I wanted to get out and meet my public.

There was no special name for this area of Jax where the Negroes lived; maybe the white people called it Niggertown, I did not know, but the residents of this large section of the city merely called it Jax. I did not know how to measure the size of a "parish," and I had been calling the members of my church "parishioners" for want of a better name. I liked the way it sounded. But since I officiated at the only Church of God's Flock in Jax, the entire city was my parish. However, on a more practical basis, I decided that the people residing within a ten-block area, within walking distance of the church, were my real churchgoers, and I greeted everyone I met on my walk with a cheery good afternoon or a "Bless you child," if the figure was less than three feet in height.

At each barbershop, drugstore, filling station, notion shop, furniture store, cafe, shoeshine stand, fortune teller, bolita stand, and other business establishment, I entered and introduced myself to the owner (if he was there) and the sales people and invited them to attend church on the morrow. I covered the neighborhood, less private dwellings and apartment houses, and everywhere I entered I was treated with great courtesy. The promises of my parishioners to attend church were very gratifying. The afternoon sped quickly by, and at six in the evening I was tired, hot, footsore and on my way home, and grateful that Jackie's Bar-B-Cue was only two blocks away from my residence. I entered the airconditioned cafe, greeted Jackie cordially, and ordered two whole barbecued chickens, a side order of macaroni salad, and a pitcher of iced tea—on the house, of course. After eating the marvelous meal, I table-hopped and invited each group of diners to church. I entered the kitchen and exacted promises from the help to attend church, shook hands with Jackie at the door, accepted a twenty-five cent cigar from him, and returned home. I stripped off my coat, sat in a rocker on the damaged front porch, and smoked the cigar. I was pleased with my afternoon's work; I had made myself known, and I had entered into the spirit of being a minister.

What more could any good minister do?

SUNDAY DAWNED THICKLY humid, sickeningly hot and overcast with a greenish-black haze, the aftermath of a big overtime night at three sawmills. I had awakened at five and, after trying for ten impossible minutes to go back to sleep, I quit fighting and got up and dressed. My collar was tight—the shirt had shrunk a full inch under Ralphine's halfhearted laundering— and the thick covert cloth trousers covered my thin legs like sheets of lead. For the first time in my life I drank iced coffee for breakfast. I was much too edgy to sit still and wait for nine-thirty. To fill in time I took a broom out of the kitchen closet, walked across the lot to the church and swept the floor clean enough to suit me, and I returned to the house for a bucket of hot water and a mop. Mopping away down the center aisle, I was surprised by a hefty, tightly corseted woman carrying an armload of lilies. The woman was the color of wet gray ashes, and she wore a broad-brimmed straw hat embroidered with red and yellow flowers.

"You drop that mop right now, Reverend Springer!" She ordered, and in surprise, I did as I was told. "I never heard of such a thing," she continued. "Here. Take these lilies and put 'em in water. I'll take care of that floor!"

"I beg your pardon?"

"Go fill those buckets with water, and put these lilies on t'other side of the altar."

Pouting with her upper lip only (this isn't easy), she grabbed the mop and began to swab the floor vigorously. In a closet by the front door I found two metal pails with green crepe paper wound tightly around the handles, and after filling them at the tap outside, I arranged the lilies on either side of the altar. They brightened the church considerably.

"The floor's good enough, Mrs.—?"

"Mrs. Kern. And I'll decide when it's good enough. I think it's a shame for a man of the cloth to scrub floors! Those windows needs washing too, and you better appoint a committee to clean this church every week, and if you don't, I will!"

At the door she gave the floor one more vicious swipe, emptied the water into a gallberry bush beside the steps, and put mop and bucket into the closet.

"Thank you, Mrs. Kern. For both your help and the lilies. They are beautiful. I am the Right Reverend Springer."

"I know. My husband said you stopped by his place of business yesterday. And he said you will get flowers every Sunday from him."

"Oh, yes," I said. "Kern's Funeral Parlor and Special Ambulance Service."

"Yes, sir. My husband has the only white Cadillac hearse in Jax, and it's in great demand. Mr. Kern is a minister, too, you know."

"No, I didn't know."

"Yes, he's been ordained for twelve years—the Church of Jesus's Rock. They don't have that church in Jax anymore, and we both attend the Church of God's Flock now."

"I'm glad," I said. "But the main thing is to love God, no matter which church you attend, Mrs. Kern."

"Amen!"

Evidently Mrs. Kern was dissatisfied with the way I had arranged the lilies and fern, because she rearranged them herself. I returned to the house and got my coat, and then smoked a cigarette on the porch of the church, where I was soon joined by Dr. Jensen.

"I thought I'd come down early, Reverend," Dr. Jensen said, "and sort of introduce you to the folks as they arrive."

"Fine. I appreciate it."

"I heard about you going around the neighborhood yesterday, Reverend, and it was a mighty fine way to do. You'll have a big crowd today, but next week it might be a different story. Folks'll be wanting to take a look at you today because you're new, but if you want 'em back next week, you will have to—pardon the expression, Reverend—give 'em hell."

"I am aware of my ministerial functions, Dr. Jensen."

I shook a lot of hands in the next half hour and met many people. They approached the steps shyly, the men with their hats in hand and in light Sunday suits of orlon, Dacron, seersucker, cord, and Palm Beach cloth with white shirts and gay ties. The women were shyer yet, in silks and nylons, but all shook my hand and welcomed me to Jax. There was no Sunday school setup for the Church of God's Flock, and a great many children attended church with their parents—little girls in white, with tightly wrapped pigtails, and little boys in plaid or solid-colored shorts with white shirts—glistening black faces, wide-eyed and well-behaved. I smiled broadly at everyone until my jaws hurt. I patted the little boys upon their closely cropped skulls. It was a relief to see Rosie Durrand climb the steps; I broke away from the crowd around me with an excuse about the music and followed Miss Durrand to the piano. The choir girls were in place, and I told Miss Durrand to have them sing their first number, *Come To The Church In The Wildwood*, when I gave her the signal. She nodded and began to play the piano softly. I entered the pulpit, bowed my head and closed my eyes. I stood in this position, arms akimbo, for three minutes, moving my lips silently and meaninglessly. I heard the shuffling and rustling and muted whispering, but I was astounded when I opened my eyes and saw the size of the congregation. Every bench was tightly packed; there was a sizeable group in the back of the church standing against the wall and blocking the open double-doors. Fans of palm straw whished back and forth in the still air, flies droned, and there was an overwhelming odor of dark perspiration, deodorant sticks, shaving lotion and musk. I held up a hand for absolute silence, got it, and prayed:

"Dear God, open Your gates and let us sinners in. There is room in Your Heart for us all. Please. Let us in!"

"Amen!" The reply surged forth from the packed house, an uncontrolled spontaneous roar. Shaken, I signaled Miss Durrand and sat down in a straight chair beside the altar. I don't know what I expected, but the sound of that multi-tongued voice scared the hell out of me.

The voices of the all-girl choir were husky, tremulous, and sweet. Miss Durrand's left hand was firm and powerful, and her rhythm was strong. The hymn was a good opener—"*Come, come, come, come, come, to the Church in the Wildwood, come to the church in the dale!*" I tapped my foot and hummed a bit until the song ended.

Standing in the pulpit again, my eyes searched and found the sloping head of the barber trustee, Clyde Caldwell. "Brother Caldwell," I said, "will you lead us in prayer?"

A pleased smile formed on Caldwell's thin lips, and he made his way from the center of the bench to the aisle where he kneeled, steepled his fingers, and rolled his eyes up to the ceiling. He prayed aloud, rapidly and confidently in a clipped voice, repeating key phrases again and again. The meaning of his prayer was as private as an abstract by Mondrian, and just as clean. ". . . washed in the blood of the lamb . . . the forces of good . . . washed in the blood of the lamb . . . worship in the holy temple of truth. . .washed in the blood of the lamb . . . sweet Jesus . . . that glorious day in Bethlehem . . . washed in the blood of the lamb . . . and that little baby, and those three wise men, and all washed in the blood of the lamb." This interminable prayer went on and on, punctuated occasionally by a member of the congregation shouting fervently, "Amen!" or "Oh, yes, Jesus!" But it was a time killer, and I let Brother Caldwell ramble on; evidently the audience enjoyed the prayer.

Finished at last, Caldwell shouted, "Amen!" and resumed his seat. His Amen was loudly echoed by the faithful. I returned to the pulpit and signaled Miss Durrand to play. The choir sang the first verse of *Onward, Christian Soldiers*. I figured that everyone knew this song, and so I shouted for the congregation to rise and join the second chorus. The little church rocked to the combined voices, and I kept the beat with a forefinger. The song ended, everyone sat down and looked at me expectantly, and I began my sermon.

"Franz Kafka was born on July the third, 1883, in Prague, and he died in the Kierling Sanatorium near Vienna in 1924. Today, thirty-some-odd years later, his effects on religious theory are still being felt in our day-to-day living. Who can read *The Trial* and blithely ignore his own tribulations? Who can read *The Castle* and still aspire to the heights of fame, glory and money without trembling? Lo, he goeth by me, and I see him not; he passeth on also, but I perceive him not.

"Kafka had a great, overwhelming, undeniable, unshakable pity for all mankind. And he expressed his pity in every line he wrote, in his every living gesture, and in the very fabric of his personal life. He loved mankind with the unselfish love that can only be given by the truly humble. 'If the scourge slay suddenly, he will laugh at the trial of the innocent.'

"Here was a simple man, and yet a complex man, a profound man who wrote like a child from the bottom of his heart. And in his writings there is a lesson for us all. There is no secret cabbala in the writings of Franz Kafka, merely basic truths that will set us free and allow us the humility we all seek. 'I will instruct thee and teach thee in the way that thou shalt go.'"

And so on for three more paragraphs. And then I stopped in the middle of a sentence. The silence chilled me to the inner marrow of my bones. My words were sailing over the heads of the congregation like a lost cloud. If I had thought that Brother Caldwell's prayer contained a private meaning, what was my sermon if it was not my own private meaning of my interpretation of what I conjectured life to be? Again I complicate matters, because I am mixed-up, confused, and leery of almost any thought that mental probing reveals.

Who was I to release my private thoughts to this innocent audience? They had crowded into this hot, miserable little church, decked out in their Sunday finery, for only one reason: Entertainment. And I was trying to make them think! How unfair of me, how unlike a minister of the gospel! The silence lengthened, and I turned in desperation to Miss Durrand.

"There will now be a solo by Miss Rosie Durrand." I abruptly left the pulpit, sat down and buried my face in my hands. Miss Durrand's voice rose in song, a spiritual I had never heard before, a crooning, lonesome wailing, deep-throated and devout. I closed my mind and drifted with the rise and fall of her deep voice and, when the song ended, I rushed to the edge of the raised platform and pointed my finger at a woman in the first row.

"You are a sinner!" I screamed.

"Yes, Lord!" she replied.

Following this pattern I pointed first at one and then another, repeating my accusation at the top of my shrill voice. In each case I got an immediate, frightened reply. Once I pointed at a child by mistake, and the poor little boy began to cry, and so did his mother. Leaving my vantage point and retreating behind the pulpit, I exclaimed, "We are all sinners before the Lord! And if we don't accept Jesus Christ as our Lord and Savior and wash ourselves in the blood of the innocent lamb, we will go to Hell!"

"Amen!"

"Yes, Lord!"

"Amen!"

"Oh, God, yes!"

"Save me, Lord!"

"Amen!"

"God save me, Lord!"

"Amen!"

"Amen!"

"Yes, Lord!"

"Amen!"

The scattered responses began to come.

And I continued.

"You love the devil! Yes, you do! I see fat men and fat women. You are gluttons, and gluttons cannot be saved! I see women with silk upon their backs and silk upon their legs. You are vain and you cannot be saved! I see men with rings on their fingers and gold in their teeth. You are acquisitive men, and you cannot be saved! I see children who have sinned against themselves in their secret beds. You are masturbators, and you cannot be saved! I see lust in the eyes of men and women and in the hearts of you young women, and you cannot be saved! I see everywhere in this church a mistrust of neighbors, a hate for constituted authority, a greediness of mind and body and soul and heart, and a love for the devil! Moviegoers, smokers, television watchers, and impure and evil thinkers! You don't love Jesus! You love the devil!"

I turned my back on the congregation and folded my arms.

"No! We love Jesus!" a frightened feminine voice stated.

I turned and faced them, lowered my voice to a whisper. "Are you willing to accept Jesus Christ as your Master?"

"Yes, Lord!"

"Oh, Yes!"

"God, yes!"

"Please, yes!"

I continued to berate the congregation. I called everything I could think of a sin against the Lord, from betting on dogs to the buying of bolita tickets, from wanting more money in pay envelopes to the failure to provide for wives and children and small animals. I listed the forbidden drinks, from 3.2 beer to 100-proof moonshine, and then I started all over again on vicious personal attacks, pointing an accusing finger at different men and women and accusing them of anything that came into my head. When I finished ticking off a sinner, I asked him if he accepted the Lord as his Savior. Not once did I get a negative reply.

As I shouted my face got hot, and I could feel a river of perspiration flow down my back. I thought of a ruse to get rid of my heavy coat.

"The devil has climbed upon our backs, and we must fight him off!" With that statement I stripped off my coat and threw it to the floor. I kicked the garment to one side. "We must fight the devil tooth and nail, with every fiber of every God-given muscle and with every strand of our hair! We must fight the devil in the caves of iniquity, in our homes, in our kitchens, on the streets, and on the beaches and on the high seas. We must band together in a mighty army of the Lord! Will you join me in this fight? Will you?"

"Will you?"

Again the responses were strong and loud. Now that I was rid of the heavy coat, I cooled off somewhat, and I lowered my voice to start all over again.

"Let me tell you a story, a story that happened only last night, Saturday night, the most devilish night in the week. A young man, now in this temple, and I will not name him, he knows who he is. A young man with money in his pocket last night, who now has nothing but sins upon his conscience for his evilness. He dressed in outrageous finery and left his home of honest, God-fearing parents last night, and his first stop on the road to Hell was a liquor store. He bought a bottle of gin. He was sober, and this evil bothered him not. He next bought a package of cigarettes. But this wasn't all. No, this sinner had other nasty thoughts upon his evil mind. He called upon a young girl, a young, sweet innocent girl of sixteen, and told her they were going to the movies. Did they go to the movies? No, they didn't. They went instead to a forest of piney woods. He tricked this young girl. He gave her a cigarette, and this innocent young girl accepted it. He offered her gin, and she drank. They sat in this quiet place and, instead of thanking the Lord for the beauty of the night, they smoked cigarettes and drank gin. But that wasn't all. Oh, no, not at all! He put his hands upon the breasts of this young girl and kissed her full upon her sweet, innocent mouth. But it wasn't a chaste or friendly kiss. Oh, no, not at all! They kissed and they drank gin and they smoked cigarettes, and then they removed all their clothes. Oh yes, they did! But they did not remove their clothes because the night was warm! Oh, no! They removed their clothes because they wanted to sin and love the devil! And they did! He kissed her all over her secret body, and she returned his kisses! And again they drank gin and smoked cigarettes and sinned, and sinned again and again until the devil had taken full possession of their bodies and their faculties and their hearts! This young man and this young woman are now in this church pretending to love God, but they do not! They have turned their backs on God and have given themselves to the devil!

"But they can be saved. All of you can be saved if you give yourself to your Lord and Master, Jesus Christ our Savior, who gave His life so that you could be saved! Yes, He gave His own life for you, and you must only give up your love of the devil to repay your Lord. Who will be saved? Who will march down the aisle to truth? Who will give himself to Jesus? Who will worship the Lord and forsake the devil? Who will come forward and take me by the hand and say, "Reverend Springer, I have seen the light, and I want to be saved!' Will you? Will you? Will you?" And I pointed my accusing finger.

"I will!"

"Oh, yes!"

"Let me love the Lord!"

"Yes, sweet Jesus!"

"I am a sinner, Reverend!"

"Let me be saved!"

"All right," I said, "I will accept your promises in the Lord's name. Form a line down this aisle and come down and shake my hand. After you shake my hand, continue around in front and up the other aisle and return to your seat. When all have been saved, and you are back in your places, turn and congratulate your neighbor by kissing him or her upon the cheek and by shaking hands. I do not want any man, woman, or child to leave this church without giving himself to our dear, sweet Jesus! If there is one man, woman, or child left who has the devil inside him, I will drive the devil out before I let that sinner leave the church! Now, come and give yourself to your Lord and Master and Savior!"

I held out my arm and shook hands firmly as the parade down the aisle began. There was noise, excitement, shouting, crying, mumbling and muttering and unintelligible speaking, but not one person in the church failed to shake my hand, including Rosie Durrand with the tears flowing down her cheeks and the frightened young choir girls. All of this business took some time, but after the group settled down somewhat and had returned to their places, I announced a hymn, and we all sang *I Waited For The Lord*, led by Miss Durrand's deep voice in lieu of a soprano, the rest of the congregation chiming in on the chorus. The strong, faithful, musical voices filled the room with song. And it was very beautiful. When the song was over, I gave a final, short prayer:

"Lead us, O Lord, into the light, and guide us through the week, and help us every day in every way to lead better, cleaner, holier lives. Amen."

"Amen!"

Following my final prayer, Dr. Jensen and Jackie Linsey each took an aisle and passed small wicker breadbaskets back and forth along the benches for the offering. When they had completed the canvassing of the standees, Dr. Jensen waved to me from the back door, and I stated: "There will be an evening service tonight at seven-thirty." As I left the pulpit I remembered that I had forgotten to mention the proposed Bible classes, but I was too tired to return for the announcement. I could do that little bit at the evening service. . .

As the members left the church, I shook hands again, standing on the porch, and accepted compliments right and left.

"You are a real sin-shouter, Reverend Springer."

"An inspiring sermon, Reverend."

"I don't know when I've enjoyed a sermon more."

"Wonderful. Simply wonderful."

Everyone had something nice to say, and they were sincere besides. Why not? They felt good, clean, washed in the blood of the lamb. I answered each compliment with the reminder, "I'll see you tonight at the evening service."

After the last member had departed, Dr. Jensen lingered and congratulated me warmly. "Inspiring, Reverend Springer. Your sermon was a joy to behold and listen to. Would you like to come home to dinner with me?"

"No, thanks," I said. "I'm exhausted and believe I'll take a little nap. But thank you very much."

"All right, sir. But there's plenty, in case you change your mind. I'll talk to you tonight."

I was exhausted. Every muscle in my body ached. As I walked across the lot, my coat over my arm, I staggered slightly with weariness. Ralphine had not put in an appearance at either the house or the church, so I assumed it was her day off. Under a faulty trickly shower, I let cold water pour over me for fifteen or twenty minutes, slipped into my shorts and flopped on the bed. My head missed the pillow; I reached for it and fell asleep before my hand touched it.

The sound of feminine voices filtered into my head, and I sat up suddenly, looked at my watch. Five o'clock. I had slept through the entire afternoon, and I could hear women talking, their muffled voices coming through the closed bedroom door. I had a headache from not eating, and my stomach growled. I slipped into my shirt and trousers and padded barefoot into the study. Mrs. Kern, Miss Rosie Durrand and a woman I identified as Mrs. Linsey from an introduction that morning were grouped smilingly around the kitchen table, which they had brought out into the study. A clean white tablecloth, a candlestick and lighted candle, and a small blue bowl of tiny red pintas decorated the table; and by a single place setting, there was a foot-high heap of fried chicken, a bowl of potato salad, and a glistening cut-glass cupful of lemon-colored jello.

"Well, now," I said pleasantly. "What's all this?"

"We brought you some dinner, Reverend," Mrs. Linsey said, following up her statement with a short happy laugh.

"That's very nice of you ladies," I said, and I sat down at the table. Miss Durrand pushed the chair under me a little bit closer to the table.

"Thank you, Miss Durrand," I said, grabbing a chicken thigh and salting it, "I wanted to see and talk to you before the evening service anyway—about the music." I smiled at the other two women.

"I done wrote out a list and put it on your desk, Reverend," Miss Durrand said.

"Thank you. Thank you very much."

"We'd better go on out and let the man eat." Mrs. Kern said sharply. "The coffee's on the stove, Reverend."

The three women left by the front door, and I did as well as I could by the chicken and the potato salad, which was very well indeed, poured a cup of coffee, and smoked a cigarette. It was time to be thinking about the evening sermon. I moved over to the desk with my coffee, opened the Bible to *Revelations* and began to make notes.

It hardly seemed possible but, if anything, the evening congregation was larger than the crowd that had attended in the morning. In the face of good Sunday evening television programs, such attendance was remarkable. But I was far from being overjoyed. Another performance like the one I had given that morning would lay me out for a week. And I didn't intend to go through that experience again, not until next Sunday morning anyway.

Clyde Caldwell was sitting in the front row with his wife, and he looked at me eagerly and expectantly as I entered the pulpit, so I nodded to him and announced: "Brother Caldwell will lead us in an opening prayer."

Again Caldwell rattled off his staccato, repetitious prayer with many "washed in the blood of the lambs" and, when he had finished, I pointed to Miss Durrand. The girls sang sweetly to her pounding piano and, when they finished two hymns, I began my sermon.

The Revelation was written by St. John The Divine. If he were alive today he would probably be classified as a schizophrenic, but there is some good writing in that book. The members of my church didn't have such a wonderful life, here on earth, particularly in Jax. They were all hardworking people, sweating for every dime, and they lived in a substandard section of the city. And they believed in the Bible. This belief was important to them, and I thought that if I could tell them about a better life to come, after their death, maybe they would feel a little better about the life they were leading on earth. Why not? St. John's revelations, however, are too ancient for present day use, and I updated them in my sermon.

"*And God shall wipe away all tears from their eyes, and there shall be no more death, neither sorrow, nor crying, neither shall there be any more pain: for the former things are passed away.*

"How does that sound? This morning, in all sincerity, many of you in this church came forth willingly and shook my hand, stating that you were saved; that you accepted Jesus Christ as your Lord and Savior. You who have been saved are the most fortunate of God's flock, for you shall have everlasting life. Nobody would want life on this globe of terror, pestilence and suffering. Who would want to work at a sawmill or mow lawns or sweep the dirt from the streets forever and forever into eternity?

"But those who are saved do not really perish. The saved are lifted to Heaven, and God personally wipes the tears away from their eyes. How fortunate you are to have such a kind and benevolent God. If you have sinned, you need but repent and give yourself to the glory that is God's, and your reward is everlasting life at God's right hand!

"You will work no more. You will cry no more. Every pleasure shall be yours forever. Your loved ones will be with you, and your enemies will be destroyed. To eat, you only need to open the freezer compartment door, and it will be filled at all times. You will sleep on clouds of downy softness. If you want to, you can sleep for a month—deep, dreamless sleep—and awake refreshed. Should you want the sunlight, it shall be yours. Should you want love, it shall be yours. And there are no time payments. You make your payments on earth, and your rewards shall be given to you in Heaven. Will your name be in the Golden Book? Only you can put it there. But it will be there if you accept God."

I talked for about an hour and, using my novelist's imagination, I put out the good word about the afterlife. The big cars, the free barbecues, the free jukeboxes, the colorful raiment, and so on; and as I got deeper into the sermon, my imagination really soared. But I spoke quietly and didn't try to frighten anyone. All in all, it was a fairly successful extemporaneous sermon.

Following my sermon, Dr. Jensen and Brother Linsey collected the offering, we sang some group hymns, and I made a brief announcement about a men's Bible class I was starting the following Friday evening, inviting all who were interested to attend.

If this congregation of mine really believed, they should have all gone home that night with a big spiritual lift. I felt empty and envied them their blind, unreasoning belief.

Dr. Jensen accompanied me to my residence, and I reheated the coffee and accepted twenty dollars from him in one-dollar bills. I shoved the money into my pocket, removed my coat, and poured two cups of coffee.

"There's some cold chicken left, if you want some, Dr. Jensen," I said.

"No, thanks, Reverend. Actually," he hesitated, "I have a weighty problem on my mind, but it's very difficult to put into words."

"I am at your service." I didn't intend to make it easy for him. I wanted him to leave. I was emotionally and physically exhausted. This Sunday, with the two long services, had been more work than I had done in a year. I wasn't used to such work, and to tell lies, like I had done, one on top of the other, with a straight face, and a sincere manner, was not the easiest thing in the world to do. Maybe, with patience, I would be able to skim right on along, but this was only my first day, and it had been a terrible day.

"You may have noticed, Reverend," Dr. Jensen said modestly, "that I am not an uneducated man. I have been to college, and I have also been to dental school in Macon. I couldn't bring myself to marry beneath me, and I didn't. I married the daughter of another dentist in Macon. A respectable man and, by our standards, a man who was fairly well-to-do. Although I am twenty-two years older than my wife, Merita, Dr. Wells was happy to have me as his son-in-law. You haven't met my wife; she will not attend church, and there are times when I believe that she does not accept the Lord. These are strong words, but after more than three years of marriage, we still do not have any children. I believe that God is punishing us, Reverend, and that He is denying us children because of Merita's refusal to accept God as her Lord and Savior."

"That may well be so," I said, sipping my coffee. "God's ways are often mysterious."

"Exactly. Another thing. Merita was trained as a dental assistant by her father, and she helped him in his office on a full time basis. Naturally I thought that she would help me in my office, too, after our marriage. Such has not been the case. She says now she is married, and her place is in the home. Not since we left Macon has she entered my new office here. If she had children to look after, I wouldn't want her in the office as my assistant. But she doesn't have any children, and she sits around all day reading confession magazines and doesn't do much of anything."

"I see. What do you want me to do about it?"

"I want you to talk to her, Reverend. Pray for her and get her to accept the Lord. I am not getting any younger, and I want to have children before I die. If you can talk her into attending church, and if she were to hear one of your inspiring sermons, I believe we would be happy together in a religious household."

"All right. I'll talk to her."

"God bless you, sir. I hesitated to ask you about this at first. I was waiting for you to get settled and so on, but I am a very unhappy man, and I couldn't wait much longer."

"That's quite all right."

Dr. Jensen reached into his inside coat pocket and removed a folded sheaf of foolscap papers. He handed the papers to me, and I looked at a listing of handwritten names and addresses.

"These are the names and addresses of our church members," he said, "in case you want to visit them. I have made a red mark by the names of those who haven't been to church in some time, and I believe you will find it to our advantage to visit these people."

"Thank you, Doctor," I said wearily. "And now if you don't mind, I'd better get to bed."

"Good night, Reverend. Again let me congratulate you on both of your sermons. I feel so much better since I have talked to you."

I opened the front door. "Go with God." I let the dentist out into the night.

Dr. Jensen was turning out to be a weird cat. What did he expect me to do about his wife? If he wasn't having any children, it wasn't God's fault. The old man was probably impotent but, like most men in that situation, he hadn't checked with a doctor. It was easier to pass the blame onto his wife. I would talk to her anyway. He was a trustee, and talk was cheap. I tossed the roster of the church members on my desk and sat down in the swivel chair. I wasn't sleepy, but I was bone tired. Feeling the way I did, I knew it would take me a day or two to recover from my all day ordeal. How much writing could I do if I felt this tired? To top it off, I would have to visit Mrs. Jensen and a couple of dozen other delinquent churchgoers on the list. I would have to get out in the neighborhood again and talk the good churchgoers into continued attendance. I would have to prepare two more sermons for next Sunday, and I also had to prepare a couple of hours of instruction for a Friday night Bible class. What time would I have left to do my own writing in the event I could think of something to write about? I was feeling discouraged when I heard the sound of fingernails scratching on the front door.

The scratching sound came again, and I opened the door and switched on the porch light at the same time. There was a young Negro standing there, and a young girl was standing directly behind him, peering fearfully over his shoulder. He wore a bright sport shirt, a pair of faded blue denim jeans and white tennis shoes. The girl was wearing a white ballerina length dress and carried a pair of open-toed slippers in her left hand.

"What do you want, boy?" I asked wearily.

"Could we talk to you a minute, Reverend?" the boy asked huskily.

"I suppose so. Come in."

"I'll wait out here," the girl whispered.

"No you won't," I ordered. "Come in. Both of you. Now what do you want this time of night?"

"We want to get married," he said, a hint of defiance in his voice.

"Married? How old are you?"

"Sixteen."

"I see. How old are you?" I asked the girl.

She put her shoes on the floor and, steadying herself by holding on to the boy's shoulder, she slipped her bare feet into them. I waited and finally she managed to whisper, "I'm sixteen, too."

"Don't you two think you're a little young to be getting married?"

The boy shook his head, stared at the floor. "Not after what you said about us this morning. We figure that's about the only way we can get right with God."

I remembered what he was talking about. Evidently my imaginary story in the morning sermon had found a mark.

"Did you have carnal relations with this girl last night?"

"Yes, sir."

I took a firm grip on the girl's arm. "Did you know, little sister," I said softly, "that you could go to Hell for such carrying on?"

She began to cry, great big blubbery tears. The boy shook her shoulder and said: "Hush! We's going to make it all right with the Lord."

"No," I said. "What's done is done. But you're both too young to be getting married. The only thing for you to do, Sonny, is to join my Bible class next Friday night and make atonement for your sins. And you, young lady, you had better get down on your knees every night and pray for your wanton soul!"

She really began to cry then, and I was surprised that such a big sound could shake loose from such a frail figure.

"The best thing for you two to do, I suppose, is to keep away from each other from now on. That way you won't be tempted to stray from God's path. However, in case she gets pregnant—"

"She won't do that, Reverend," the boy broke in hastily, "I used me a safety."

"In that case, you just keep it in your pockets from now on. And if I ever hear about this kind of goings-on between you two again, I'm going to give your names out in church. Right out loud for everybody, do you hear?"

"Yes, sir. But we're trying to do right. I'm ready to marry her."

"You don't have to get married. Just promise you'll be good from now on."

"I promise," he said.

The girl dropped to her knees and grabbed my hand. "Please don't tell my daddy on me, Reverend!" she said through her tears. "I won't do it again!"

"In that case," I opened the door. "Go with God." I ushered them out and put a fresh pot of coffee on the electric burner.

Jesus, dear sweet Jesus!

THE NEXT MORNING, Monday and a new week, I sat around in my shorts drinking iced coffee after breakfast and pondering my new profession. I was not nearly as tired as I had thought I would be, and after thinking over the events of the preceding day, I realized that—on the whole—I had been quite successful. My spirits were high, and I had a warm feeling inside my chest.

Naturally, I didn't feel as elated as when I had first received the bound copy of my novel, but that had been my first taste of success. My new success as a minister, however, was something else again. An alien field and a difficult assignment, and I had conquered it. As any book on management states, ". . . the happiest employee is the man who has a feeling of personal worth." This is the feeling I had. Whether I had intended to make people happy or not, I had made a lot of people happy by my rabid morning sermon, and I had made more people happy in the evening by giving them something to think about, something to dream about when their trials and tribulations were piled unbearably high. What difference did it make that I personally believed in nothing I had said? Abbot Dover had been right when he had told me that the most successful ministers believed the least. A great man, Abbot Dover.

Of course, I had many things to do in the next few weeks, and I wouldn't get much writing done, but on the other hand, wasn't I meeting people and having experiences I could write about later? Of course. Sitting for a full year in the ivory tower at Ocean Pine Terraces had put me out of contact with people. Readers want to read about people, not things. I would get back to writing, all in good time. And I would be a better writer for my experience. Indubitably.

Taking up the membership roster on my desk, I filled a notebook with the names and addresses of delinquent members and set out on my rounds. The morning sun was blistering, and my black suit was smothering me. I was bringing lost lambs back to the fold.

The first name on my list merely said, *Tom the Ragman, (alley behind the Afro Hotel)*. The hotel was easy to find; it was located on Jefferson Avenue, and the exterior was painted a violent purple. A vertical neon sign perched on a narrow marquee in front of the main entrance spelled out AFRO HOTEL in glowing, alternating green and red letters. I entered the shabby lobby, continued down the hall and let myself out the back door into the alley. Catty corner from the back entrance and across the alley, there was a ramshackle two-car garage and, in the interior, was my errant sinner—Tom, an aged Negro engaged in the tying of bundles of newspaper.

I removed my straw floater as I entered the garage and said: "Are you Tom the Ragman?"

"Yes, sir!" the old Negro said courteously. He shuffled closer until he was less than two feet away from me. "What do you want with old Tom?" he asked defensively. "I ain't done nothin'."

"I don't want you, Tom," I said. "God wants you. Jesus Christ has you on his list as an unrepentant sinner. Yesterday I looked for you in church and couldn't find you. Why have you forsaken God, Tom?"

"I didn't know the Church of God's Flock had a new minister, Reverend. Otherwise I would have been there, right up in front."

"You're lying, Tom. Everyone in this section of Jax knows of my arrival, including you."

"Seems to me I did hear something about it, Reverend. But I suppose it slipped my mind." He began to whine. "I'm an old man, Reverend, and I don't see so good, and I don't remember so good. . ."

"That's why I came to see you, Tom. You're an old man and you haven't accepted Jesus Christ as your Lord and Savior. You have many evil sins upon you, and you must be washed clean in the blood of the lamb. I'll pray for you, Tom, and I'll expect to see you in church next Sunday."

"I'll be there, Reverend, don't worry. You can look for me next Sunday, and I'll be there. Thank you for reminding me, Reverend."

I was wasting my time with Tom the Ragman. He was too far gone to be saved. Tom would have promised anything to get rid of me. Why badger the poor old devil?

"Goodbye, Tom. If I can help you in any way, you let me know now, hear?"

"Yes, sir, Reverend. I sure will."

"God loves you, Tom."

"I know he does, Reverend. God loves all of us and watches every sparrow."

I left the old man to his newspapers and reentered the hotel. The hotel clerk had missed my entrance through the front door, but his eyes widened when he saw me enter the lobby from the rear hallway. I strode purposely to the desk.

"What's your name?" I asked the clerk. He was a young man, the color of anthracite, flamboyantly attired in a solid-blue shirt, a yellow tie and a yellow-and-black tattersall vest.

"Toby Harris, Reverend," he said politely. "What can I do for you, sir?"

"I understand you have girls in this hotel," I announced casually.

"Oh, no, Reverend!" He was obviously lying, and his dark eyes rolled up in his head, giving his fat round face a mock piety.

"I've heard differently," I said. "And I want it stopped. The Afro Hotel is a veritable den of iniquity. Where's the manager?"

"He ain't in now, Reverend. I don't know when he'll be back."

"You tell him I want to see him at church. And that goes for you, too."

"Yes, sir. I'll tell him."

"See that you do."

"Yes, sir. I won't forget."

I examined the magazines in the rack next to the desk, pulled out a well-known national publication featuring a semi-nude photograph on the cover.

"Does the manager of the Afro Hotel sanction this kind of trash?" I threw the magazine on the desk. "Or this?" I tossed another lurid magazine on the desk. "Or this?" I found another sensational magazine.

"Oh, no sir, Reverend!" the clerk replied piously. "I don't know how them magazines got in our rack. The man who brought them last night must have made a mistake."

"I don't like to see magazines like this," I said sternly. "They inflame the passions and thwart the soul. Do you think Jesus would read magazines like this? Well? Do you?"

"No, sir. He sure wouldn't!" Sweat was pouring from the clerk's face. He vaulted the desk clumsily and began to gather all of the magazines from the rack, piling them onto the desk in confusion. I'll get rid of these right away, Reverend."

"See that you do!"

As he emptied the rack, I left abruptly, turned right and walked down to the corner drugstore for a Coca Cola. I was amazed. There didn't seem to be any limit to the power of a man with a backward collar! I sipped my large Coke, and the fountain girl timidly placed the check on the marble counter. A moment later, the proprietor of the drugstore, a short, fat man with a golden smile, sat down on the next stool and tore the check into quarters. He turned to the fountain girl with his golden teeth exposed and said: "The Reverend Springer can't pay for anything in here, Ellie May."

"Thank you, Brother—?" I recognized the proprietor as a churchgoer, but couldn't remember his name.

"Lyle, Reverend. Jim Lyle."

"Thank you, Brother Lyle."

"I enjoyed your sermon yesterday, Reverend Springer. It was wonderful."

"I hope you took my words to heart."

"I did, Reverend, I did." He returned to his cash register behind the tobacco counter. After I finished my Coke, I decided to push things to see how far I could go. I wandered slowly around the drugstore and gathered up a new razor, a toothbrush, toothpaste, a package of blades, three bars of soap, a small flashlight, a ballpoint pen, and a Zippo cigarette lighter. I piled this loot on the tobacco counter.

"How much is all this?" I smiled at Brother Lyle.

"To you, nothing," Brother Lyle said hoarsely.

"Thank you, Brother Lyle."

He began to put the items into a paper sack, and I said, "I'll need a couple of cartons of Camels while you're at it."

"You bet, Reverend." Two cartons of cigarettes were added to the full sack.

"God bless you, Brother Lyle," I said, taking the sack from the generous proprietor.

"Thank you, Reverend." He was no longer able to smile, I noticed.

I returned home, ate two bowls full of turnip greens, a slab of cornbread, drank a glass of buttermilk, and smoked a cigarette. I examined my roster of delinquents—Mrs. Merita Jensen was near the top of the list. Why not get it over with?

Dr. Jensen lived in a salmon-colored, four-apartment, double duplex—two families below, one above, and one for rent—and the bottom right apartment, the lushest of them all, with greener grass in front, and more bushes, and more inlaid tile, and a side entrance from the garage into the back of the apartment, was his. As I rang the doorbell, I hoped that Dr. Jensen had pulled enough teeth that year to provide air-conditioning in his home. I was somewhat taken aback when the door was opened by a sullen-lipped, dish-faced young woman with a pair of bare feet resembling black cowhide suitcases. "*Why does Jensen bother?*" I thought.

I said, "Good afternoon, Madame. I am the Right Reverend Deuteronomy Springer."

"You lookin' for me, Reverend, or Miz Merita?"

"Mrs. Merita Jensen."

"Come on in, Reverend. I'll tell her you is here."

I entered the apartment and waited in the living room. It was not air-conditioned after all, but was quite cool just the same. I laughed to myself about mistaking the maid for Mrs. Jensen. I still had a lot to learn about status among my parishioners.

The living room was moderately furnished; utilitarian is the word. There was a three-cushion couch, an easy chair, a television set, several end tables, table lamps and a couple of floor lamps. There was a seascape reproduction on the wall above the imitation fireplace and a photo in a heavy silver frame upon the mantle. I picked up the mount and examined the face in the photograph. Could this be Mrs. Jensen? The photograph had been taken with only a key light across the black snapping eyes, without any back lighting, and it was evident that the photographer had done his best to show the woman's features to her best advantage; but this woman would be beautiful under any kind of lighting, or without any lighting at all. There was an inner beauty to the face that didn't seem quite proper, and there was a half-smile on her full lips that was more bored than amused. Her hair was combed straight back from a high broad forehead, and a wide, jeweled silver comb jutting up from the thick knot at the back of her head gave the Negro woman a Latin appearance. And what a beautiful Negro she was! I heard a step in the hallway and turned as Merita Jensen entered the room. The photograph had been unkind to this young woman; no black-and-white still could have caught the delicate coffee-and-heavy-cream coloring of her face.

"I was admiring your photo, Mrs. Jensen," I said. "It's a good likeness."

"Photographs usually are good likenesses, aren't they, Reverend—or is it Doctor Springer?"

"The Right Reverend, I mean, Reverend is fine."

"My husband said you would call, but I didn't expect you so soon. You came to pray over me. Is that right?" Her voice was musical, but she failed to hide the underlying amusement so evident in her manner and smile.

"You appear to find prayer amusing, Mrs. Jensen," I said coldly.

"Oh, I don't know," she laughed. "I've never been prayed over before by a white man. My husband has prayed for me often, but husbands hardly count, do they?"

"I don't want you to consider me as a white man," I said defensively. "I would rather you thought of me as your pastor."

"The way you're staring at my legs, Reverend, I believe I'll consider you as just another man." She moved to the doorway and called, "Ruthie!" Turning in the doorway, she smiled at me. "Please sit down, Reverend. I'm going to have a gin and tonic, but I suppose you would rather have tea?"

"Sometimes," I faltered, "a gin and tonic is very refreshing on a hot day."

I had been staring at her legs, but it was hard not to stare. Mrs. Jensen was wearing a pair of white short-shorts, and these had been rolled up a full turn, and she seemed to be all legs and breast, like a young robin. Ruthie slewfooted down the hall, and Mrs. Jensen ordered gin, ice and quinine water, then joined me on the overstuffed couch. After curling her long legs beneath her buttocks, she leaned toward me, her breasts taut against a sheer white blouse.

"May I have a cigarette, Reverend?" Her smile was dazzling. For a moment I thought of telling her I didn't smoke, but she was way ahead of me. "You do smoke, don't you, Reverend? How did you get the brown stain between your fingers?"

"Of course I smoke." I brought out my cigarettes, lighted two, and passed one to Mrs. Jensen.

"I have to hand it to you, Reverend," Mrs. Jensen laughed merrily. "You're a cool one all right. For a moment there I thought butter wouldn't melt in your mouth, but here we are—" Ruthie entered with a tray, and the dentist's wife mixed two tall drinks.

"What do you mean," I asked, taking a beaded glass, "butter wouldn't melt in my mouth?"

"Never mind. Let's get on with it. Just what did my giant-brained husband tell you about me?"

"Dr. Jensen is perturbed about your failure to accept Jesus Christ as your Savior. Frankly I, too, would like to see you back in the fold of God's flock, Mrs. Jensen."

"Why not call me Merita. What's your first name?"

"Deuteronomy." I felt like a fool giving her this name, but what else could I do? Her ringing laughter added to my discomfort.

"Deut Springer. That's all right. Here, have a warm-up." Merita added two fingers of gin to my half-emptied glass.

"Thank you. That will be sufficient."

"Sufficient for what?" She smiled.

"Another thing is worrying your husband, Merita." I said solemnly. "And that is your failure to have children. I didn't talk to him much about this problem, but now that I've seen you, I don't see why a healthy woman like you couldn't have a dozen if you wanted them."

"That's your answer, Deut."

"I beg your pardon?"

"If you wanted them, you said. I don't want any children, especially Fred Jensen's children." She laughed prettily, took a long swallow from her glass. "And I know a perfect way to prevent them. Next question."

"Dr. Jensen wants a God-fearing household, Merita, and I know it would please him if you came to church. Evidently he provides well for you; certainly you owe him this courtesy—"

"Preach to me, Deut. Sell me the idea, if you can," she said flippantly.

"Shall we pray?" I put my drink down on the end table, snuffed out my cigarette, and dropped to my knees on the floor.

"Dear God," I began, "help this poor unfortunate girl to see the error of her ways. Guide her, comfort her, and teach her how to love Thy name. Lead this poor lost soul out of the wilderness and bless her, Oh Jesus—"

"Cut it out now, Deut," Merita said angrily. "I don't like that kind of talk!"

"Get down on your knees, woman, and pray to your God to forgive you!"

"No!" Merita leaped to her feet hurriedly, and she would have left the room, but I caught her by the arm and jerked her to the floor. On her knees she faced me, and I slowly forced her arm up behind her back.

"Pray!" I said loudly, my mouth two inches away from her lips.

"No!" she screamed. "You're hurting my arm, Reverend Springer!"

"The Lord's Prayer. Repeat after me. Our Father, Who art in Heaven—say it!"

"Our Father, Who art in Heaven," she whispered softly.

"Hallowed be thy name."

"Hallowed be thy name."

"Thy kingdom come—"

"Thy kingdom come. . ." Merita's eyes were closed and she was breathing heavily through her mouth. I loosed my grip on her wrist, and she let her arm fall. She swayed toward me, her eyes still closed, and I cupped her breasts with my hands. I held them gently for a moment, and then I kissed her on the lips. Her arms wrapped around my head, and she returned my kiss hard.

I jerked my head back, pulled her arms away and got to my feet. My legs were trembling, and I took a short drink right from the bottle. I picked up my hat and placed it on my head. Merita opened her eyes and laughed wildly as I stumbled toward the door.

"Wheee!" she wailed. "That was fun! Come on, Deut, let's pray some more!"

"Don't worry, baby," I said, a wide grin on my face. "We will. We will."

Out on the street again, I seemed to be on fire. This was a woman! And I had to have her; she was much too good for old Dr. Jensen. But there is a time and a place for everything, and I would pick my own time and my own place. . .

No more calls today, I thought. Another call like that one would be the very end. My legs were like rubber bands, and I couldn't control the violent shaking of my hands. Although it was only six blocks to the church, I caught a taxicab home.

I paid the two-bit fare, crossed the lot to the house and saw a visitor on the porch. He was dressed in black, like me, but his suit was made of thin pongee, and he wore a regular white dress shirt and a gray tie. As he got out of the rocking chair to greet me, I saw that he was wearing old-fashioned high-top shoes and white cotton socks.

"Dr. Springer," my visitor stated in a deep gravelly voice.

"Reverend Springer," I corrected him.

"I'm Dr. Theodore Heartwell," the middle-aged Negro announced pompously, "The head of the Jax Colored Church League. I'm the pastor of the Southern Baptists of Saint John."

"Glad to meet you, Dr. Heartwell," I said jovially. "Come on in and have a glass of iced tea."

"No thank you, Reverend, although I would like to very much. I have several more errands to run. A very serious problem has come up and, although you are a white man, you are the pastor of a colored church, and I am inviting you to attend our meeting tonight at my church."

"What kind of meeting is it?" I hedged.

"A crucial meeting. An important meeting. And a meeting that concerns us all, white or black."

"All right, Dr. Heartwell," I said. "If you put it that way, I shall be there. What time?"

"Eight p.m. But do not come through the front door. The church will be dark, and there will only be the one back entrance open. The meeting will be held in the basement."

"It sounds like a secret meeting."

"It is, Reverend Springer. It is."

"I'll be there." We shook hands solemnly and he departed, carefully picking his way through the weeds of the lot. I wondered if he had smelled the gin on my breath, and then I laughed. The hell with him. It was tough enough to keep my own church members satisfied without worrying about the other Negro preachers in the community. I would go to the meeting, however. I had a lot to learn about Negroes, a lot to learn.

I entered the house, stripped off my coat and shirt, and asked Ralphine to fix a pitcher of iced tea. What I needed at that moment was a shower, a long, cold shower. . .

THE SOUTHERN BAPTISTS of Saint John Church was an impressive structure compared to my small church. The building had been constructed of red brick and had an imposing front Gothic entrance, with a massive door tall enough and wide enough to admit a horse and rider. Two iron knockers had also been provided by the medieval-minded architect, one at waist level and the other presumably for a churchgoing horseman. Except for the entrance, however, the rest of the building was an oblong brick box completely devoid of decoration. To the right of the building, enclosed by a ten-foot high chicken-wire fence, there was an outside combination tennis-basketball court. Strung above the clay court were a couple of dozen unlighted Japanese lanterns. A tattered homemade poster by the sagging wire gate announced:

CHURCH BIZARRE TUES.
DANCING WATERMELLON FUN!

I had missed the fun; the "bizarre" had been held the previous Tuesday. I cut across the court, jumped over the drooping tennis net and made my way around to the back of the darkened church. As I lowered my head to see better on the unlighted stairway, a hand reached out and grabbed the lapels of my coat and jerked me down the last two steps. I was lifted bodily and shoved against the rough brick wall.

"Hey!" I protested.

A match flared for a brief second, and I saw two white eyes somewhere behind the long arm, and then a voice said: "Sorry, Reverend. Go on in." The hand released me, and I dropped six inches to solid concrete, pulled down my coat and pushed through the swinging door to the basement.

I stumbled down the dark hallway to where a light came through an open door and was met by Dr. Heartwell, who clasped me warmly by the hand and led me inside still holding tightly to my hand. There were three other Negro men in the room, and they sat on metal folding chairs around two card tables that had been pushed together. A gray-haired Negro woman, who was wearing a heavy cloth coat with an unidentifiable fur collar, despite the heat, sat to one side of the conference table. Both of her shoes had been slit at the great toe, and large bunions protruded through the gaps.

Dr. Heartwell introduced me to the other ministers present, and they each solemnly shook my hand. Evidently this was a grave, clandestine meeting, and I kept my voice lowered to the same conspiratorial pitch as the rest of them. I was wary of this holy little group. My experience with ministers had been limited to a few Unitarian sermons years ago, to my recent contact with Abbot Dover, and to the brief meeting earlier that afternoon with Dr. Heartwell. The good bald Abbot at Orangeville had stated that all ministers were phonies, or words to that effect. In a way he had reaffirmed my own personal opinion of this profession, and my own actions, sermons, and activity since getting my own church had really convinced me. I was a phony minister, but none of the laymen I had met could tell the difference. Could these four intelligent-looking Negro ministers tell the difference? Or were they phony too?

Dr. Heartwell sat at the head of the low tables. Seated next to him was the minister of the Afro-American Christian Church, a neat wiry man with a thin, pinched face and no lips. His name was Dr. Harry David. Across the table from Dr. David sat the Right Reverend Jason McCroy, Pastor of the Church of the Divine Spirit. He was a heavy-jowled man of forty-odd, wearing a pair of steel-rimmed glasses on a black cord attached to the lapel of a black frock coat. When he talked he punctuated the end of each sentence with a thump of his forefinger on the card table.

Opposite me was the last minister of the Colored Church League, a young Negro in his twenties with a face the color of faded yellow parchment. A thin wisp of a black mustache rode his wide upper lip like a wet and clinging dust mote. He had the simple title of Reverend Warren Hutto and was without a church of his own. Dr. Heartwell had introduced him as his assistant, and "my good right arm."

Dr. Heartwell drummed on the card table with his fingers. "We don't know what exactly will come from this meeting, Reverend Springer, but before we start, I want you to listen to Mrs. Bessie Langdale's story. We have all heard it; she is a member of my church in good standing, and her story is truthful."

It was a sad story. Bessie told it hesitantly, and once she cried for a few moments before she could continue. Bessie had gone downtown that morning to buy some material to make drapes for her oldest married daughter. She hadn't been able to find what she wanted, and she had gone everywhere under the sun, walking all over town. She had picked up a few toys for her grandson, Robert, in Kresses, and then she had waited for the bus. After her exhausting day in town, she had been lucky enough to find a seat on the bus next to the window. Now the seat was in the back, but not all of the way to the back. But this was all right at first. Negroes sit from the rear to the front, and white people sit from the front to the rear. After a few stops, however, the bus began to get crowded, and a white man wanted to sit in the empty aisle seat. According to law, the white man had priority on seating and was not allowed to sit beside a Negro. The bus driver had said to her, "Get up, Auntie, this gentleman wants to sit down." Bessie was very tired, and she didn't know what made her do such a thing because it wasn't like her at all. She was a Christian, God-fearing, law-abiding woman, and she had followed the law and had done right for all of her sixty-three years on God's green earth. But it just didn't seem right. Here was this empty seat, going to waste, and she would have to stand up, tired as she was, so this white man could sit down. Maybe, if there hadn't been that empty seat going to waste, she would have got up when the bus driver told her to, but the thought of giving up her seat when it wasn't necessary had just been too much for a body to take. She had told the driver, "No. I won't get up!" Everything had happened so fast then, she could hardly recollect what did happen. The driver stopped, a policeman dragged her out of the seat and shoved her into a police car, and she was booked at the police station. She was supposed to appear in court the next morning for committing a misdemeanor and disturbing the peace.

That was the story, and it took Bessie some time to tell it.

It was obviously the truth. I believed it. But what did they want me to do?

"Did they give you your bus fare back, Mrs. Langdale?" I asked.

"No, sir! Nothin'."

"I have no further questions." I sat back in my chair and lit a cigarette. Smoking displeased Dr. Harry David; I could tell by his eyes.

"Gentlemen," Dr. Heartwell began to make a speech, "this isn't a very pretty story. It is an ugly story—"

"Are you beginning the official meeting, Dr. Heartwell?" I interrupted.

"Yes, I am." He sounded annoyed.

"Then don't you gentlemen believe it would be well to start with a short prayer? I'm certain we'll all feel better with God."

"An excellent idea," chimed in Dr. David, with sharp, clipped syllables.

"All right," Dr. Heartwell said. "Dear God, Omnipotent Master with infinite wisdom, may You guide our thoughts and words this evening and provide us with Your wisdom. For Yours is the power and the glory forever and forever, Amen. And it is a story that happens daily in Jax and in every southern city that knows the yoke of oppression, where brother does not recognize brother. We have all listened to Mrs. Langdale's story about the harsh treatment she received today, and as far as I am concerned, this is the breaking point. Something must be done." He sat down.

"What, exactly," I asked, "will happen to Mrs. Langdale when she goes to court tomorrow morning?"

"I can answer that," Reverend McCroy said. "The misdemeanor charge will be dropped, and she'll probably be fined ten dollars for disturbing the peace. Since the Supreme Court decision in our favor, the judges invariably change the charge to something other than a Jim Crow law." He thumped the card table with his thick forefinger.

"If it is money," I said, "I can certainly chip in a few dollars for her fine. But I believe you have something else in mind."

"Yes, we do." Dr. Heartwell said. "We were discussing the situation before you came, Reverend Springer. We were thinking that perhaps Mrs. Langdale should go to jail rather than pay her fine."

"That's great," I laughed, "just great! What will that accomplish for Mrs. Langdale? She'll spend ten days in jail cooking greens and grits for prisoners, and then she'll be released. From that time on there will be a jail record on file against this good woman for disturbing the peace. Is that what you want, gentlemen?"

"There is wisdom in your supposition, Reverend Springer," Dr. David said, "but don't you believe that some kind of moral protest is in order? Without publicity, we will never have our rights. The Supreme Court is on our side, but—"

"The Supreme Court is on everybody's side," I said flatly. "No, gentlemen, you won't achieve anything by letting Mrs. Langdale cook for the jailbirds. If you want to sacrifice someone to a cause, sacrifice yourselves! I'm with you. The Church of God's Flock believes that the white man and the black man can and will love one another if they are only given the chance. And as the pastor of the Church of God's Flock, I am willing to fight for this belief. Let us take a lesson from some of the other southern cities that have won the bus segregation fight. It takes time. It takes money. It takes patience. And it takes love. No violence. Patient, passive resistance. You have an organization here called the Colored Church League. This name doesn't inspire me to resist anything, and it won't inspire anybody else either. Let's form a new group right now and call it the League For Love! We can appoint Mrs. Langdale as the honorary president and have her speak at each Negro church in Jax, night after night. If they'll stand for it, we can have her make the same talk to the white churches in Jax. To start off tomorrow with some publicity and a protest, all of us—Dr. Heartwell, Dr. David, Reverend McCroy, Reverend Hutto and myself—we'll ride the same bus, and we'll sit in front. We won't move, and we'll let them arrest us. Tonight, right after this meeting, I can call the morning newspaper and announce our intentions. They'll print it because a protest by the major colored church ministers is news. The League For Love, gentlemen! And then, following our arrests, we'll organize a bus boycott right in this room. Organize car pools, assign the drivers, collect the funds and donations, organize nightly meetings in first one church and then another. But the key, gentlemen, is nonviolence!"

I sat back. If these ministers were phonies, and I believed they were, there would be some adroit hedgehopping in about one second. There was a dead silence around the table.

"I am fifty-three years old," Dr. David said quietly, "and I have a weak heart—"

"One out!" I laughed.

"But I am willing to spend the rest of my life in jail if it will help end segregation." Dr. David stared at me and continued to speak in a clipped, quiet voice. "You are a white man, Reverend Springer, and you have nothing to lose in this fight. But you speak well, you think fast, and we need a man like you. I think your plan has merit. But despite your talk of nonviolence, there will be violence. Can we risk it? We are a hot-blooded race, and southern white men have generations of prejudice on their side. We both—white and black—believe we are right. However, if we can get our people to turn the other cheek regardless of bloody heads, beatings, bombings and other violence, which will come, believe me, we shall win this fight. I'll cast my vote for your plan, Reverend Springer."

"I am willing to take a protest bus ride tomorrow," Reverend McCroy stated, with an angry laugh. "And a few days in jail or a ten-dollar fine won't hurt me very much. But what about you, Reverend Springer? They won't arrest you. You're a white man, and you can choose any bus seat you desire."

"I was expecting that. I am morally obligated to ride the bus. I have an all-Negro church, and I love every member of my flock. To insure that I go to jail with you all, you merely have to tell the arresting officer that I put you up to it. That will qualify me, I believe, as a disturber of the peace."

"I don't think we have to do that," Dr. Heartwell protested.

"I insist," I said firmly. "I take it, then, that you also approve of the plan, Dr. Heartwell?"

"Yes. Why not? I don't have an alternate plan to offer, and right now I'm rather ashamed of myself to even think that I proposed to let Mrs. Langdale languish in jail and fight our fight for us."

"Don't worry about me, Dr. Heartwell," Mrs. Langdale said spiritedly. "I'll do anything you say. If you want me to ride the bus with you all in the morning, I'll go to jail, too."

"No, Mrs. Langdale," I shook my head. "You'll be an excellent symbol and president for the League For Love. Go ahead down in the morning and pay your fine. Don't say anything to anybody, and we'll make the arrangements for the church meeting here tomorrow night." I turned to Dr. Heartwell who was frowning bleakly at the wall. "You have the largest church, but we can use mine instead. It's up to you."

"Sorry," Dr. Heartwell said, "my mind was way off some-where. Certainly we'll use our church here, and we'll all take turns speaking—if we aren't in jail."

"At the least," I said, "you'll all be out on bail. But we haven't heard from Reverend Hutto yet. What's your opinion, Reverend?"

"Dr. Heartwell speaks for me," Hutto said, fingering the smudge on his lip.

"No," I said emphatically. "You speak for yourself here. Do you want to go along or not?"

"It doesn't make any difference to me," Hutto shrugged. "I'd just as soon go as not. But somebody's got to contact a lawyer, answer the telephone here, and start rounding up an audience for the evening meeting, get some music ready, decorate the church, have some banners made on this League For Love business, and—"

"Whoa!" I laughed. "You've got quite an assistant there, Dr. Heartwell."

"I think so," Dr. Heartwell agreed, smiling fondly at his associate.

"All right, Reverend Hutto," I continued. "I believe we can spare you, and there is a lot to do. Does everybody agree?"

Both Dr. David and the Rt. Rev. McCroy nodded.

"I'll need some paper and a pencil then." I smiled at Reverend Hutto.

"I have a pad right here—"

"Then take this down verbatim, so I can phone it in to the newspaper." I began to dictate: "Yesterday, because of two sore bunions, segregation on busses ended forever in Jax, Florida, according to the Right Reverend Deuteronomy Springer, Pastor of the First Church of God's Flock. When a God-fearing, Christian woman of sixty-three years of age is made to stand up on a bus because a white man wants to sit down, it is time for the ministers of the gospel to end such evil—"

There was more of the same. A lot more.

THE NEXT MORNING at seven-thirty, tired and sleepy after a long session with my fellow ministers of the League For Love, talking, talking, talking, I waited patiently at a city bus stop at the corner of Lee and Broadway in downtown Jax. This was the point where we were to meet and, while I waited for the other ministers, I talked to the combination reporter-photographer assigned to the story by the *Jax Daily Advertiser*.

"How come you want to get mixed up with all these niggers, Reverend? I'm really interested, because I can't see it." A Speed Graflex dangling from his right hand, a cigarette dangling from his lip, and coarse straw-colored hair dangling over his damp forehead, the *Advertiser* man was working hard to look like a reporter. Both of the patch pockets of his gray Palm Beach jacket were bulging with flashbulbs, and he had loosened his blue-and-red hand-painted necktie and the collar of his shirt to create a careless effect. He had only succeeded in looking sloppy. He was about twenty-six or -seven, and it was quite evident that he had shaved his sharp, inquisitive face that morning with an electric razor. You can always tell.

"Why do you ask—off the record, or for publication?" I countered.

"I was just wondering." He shrugged—a slow, exaggerated gesture—spat the cigarette into the gutter without touching it with his hands. "I'm used to this race business. I'm not from this hick town; I'm from Atlanta. This stuff wouldn't go in Atlanta. We know how to keep niggers in their place up there."

"And what, exactly, is their place?"

"They're black apes, Reverend, that's all. All any of 'em are interested in is a bottle of gin and a place to lay down. They all got one big ambition though, and that's to rape a white woman. That's why you got to keep 'em down. Lazy, good-for-nothing apes! The only thing a nigger really understands is a good swift kick in the ass."

"I don't agree, Mr. Ames."

"You're from the North, that's why." He spat into the street. "I could spot that accent as soon as you started talkin'."

"I don't have an accent."

"That's what I mean. Go ahead, Reverend, get mixed up with these people. Wait till you've lived down here as long as I have. I know 'em. You can't love a nigger. They won't let you. You're white and they're black, and the two colors don't mix. My daddy had a nigger servant for twenty years. Treated him like a king. My daddy thought more of that old nigger than he did of us kids. Well, you may not believe this, but it's true. Daddy had a stroke, paralyzed the whole right side of his body, and he couldn't talk. We all thought it was fine that we had old John to look after Daddy and all. He had to be treated like a baby, couldn't do nothin' for himself. Know what that nigger did?"

"How would I know what he did?"

"Daddy was layin' there paralyzed, and old John knocked out his gold inlays and sold them for old gold! That's right. We wouldn't never have found out about it if the pawnbroker hadn't got suspicious and called the house. Mama went down and identified 'em, and they were Daddy's inlays all right. That's how John repaid my daddy's love. How would you like to be paralyzed and have somebody come along and knock the gold right out of your teeth?"

"I don't think I'd like it, Mr. Ames. By the way, when you go back to the paper, I want you to give my thanks to the editor for the fine coverage he gave the story this morning."

"Okay, Reverend, I'll do that little thing. I can see I'm not gettin' through to you." Ames moved away and leaned against a lamp post. "The *Advertiser* is goin' to feel pretty bad about runnin' that story if them nigger preachers don't show up for the bus ride." He laughed heartily, choked up a gob of yellow phlegm and spat into the gutter. "I doubt if they will show up. You show me a nigger, and I'll show you a coward."

Ames was wrong. Dr. Heartwell drove up a few moments later in a big 1939 Buick town car and parked across the street. While Ames maintained his position at the lamppost, I crossed the street and joined Reverend Heartwell at the parking meter. He squeezed two nickels into the spring slot.

"Good morning, Reverend Springer," he greeted me, smiling.

"Do you think two hours will be enough?"

"I really don't know. But why take a chance? Put in a quarter."

As they climbed out of the car, I greeted them: Dr. David, Reverend McCroy and Tommy Heartwell, Dr. Heartwell's giant-sized son, the man who had lifted me off my feet for inspection the night before in the basement of the church. We gathered together in a small cluster to go over the plans one more time.

"Tommy wanted to come along, too," Dr. Heartwell explained. "I tried to discourage him, but he insisted."

"There might be some trouble," Tommy grinned broadly, grinding the knuckles of his huge right fist into the palm of his left hand. "And just in case there is, I'd like to get me in a couple of good licks."

"No!" I said sharply. "That's exactly what we don't want. One tiny spark of violence on our part, and we will lose before the start. The entire theme of our campaign is love! Turn the other cheek."

"Suppose I turn the other cheek, and it gets slapped too?" Tommy grinned. "Isn't it my turn?"

"No," I replied. "You have to stay out of it. But you can follow the bus in the Buick. That might be a good idea. And then, after we're arrested, you can drive over and tell Reverend Hutto to get down to the courthouse with a lawyer."

"All right," Tommy reluctantly agreed.

Our plan was to get on the eight o'clock bus, and I had so informed the editor of the *Jax Daily Advertiser*. The *Daily Advertiser* and the *Morning Advertiser* were the only two newspapers in Jax and, for all practical purposes, they were the same paper except for the time of issuance. The *Morning Advertiser* had given my story space on the front page with considerable carryover to page three. I expected a very big play, with photos, in the evening *Daily Advertiser*; and through the resultant publicity, I anticipated a large church meeting and, as an aftermath, an all-out bus boycott by Negroes.

On my part, I had no personal motives, nothing to gain one way or another. I didn't believe in what I was doing, and I didn't disbelieve in it either. I was indifferent. But the plan was interesting, almost exciting, and I wanted to see how it would work out. My fellow ministers were all very calm about the situation. If they were inwardly excited, I could not tell it from their outward expressions or actions. If anything, they were run-of-the-mill martyrs. These Negro ministers were men with a painful, incurable disease. They had tried cure after cure only to find that their disease persisted, and they felt in their hearts that not even death would wipe out the cause of their illness. Like victims of malignant cancer they would always be willing and eager to attempt any cure, no matter how extravagant and impossible the claim might be. Another straw to clutch at. Another skirmish, another brush with the law might bring a slight concession or gain to their neverending fight to gain equality. Most likely, they would lose. They fully expected to lose, but they were still willing to go through the motions. I found such an attitude very refreshing.

My many years of deadly, stultifying employment, which demanded constant repression of all emotional feelings, had frozen my face into a waxy, defensive mask. Only my voice was alive, and my face rarely reflected any of the verbal excitement, laughter, passion, or sadness my voice could summon at will. Once, at a party in Columbus, the host had brought out a tape recorder and had recorded the conversation of the guests for a fifteen minute period. When he played the tape back for us all to hear and enjoy, I had listened from my place by the fireplace, looking into a mirror. As I watched my face and listened, the animated voice that belonged to me told a filthy joke and was punctuated by the laughter of the other guests. My solemn, fixed expression in the mirror was the same expression I had had when I told the story. I knew this, and I wondered how anybody could laugh at any joke, no matter how funny it was, when he was also looking at a frozen, emotionless face. And I was amazed, too, at the ability of my reedy, thin voice to convey emotion that didn't match my expression. If a stranger had been asked to choose the face that went with my recorded voice, I would never have been identified. My voice was an independent organ I didn't fully own or control. Sometimes I talked and listened to myself at the same time, quite interested in what the voice had to say. There was a husky tenderness at times, which was quite effective and, although my voice was highly pitched for a man, it wasn't squeaky; and within its narrow range, there was a straightforward, confident sincerity that was most impressive.

Because of my expression, I had gained a reputation as a good listener. I had listened to hundreds of tales of woe, marital arguments, chunks of gossip, rambling, boring accounts of vacation trips, anecdotes, plans for impossible futures, and trite, domestic revelations over the years. When it was my turn to talk, my voice consistently said the right thing—a murmured, sincere condolence or a cheering word of advice slipped readily through my lips, independently, and without effort or thought. There had been times when I had suspected a friend of embroidering a story, or adding details calculated to shock me into changing my expression, but I may be wrong about this. As a minister, my expressionless face was a definite asset to me. Who would ever suspect this persuasive voice of belonging to an insincere person?

A small mixed crowd had gathered at the bus stop, and they watched curiously as Mr. Ames took a couple of group shots of the League For Love standing by the bus stop sign. Mr. Ames then wrote our full names down in his reporter's notebook and made a small diagram in the notebook showing our positions from right to left in the photographs he had taken.

"I always do this," Ames said to me. "It takes a little more time, but since I started this system, I've never made a mistake in the cut lines under a picture."

"A very judicious precaution," I complimented the reporter.

The flat-nosed, green-and-white city bus lumbered into the reserved slot, and Ames took another shot of us entering the door. There was a white policeman in the front seat, and we had to wait a couple of minutes before he could raise the window and stick his head out. The policeman wanted to get his face into the photograph and, after it was taken, he wrote his name on the inside of a matchbook cover and gave it to Ames. While Ames re-inscribed the policeman's name in his notebook, we clambered aboard and took our seats. Dr. Heartwell and I sat in the seat behind the driver, while Dr. David and Reverend McCroy sat directly behind us. The remainder of the bus was empty except for the policeman in the front seat opposite me and the photographer-reporter sitting behind him. The driver, an affable sort who wore his chauffeur's cap at a jaunty angle, turned and smiled, winked at the policeman.

"Is everybody comfy?" the driver asked.

"Move it out, Roy," the policeman said. "I reckon we're ready."

The driver shifted into gear, and the bus whirred down Lee Street. As the bus filled with white passengers, the driver would be forced to ask the Negro ministers to move to the rear. That was the law. When they refused, the policeman would be forced to arrest them. That was our plan. I was already disobeying the law by sitting beside Dr. Heartwell but, evidently, the policeman had decided to ignore the violation. We drove on. One block. Two blocks. Three blocks. The third corner was a bus stop, and there were several Negroes waiting, but the driver didn't stop. I leaned forward and tapped him on the shoulder.

"Driver," I said, "Why didn't you stop back there? There were passengers waiting."

"Is that right?" he asked. "That's funny. I didn't see anybody. I'll stop at the next corner."

At the next bus stop there were two white men, one white woman, and one Negro woman. The driver stopped, opened the folding door, and courteously tipped his cap.

"Are there any nigger lovers here who would like a bus ride?" he addressed the white trio.

One of the men laughed, and the other man and the woman smiled broadly. The Negro woman poked her mouth out, but said nothing.

"Not me," one of the white men said. "How about you, Mr. Sawyers?" He addressed his companion.

Mr. Sawyers shook his head and laughed, "Not me. I'd rather walk!"

The white woman, a matronly type in her early forties, giggled.

Our driver shrugged comically, closed the door, and drove on. He turned and grinned at the policeman.

"Don't look like anybody wants to ride with these niggers, Officer."

The policeman laughed. "Try again, Roy. There must be more than one white man in Jax who loves niggers." The remark was for my benefit, and he glanced in my direction to see how I would take it. Naturally, I took it very well.

Roy, the bus rider, made four more stops, and each time there was a similar reaction by the waiting passengers. None of them would get on the bus, and they all smiled or laughed as though they shared a secret joke with the driver. The Negro passengers didn't climb aboard either. The presence of the policeman, I concluded, frightened them, and they didn't want to get "mixed up" in anything. The reaction by each group of waiting passengers was too pat. They couldn't all have been informed of our plan for disturbing the peace, and even if they had been briefed, many of the white men should have been delighted to see us get arrested. At the next bus stop, as soon as the driver had stopped, I got to my feet and stood by the door. Roy reluctantly opened the door for me, and I jumped out. My suspicions were confirmed.

The destination sign behind the glass didn't read 132ND STREET; the driver had flipped the cards after we had climbed aboard, and it now read NIGGER LOVER SPECIAL. No wonder none of the white passengers had wanted to ride! As I stood on the curb looking at the destination sign, a flash bulb exploded. Mr. Ames had followed me out, gotten behind me, and had taken a photo of me staring up at the ridiculous sign. This news photo was later picked up by the Associated Press and subsequently appeared in almost every major daily in the United States via wire photo release.

I shrugged, beckoned to Dr. Heartwell and the other ministers to come out and join me on the curb. After they had seen the sign, they walked silently down the street to where Tommy Heartwell was waiting with the Buick. I followed them, and great guffaws broke out behind us as Mr. Ames, the policeman, and the driver released their suppressed laughter. We had been very neatly tricked.

For a few minutes, we sat in the car and tried to come up with an alternate plan. Tommy Heartwell was sullen and angry and wanted us all to split up and each ride a different bus.

"They can't take four busses off their regular runs and make them nigger lover specials," he said angrily.

The other ministers favored Tommy's idea, but I talked them down.

"No," I said, "let's call it a day. We failed because I came along in the first place, but I have a hunch we will come out on top. Our main reason for getting arrested was to get publicity, and we will. The paper this evening will give this story a good play, and they will ridicule our efforts. I believe that ridicule will work for us rather than against us. You can make fun of almost anybody, but when you take a poke at religious leaders, regardless of their race or creed, you are attacking American fundamentals. Let's just go ahead and hold our meeting tonight, announce the bus boycott and see what happens."

The rest of the day we devoted to making the rounds of our respective church memberships and passing out the word to attend the evening meeting.

When the story appeared in the *Daily Advertiser*, under Dick Ames' byline, I read it quickly. Regardless of the way Ames talked, he could really write, and the story was a clever and humorous monologue in Negro dialect. Even though I was the butt of the joke, I enjoyed the story enormously.

I suppose white people all over Jax were reading the story and laughing, but Negroes wouldn't think it was funny. There were two photos on the front page accompanying the monologue: the group picture with an overline reading *The League For Love*, and the one of me alone with the bus. A cut line gave our names and the churches we represented, but my name was preceded by the title *Nigger Lover*. Directly beneath the two-column story, the photograph showing me looking at the plainly revealed bus destination sign had an overline stating *Going My Way?* I looked ridiculous in the photo; tall, thin, and with an overlarge, flapping coat and a straw hat, I resembled a misplaced scarecrow. To anyone who didn't know me, my face had a stunned, almost stupefied expression, as though I had suddenly been hit over the head from behind with a blunt instrument.

I tore the article and photos from the page, folded the clipping and placed it in my wallet. I wadded the rest of the newspaper together and tossed the ball into my waste-basket. I was very tired and hadn't as yet prepared any notes for my talk that night. Ralphine had left boiled turnips, turnip greens and a platter of cornbread for my supper, and she cooked these items very well. But I wasn't keen on my meal. The novelty of Ralphine's cooking had worn off quickly. This was only Tuesday, but it seemed like I had been tearing around for weeks instead of just a few days, and the evening meeting promised to be a long one.

I forced down a small helping of greens, ate a slab of cornbread and finished off my supper with two cups of instant coffee. Over the coffee, I made a few notes for my speech and then walked the six blocks to the Southern Baptists of Saint John Church.

The street in front of the church was a teeming black mass of people. At the basketball court I meant to cut across and enter through the basement, but I was spotted by several men who joyfully shouted my name. A moment later I was surrounded by men and women who tried to shake my hand. My back was pounded unmercifully by well-wishers, and I was lifted off my feet, hoisted to a pair of shoulders; and riding high above the crowd, I was carried through the wide high doors into the church. Every seat was filled, and the walls were lined with standees. A great roar came from the crowd when I appeared, and I was hustled down the center aisle to the pulpit. A large white banner, three feet high and twenty feet across, was strung across the back wall behind the altar, and it proclaimed in red, block letters THE LEAGUE FOR LOVE!

Dr. Heartwell and his right-hand man, Reverend Hutto, were seated on the platform behind the altar. To their left Dr. David and the Right Reverend McCroy were seated behind a card table and, in the center of the group on a raised platform, Mrs. Bessie Langdale occupied the place of honor. Dr. Heartwell got up quickly and wrung my hand.

"You were right, Reverend Springer," he said warmly. "We're going to win! I want you to start the meeting with a prayer, and then you will be the last speaker on the program."

"Fine," I agreed.

I entered the pulpit and a cheer arose from the crowd. I waited for silence. When the talk died and the whispering stopped, and when the rustling ceased altogether, I prayed:

"Dear God, what we say here tonight, what we do here tonight, is in Your hands. Listen to us and guide us in our fight to leave the wilderness. Teach us, help us to love our neighbor and make us brothers. Help us love our neighbors as we love You. Teach us to live side by side in love. Be our judge and jury, and if we are right, let us win. Dear God, in Your infinite wisdom, teach us how to love! Amen."

"Amen!" Came the multi-tongued echo from the assemblage.

I sat down in a metal folding chair next to Mrs. Langdale and shook hands with her. She was trembling with stage fright, and I calmed her by saying, "Don't worry, Bessie. God is on our side."

Another great roar greeted Dr. Heartwell as he entered the pulpit. He played the assemblage like a virtuoso playing a violin. As he outlined the bus boycott to the enthusiastic crowd, he sprinkled in biblical precedents the way a famous chef adds salt to a dish prepared for a gourmet. He didn't overstate anything, but his approach reached the emotions of the audience, and they fully understood and endorsed the boycott with their applause when he had finished.

Dr. David was next. His talk was a sincere eulogy and a moving tribute to Bessie Langdale. In a dry, clipped voice he told of her struggle to raise two daughters and a son by washing clothes and doing day work in Jax over the past thirty years. He told of her humble origin on a tenant farm, of the hunger she had suffered in the Great Depression, about her son in the Air Force who had been promoted to Airman First Class. He paid tribute to her two married daughters, both mothers, who were raising children in the hope of a better world.

Dr. David was a good speaker, and from my chair I saw tears coursing down the cheeks of both men and women in the audience. This was understandable: Bessie Langdale's life paralleled the lives of the majority of the people in the church. He introduced Bessie and then sat down.

Bessie Langdale was a large woman. Her great buttocks protruded like a circular shelf, and she wore a homemade evening dress of red silk. There was a white orchid corsage pinned to a red velvet sash that encircled her massive waist, and she wore a floppy black straw hat. Six imitation cherries had been sewn to the brim. She was so frightened, I thought she was going to faint. She stood in the pulpit, clutching the sideboards with a death-like grip. Her lips opened and closed rapidly but no words came out. I left my seat and put my arm around her, hugging her hard. I looked out at the audience.

"Tell her that you love her!" I shouted.

"We love you, Bessie! We love you!" the voices shouted. Bessie began to bawl. Great rasping sobs shook her body, and her brown face contorted as the tears streamed down her face. As though a secret tap was turned on, everybody in the audience began to cry at the same time. It was amazing. And through the sobbing, choking tears, a chant began, a unanimous chant that mounted in tempo and volume until the pine rafters across the ceiling trembled.

"Love you! Love you! Love you! Love you!"

I had to lead Bessie back to her seat. We had planned to have her tell her story about the arrest and fine she had suffered, but this spontaneous demonstration was much more effective.

As the chant died down there was a flutter of handkerchiefs, mostly red and blue bandannas, and a great blowing of noses. The Right Reverend Jason McCroy had brought his ten-man

male choir over from his Church of the Divine Spirit, and he
signaled them to stand up and sing. The choir was uniformly
dressed in white Palm Beach suits and bright red silk neckties.
Reverend McCroy led the choir through three choruses of *The
Battle Hymn of the Republic* and, on the fourth chorus, he made
a gesture to the crowd with both hands for them to stand and
join in. The stirring song swept through the group as though it
came from a single voice attached to a single heart. He had to let
the audience sing the chorus three more times before he could get
them to stop.

Reverend McCroy then made an impassioned appeal for funds
from the pulpit and, while he pleaded, cajoled, begged and demanded money, Reverend Hutto and a group of small Negro
boys passed through the audience three times, collecting a larger
amount each time.

I dosed the meeting with another prayer about love; the choir
sang another hymn, a repetitious spiritual; Dr. Heartwell said a
short prayer, and the meeting was over. I didn't make a speech as
I had planned; I didn't think it necessary.

The League For Love assembled in the basement and, after we
counted the money, we discovered we had taken in $962.43. We
elected officers: Dr. Heartwell was president, Reverend McCroy
and Dr. David were vice-presidents, Reverend Hutto was secretary, and I was treasurer. I could have been the president but,
after I informed the League that I had once been an accountant
and that I was familiar with business law, they let me have the
post of treasurer without further argument.

Bessie Langdale, of course, was our honorary president without administrative duties. She was almost in a state of shock from
her emotional experience in the church and, before we had our
meeting, Dr. Heartwell told Tommy to drive her home.

I walked home and, after I entered my house, I undressed without turning on any lights. I was completely exhausted. In my underwear I stretched out wearily on my bed and tried to sleep. But
I couldn't sleep; my thoughts were centered on Merita Springer.
Her face and figure were in my head like a color photograph. My
mind dwelled fondly on her sharply defined widow's peak, the
way her hips swelled out from her narrow waist, the maddening
firmness of her breasts, the wonderful contrast of her golden legs
and the white shorts she had worn. . .

An automobile stopped in the street outside, and I heard several loud male voices. I listened. These were not Negro voices, and there was a sharp, barking laugh, a nasty laugh. Barefooted, I crept from my bedroom into the study. Through the window I could see several dark figures in the empty lot between my house and the church. They were doing something, and I heard a man curse viciously as he stumbled over a pile of tin cans.

Matches flared in several places, and then a large cross began to burn in the center of the lot. The cross was at least ten feet high, and the crossbar was about four feet in width. The cross burned well with an uneven, bright blue flame. Evidently rags had been wound around the wood and soaked either in alcohol or gasoline. The dark figures returned to their car, a convertible parked in the street. A rock bounced across my front porch and then hit the door. The men climbed into the car and, as it drove away, one of the passengers smashed a bottle on the sidewalk in front of the church.

I locked the front door with the slide bolt and returned to the window. I watched the flaming cross until nothing was left but a dim glow of embers on the ground.

Then I went to bed and fell asleep immediately.

BY EIGHT-THIRTY the next morning, the bus boycott by Jax Negroes was approximately forty percent effective, so far as we could determine. Dr. Heartwell was discouraged, but I was astonished by our success.

"Give it a few days, Doctor," I told him. "We've only had one big meeting, and it takes time to get out the word. We haven't got our car pool fully organized yet, and these people have to get to work some way. By Monday the boycott should be one hundred percent."

"I certainly hope so," Dr. Heartwell grumbled.

"Where is your faith?" I smiled and patted him on the shoulder.

"My faith is in the Lord, but if we want to win, I suppose we had better get to work!"

"Now you're talking," I said cheerfully.

The basement of the Southern Baptists of Saint John Church had been converted into a GHQ by the members of the League For Love and with the help of many willing volunteers. There were ample desks, chairs, typewriters, and a dozen or more desk and floor lamps had been connected to the limited wall sockets by a maze of extension cords. A desk had been reserved for me in a back corner, and there was a stack of telegrams and air mail special delivery letters brought in earlier that morning, waiting to be opened.

Dr. Heartwell's church was centrally located in the Negro district of Jax, and the basketball-tennis court outside was in use as a motor pool. Assorted vehicles had been pressed into service: one panel delivery truck, two flatbed one-ton trucks, three half-ton pickups and several large, vintage Buick and Cadillac town cars, including the big 1939 Buick owned by Dr. Heartwell and driven by his son, Tommy, were in constant shuttle. These were not enough, of course, to handle the waiting mass of patient passengers, but news of the bus boycott was spreading quickly by telephone and word-of-mouth, and car owners who were not in the pool stopped constantly at the curb and filled empty seats with passengers.

Reverend Hutto, with his gift for organization, had a desk by the entrance to the large basement room. A large city map was tacked to the wall behind his desk, and he had it divided into various zones. There seemed to be ten or more people about his desk, and he was quite capable of carrying on a conversation with all of them at the same time. Two illegal extension lines had been wired in, brought down from Dr. Heartwell's upstairs office, and telephones had been connected—one on the doctor's desk and the other on Reverend Hutto's. The room was crowded with volunteers, men and women. There was a great deal of noise and confusion and a lot of coffee drinking.

Pleased by all the activity, I circled the room, smiling encouragement, slapping backs, shaking hands, and then sat at my desk to go through the wires and mail. A young girl in pedal pushers and a tight orange sweater brought me a cardboard container of coffee and tiptoed respectfully away. The coffee was too sweet, but I drank it anyway.

Some of the wires and many of the special delivery letters were addressed simply to *Nigger Lover, Jax, Florida*. But when I read them, they seemed all right. The wires were not too strongly worded, although they expressed dissatisfaction with my boycott activities, but the letters were vitriolic indeed. I wondered how anybody could get so worked up about such a basic problem. After reading the wires and letters addressed to Nigger Lover, I turned to the remainder of the mail. These wires and letters addressed to Reverend Deuteronomy Springer ran about fifty-fifty between hate and love messages. Two letters contained five-dollar bills, one included a twenty-dollar bill, and there were several letters containing singles. I decided to retain this money to supplement my income, and I slipped the bills into my wallet. This early mail was from southern states, and all of it was special delivery. When the regular mail began to roll in from conscience-stricken northerners and the far western states, the take would be better.

After composing a short, blanket-letter of thanks, I gave the handwritten message to one of the volunteer typists with instructions to send it out to all of the correspondents who had included return addresses.

Dr. Heartwell called me. "You're wanted on the telephone, Reverend Springer."

I picked up the telephone. "Hello," I said. There was no reply. "Hello," I said again. "This is the Right Reverend Deuteronomy Springer." From the other end of the line came an overly pro-longed hawking in a throat, followed by a sharp report as a gob of spittle hurtled into the distant mouthpiece. "Hello," I said. The receiver was banged down at the caller's end with a click painful to my ear. I racked the receiver and replaced the telephone on Dr. Heartwell's desk. After telling him what had happened, I advised him to screen all future calls before calling me to the telephone.

"I'm very sorry," he said. "If I had suspected anything like that I wouldn't have called you."

"Such things don't bother me," I said, forcing a smile. "They are to be expected. It is just that I don't like to have my time wasted when there are so many things to be done."

I told Dr. Heartwell about the burning cross in the lot in front of my house the night before.

"The fight begins in earnest." He nodded, grimly.

"No, Doctor," I said sternly, "the word 'fight' has no place in our vocabulary. Love begins! Love for God and love for our fel-low man."

At that moment the Right Reverend Jason McCroy came into the room and announced excitedly that four of the six Negro taxicab companies he had visited that morning had agreed to lower their basic rate of twenty-five cents for the first half mile to fifteen cents instead, and they would maintain that lower fare until the boycott had been won. In the general excitement, I re-turned to my desk to set up a bookkeeping system for the League For Love funds.

The money collected at the mass meeting the night before had been stored in a thick 1893 safe, and this safe was in the corner behind my desk. The combination to the safe no longer worked, but there was a welded hasp and a Yale lock securing the door, and I had the two keys in my possession. A cigar box would have provided almost as much security for the money as the safe, but at least the old safe was fireproof, and it was all we had. I gave one of the keys to Reverend Hutto and advised him to keep his addresses and rosters of volunteers locked up when he wasn't using them to prevent their loss. I began to make entries in the ledger. As I worked out a fairly simple double-entry bookkeeping system, which would also lend itself to needed complications in the event of audit, a brief, sardonic laugh escaped my lips.

I was right back where I started. Sam Springer, Accountant, hunched over a desk with a soft number two pencil clutched in his hand, ready to work over a set of figures and a cost estimate of boycott expenses. But here the similarity stopped, because there would be no take-home check of $78.35 when Friday night rolled around—I was doing this tedious work for love instead of money. And when Friday did come, instead of a weekend of quiet boredom watching television and drinking beer in a small apartment with a fat, dull wife for a companion, I had a Bible class to teach, sermons to prepare, and two exhausting sessions in church with a crazy congregation unable to get its fill of religion.

It was best not to think about the bookkeeping; why not look on the bright side? Wasn't this bus boycott an exciting experience? No. Wasn't I a successful minister of the Gospel? Not really. Were not the wires and the letters I had received fascinating? No. Surely the people I was allied with in the League For Love were wonderful people? So what? Well, what about Merita Jensen? Yes. Yes. Yes! Merita! My pencil poised in mid-air, several escape plans—all of them including Merita Jensen—began to form in the dark shadows of my imagination. . .

"Reverend Springer? Reverend Springer?" a persistent voice repeated.

Annoyed, I looked up and into the troubled face of Dr. Fred Jensen.

"Well, well," I said, "what brings you to this nest of confusion, Dr. Jensen?"

"Do you mind if I sit down, Reverend?" Dr. Jensen asked testily.

"Not at all. Drag up a chair."

Dr. Jensen sat down in a metal folding chair, bit his thick upper lip and frowned. As he began his little talk, he kept his eyes averted from mine.

"I've just come from a meeting with my fellow trustees. Mr. Caldwell, Mr. Linsey and myself have decided unanimously that you should withdraw immediately from this bus boycott business. It's an illegal enterprise, and we don't want the Church of God's Flock's name connected with it. We are businessmen here, and Jax is our home. We must get along with white people. This business—" Dr. Jensen waved his arm to include all of the people in the room and shook his head—"can only lead to serious trouble. We didn't hire you as a rabble-rouser. You are supposed to work for us as a minister of the Gospel—"

"Just a second, Doctor!" I said sharply. "I don't work for you, period! I work for the Lord! You didn't hire me, and neither did Linsey or Caldwell hire me. I was appointed to my church by the titular head of the Church of God's Flock. This is a permanent appointment, and I fully intend to spend the rest of my life as the permanent pastor!" I ran my fingers through my hair, lowered my voice. "I suppose it is my fault for not setting you straight in the first place. But I alone have the authority to commit the Church of God's Flock to any enterprise I consider worthy. Not you or any other trustee can override my decision. Our church is committed and, as a member, that includes you and your fellow trustees. I expect you to work for the boycott, encourage it, and get behind it one hundred percent."

"I'm sorry, Reverend Springer," Dr. Jensen said apologetically. "I guess we labored under a misapprehension."

"That's quite all right," I said, "Anybody can make a mistake. Now, about the boycott. This defiance of the law may seem like bad business to you, and I agree that it may sound petty. But it isn't a petty cause; it is a great cause because it will be a major stride forward in the overall goal of racial equality. You have a large Buick automobile, and you don't ride the bus. Others do. But you must, in God's name, support the boycott."

"I'm for racial equality, Reverend. All of the trustees are; we just didn't want to get in any trouble with the law—"

"The law is wrong, and we must change it. The Bible says so. You are a good Christian man, and you must follow the teachings of the Lord."

"Yes, sir. I'll tell the other trustees. If there is anything I can do myself—"

"Of course." I smiled and called to Dr. Heartwell. He came over to my desk. "You know Dr. Jensen, don't you?"

"Of course." The two men shook hands.

"Dr. Jensen came in to make a contribution to the boycott fund."

"That's wonderful!" Dr. Heartwell exclaimed. "We are grateful for any amount you care to give us."

Dr. Jensen took his checkbook out of his inside coat pocket, and I handed him a ballpoint pen.

"How about twenty-five dollars?" Dr. Jensen asked apprehensively.

"Better make it fifty. Pay to the order of the League For Love."

I accepted the completed check. Dr. Heartwell thanked the dentist again and returned to his desk. I got to my feet before Dr. Jensen sat down again.

"I haven't forgotten your personal problems, Dr. Jensen," I said softly. "I visited your wife, and I intend to see her again."

"She told me you stopped by."

"We prayed together," I pursed my lips, "and that was a good beginning."

"She didn't tell me she prayed!" Dr. Jensen was genuinely surprised.

"Your wife needs God's love," I said simply. "One of these days she will be a mother. You must pray for her and talk constantly to her about the Lord. I know that in her heart she will appreciate it, regardless of what she outwardly expresses."

Moved, Dr. Jensen wiped his eyes with a silk handkerchief. "I thank you from the bottom of my heart, Reverend."

"I will do everything I can. It's my duty as your minister. Do you have your car with you?"

"Why, yes. Can I take you anywhere?"

"No. But Reverend Hutto can dig up a load for you." I marched the dentist over to Hutto's desk, introduced them, and Hutto added Dr. Jensen's Buick to his growing list of available automobiles.

By noon my bookkeeping work was completed, and I had added a few contributions to the fund, which had been brought in by many people in person, and some donations that came in by regular mail at ten-thirty. Many of the encouraging letters and monetary contributions mailed in were from white people residing in Jax. Actually, the bus boycott did not seem to be a hopeless cause. There were a great many white Floridians who were sympathetic, convinced that segregated seating was morally wrong. I locked the safe looking forward to a walk home in the fresh air and a spot of lunch.

A block away from the church, a small colored boy jumped out from behind a jacaranda tree bordering the sidewalk and confronted me.

"Reverend Springer?" The boy was frightened and wore a pair of blue denim shorts, cut down from regular jeans. He held a sealed envelope in his trembling right hand. "Yes, boy. What is it?"

"They said you'd give me a quarter," he said as he shoved the envelope into my hand.

"Who told you that?"

"The quarter's inside."

I unsealed the envelope, removed the coin and handed it to the boy. He popped the quarter into his mouth, turned and ran down the street as fast as his pipe-stem legs would carry him. A folded slip of paper inside the envelope stated: "*Call AD7-3146. To your advantage.*" The note was unsigned.

I continued my walk home. I was interested in the message, but I was also hungry. Ralphine had set the table with some hot string beans and potatoes, cornbread, and buttermilk.

"What about that cold fried chicken, Ralphine? Any left?"

Ralphine cackled crazily. "I done ate that this morning."

"Well, how about some steak tonight? Think we can manage it?"

"Ministers don't never get no steak!" She broke into a fit of cackling, raised her thin arms over her head, and then beat at her legs with a mad rhythm. "Whooee!" she whooped. "No, sir! Ministers don't never get no steak!"

I took two singles out of my wallet, placed them on the table. "You just see if you can buy me a steak with this," I said. "Once in a while I like a little meat."

Wheezing and cackling, Ralphine snatched up the bills and put them in her apron pocket. Dragging a broom behind her and muttering madly to herself, the old crone shuffled out of the kitchen into the study to do a little sweeping. If Ralphine had suddenly mounted the broom and flew away into the sky, I wouldn't have been surprised.

Instead of taking a much needed nap following lunch, I ambled down to the drugstore on the corner and entered a pay telephone booth. After dropping a dime in the slot, I called AD7-3146. The telephone rang several times before it was answered, but I waited.

"Hello," a voice said. "Price's Garage. Sorry to have kept you waiting, but I was gassing up a car out front and just now heard the ring."

"That's quite all right. Who is speaking?"

"Eddie Price."

"This is the Right Reverend Deuteronomy Springer. Did you send me a message by a little colored boy?"

"Oh! Yes, I did. We've been expecting you to call."

"What's on your mind."

"I want to talk to you. There's a man over here who wants to meet you."

"That's nice. But he can meet me at the Southern Baptists of Saint John Church."

"The gentleman who wants to talk to you prefers to remain anonymous."

"I see. What does he want to talk about?"

"I want to talk to you, too, Reverend. It's about the bus boycott."

"Very well. Where is your garage?"

"Do you know where Montgomery Street is?"

"Not exactly."

"Do you know how to get to Flagler Park?"

"No."

"Well, are you driving?"

"No."

"Where are you now?"

"Why?"

"Well, if you can take a Flagler Park bus, I'll tell you where to get off."

"I'm not riding busses these days."

There was a laugh at the other end of the line. "All right. Take a cab and tell the driver to let you off at Montgomery and 36th Street. I'll meet you, and I'll pay for your cab."

"Okay, Mr. Price. You can expect me."

I took a taxicab to the designated meeting place, but there was no one there. I paid off the driver and, as soon as he drove away, a man wearing overalls crossed the street and joined me. He was a thin, wiry little white man with grizzled gray hair and a pale thin face spotted with freckles. He was younger than he looked, because the dark stubble of beard on his cheeks and chin was coal black. This was the first white man I had talked to in a long time, I thought.

"I'm Eddie Price," he said.

"The cab fare was ninety cents."

"Oh! Sure." Mr. Price pulled a dollar out of his pocket and handed it to me.

"I don't have any change."

"That's all right. Follow me, Reverend."

Instead of following him I walked at his side, and in the middle of the block on Montgomery Street, we turned into a low one-story garage building. Outside there was a single gas pump. Price took a crudely lettered GONE FISHIN' sign down from the wall and hung it over the top of the pump. He rejoined me at the entrance and then pulled down the reinforced door. Dim overhead lights burned in the rafters of the garage, and there were six automobiles of different makes parked along one wall.

"The office is over there," Price said, pointing.

We crossed the grease-spotted concrete floor and entered the small office in the far corner of the building. The office was a poorly constructed addition of beaverboard: two walls jutting out at right angles from the corner, and a dutch-door entrance.

Seated behind a cluttered and messy desk was a middle-aged man wearing a gray seersucker suit, a blue necktie and a white shirt. In contrast to Eddie Price, he resembled a banker. He stood up as I entered the office and waited until Price closed and latched both the top and bottom halves of the dutch-door before he spoke.

"How do you do, Reverend Springer. My name is Corwin, and I represent the Jax Intertransit Omnibus Company."

"How do you do, Mr. Corwin."

"Eddie here," Corwin added, "is chairman of the Citizen's Committee of Jax."

"Evidently you gentlemen want to talk business," I said, hoisting myself onto the desk. I sat stiffly, watching both of them warily. Corwin winked at Price, nodded his head sagely.

"Yes, you can call it business. You look like a reasonable man, Reverend, and I think we can come to terms."

"Just a minute," I said. "Before we go any further, I want you to know that I'm not the head of the League For Love. I am only a member, and any decision must be made by the group as a whole. Not by me."

"We don't talk business with niggers," Price said.

"That's right," Corwin said firmly. "We don't. But then, I don't think we have to talk to niggers. I think we can stop this bus boycott right here, just among the three of us. Don't you think so, Eddie?"

"I certainly do, Mr. Corwin."

"I came to listen," I said, lighting a cigarette. "Let's hear it."

"I'm going to get personal then," Corwin said bluntly. "How much are those niggers over there paying for you to stir up trouble?"

"As yet, the question of salary hasn't come up. As a minister of the Church of God's Flock I am paid eighty dollars a month."

Price spat on a rubber mat in front of the door. "I pay two mechanics eighty bucks a week apiece!"

"Naturally," I said coldly. "Unskilled labor should be paid a larger weekly wage."

"Cut it out, Eddie!" Corwin said sharply. "Eddie didn't mean to belittle your profession, Reverend. As a minister you are preaching the Good Book, and both of us admire you for it. But you're entitled to a living. Look at your clothes! You need a new suit, your collar is frayed, and even a new pair of shoes would come in mighty handy. Right?"

"I suppose." I shrugged.

"Now, look," Corwin continued. "We're all good Christians here. I'm a Methodist, and Eddie here is a Presbyterian. But we're Southerners, too. We've lived around niggers all our lives, and you haven't. As soon as I heard your accent—"

"I don't have an accent."

"That's what I mean. As soon as I heard you talk, I knew you were from up North. We take care of our niggers down here. Good care of 'em. We always have and we always will. We know them and we love them. We need them and they need us. If it wasn't for niggers, there is one hell of a lot of work we would have to do ourselves. Right, Eddie?"

"Yes, sir."

"Now you come down here and start stirring 'em up; get our niggers all excited, and they get confused. They don't rightly know what to do, you see. You start out on something like this bus boycott, telling niggers they got a right to sit any place they like, first thing you know—Bang! Trouble. As I said before, Reverend, you look like a reasonable man. You don't want any of these niggers in trouble, and neither do we. A lot of 'em are getting mighty biggity these days as it is. Eddie here, I know, spends a good many hours every week, when he could be working at his business, holding meetings, making night visits and all with the

Citizen's Council. He doesn't want to do that, and neither do I."
Mr. Corwin spread his hands out, palms up. "But we have to do
it. The Negro has a very definite place in the South, and we must
keep him in it."

"How would you like to have your sister marry a nigger?"
Price asked me belligerently.

"My sister was run over by a car when she was nine years old,"
I said. "What she does now is in God's hands."

"I'm sorry," Price said contritely. "But what I mean is: that's
what they want! Niggers all want to marry white women, and if
you let 'em have so much as an inch, that's what'll happen, just
as sure as you're born. We can't let that happen."

"I didn't know that," I said. "None of the colored men I've met
have expressed such a desire."

"Oh, they don't say it!" Price raised his voice. "But you just
look at what happens when they get a little money up North.
They marry a white woman every time!"

"Eddie knows what he's talking about." Mr. Corwin nodded
sagely. "He's made a study of race problems for many years, and
he knows 'em. When they put Eddie up for Chairman of the
Council, I gave him my vote, because I knew that Eddie knew the
problems we faced."

"I appreciated that vote of yours, too, Mr. Corwin!"

"And I was glad to give it to you, Eddie."

"Suppose we talk business," I suggested.

"All right," Mr. Corwin agreed. "Let's. All we want is a normal
situation again. We'll keep your name out of it, and you won't
have to do or say a thing. Just quietly drop out of the—what
do you call it? League For Love—and start preaching the Good
Book the way you're supposed to do at your own little church.
That's number one. Number two, this is an easy thing for you to
do. Deliver a copy of the rosters of the people who are in your car
pools and on the volunteer lists to me or Eddie. If you will do this,
I'll give you five hundred dollars right now, and upon delivery, I'll
give you a thousand dollars. There it is. That's our proposition.
We'll take care of the boycott by visiting these people on the list
and talking to 'em. Eddie knows what to say. I promise you that
there'll be no violence whatsoever."

"Five hundred now and a thousand later?" I asked, thinking
the proposition over.

"That's right," Eddie said. "One thousand upon delivery."

"Let's make it a thousand now and another thousand on delivery," I suggested.

"That is a fair figure, and I agree with you, Reverend," Mr. Corwin said affably. "To end this boycott peacefully, I'd be willing to pay any amount of money but, unfortunately, the Inter-transit Company didn't authorize me any more."

"All right," I said. "Give me the five hundred. I'll see what I can do about the rosters. But they're kept in a safe, and it may take a day or so."

"Speed is essential." Mr. Corwin frowned.

For some time I had heard a faint, whirring sound, and when we stopped talking for a moment, I traced the noise to the inside of the desk. I slid down from my seat atop the desk, squeezed by Eddie and, before Mr. Corwin could stop me, I jerked open the file drawer of the pine desk. A tape recorder whizzed away; a blinking green light in the center indicated that the machine was recording. The microphone was in the tray of the partly open top pen-drawer, and Mr. Corwin had effectively shielded both mike and dangling cord from view throughout our conversation by leaning forward and resting his hands on top of the desk.

"You boys have been bugging me, I see," I said quietly.

"Just protecting our investment," Mr. Corwin said easily.

"Give me the tape or it's no deal," I said.

"Let's put it another way." Eddie smiled happily. "We keep the tape, you get us the rosters, and then we'll give you the tape. But let's forget about the fifteen hundred dollars, shall we?"

"Okay," I said. "Your company just lost a bus boycott."

"Get out, nigger lover!" Eddie said contemptuously. He turned away from me, unlatched the top half of the dutch-door and pushed it open. The bottom half was latched on the outside. As he bent over to raise the latch, I picked up an empty Coca Cola bottle from the desk and swung it hard against the base of his skull. Eddie didn't move or make a sound; his body merely hung limply over the bottom section of the door which remained latched.

With the bottle firmly gripped in my hand, I wheeled on Mr. Corwin who was still in this same position behind the desk. His pale blue eyes were opened wide, and he stared at me disbelievingly. As I looked at him, he raised his hands to protect his face.

I slowly advanced, and he backed up against the beaverboard wall. Without taking my eyes from his face, I reached down and switched off the recorder, jerked both the spools off the spindles with my left hand, and dropped them into my coat pocket.

"How about the five hundred dollars, Mr. Corwin?"

"You killed him, Reverend! He's dead, I know he is!"

"No. A man can take a pretty good blow at the base of the skull. Now, if I had hit him on top of the head, he might be dead. But he isn't dead. What about the five hundred dollars, Mr. Corwin?"

"The company didn't give me that much," Mr. Corwin stammered. "I got three hundred this morning, and Mr. Keene didn't want to give me that. He didn't think I could bribe you."

"I bribe easily," I said. "Give me the three hundred."

Mr. Corwin fumbled his wallet out of his hip pocket, his fingers trembled so violently he couldn't get the money out. I took the wallet out of his hands and removed the money.

"Some of that money is mine!" he protested.

"It still doesn't add up to five hundred," I told him reasonably. "And now let's talk some more. I have the tape. You don't. One blubbering bleat out of either you or Mr. Price, and you're through. You know that, don't you?"

Mr. Corwin nodded. "What about the rosters? You'll get them for us, won't you?"

"Just as soon as you can dig up twelve hundred dollars in cold cash. Goodbye, Mr. Corwin." I pulled Eddie's limp, wiry body away from the top of the door, and let him fall to the floor. He groaned and rolled his head back and forth, brought his hands up to his face. "You see," I said, "he's all right."

As I unlatched the lower door, I kept my eyes on Mr. Corwin's face; then I backed out, closed the door and latched it again.

"I'll really be in trouble if I don't get those rosters," Mr. Corwin called out to me when I was halfway across the garage floor.

"Just give me a ring when you get the money," I shouted back cheerfully. "Right now you'd better take care of your chairman!"

Near the entrance to Flagler Park, I hailed a taxicab and climbed inside.

"Where to, Reverend?" the driver asked respectfully.

I looked at my watch. One-thirty. So much had been going on, I had thought it was much later.

"To the nearest telegraph office," I told the driver. My right hand felt numb, and I flexed my fingers. The Coca Cola bottle dropped to the floor of the cab as I opened my hand. I had been holding the bottle in a death grip since leaving the garage, and I hadn't realized it. The incident in the tiny office had been rather tense at that. Amateurs, I thought. If they had wanted to bug me, they could have done it easily in that messy, disorderly office. They could have run an extension microphone in from the open garage and hidden it in a dozen places. But that was the trouble with all of us: we were all amateurs. I was an amateur preacher; Eddie Price and Mr. Corwin were amateur boycott breakers; and the League For Love was working in the dark. We had organized hastily, and we were without a long-range plan of any kind, meeting each crisis as it came along hurriedly and without thinking it out. Amateurs.

I counted the money Mr. Corwin had given me. Three hundred and twenty-seven dollars. Not bad, but why all the gobbledygook about fifteen hundred bucks? Did they really have that much dough to spend for just a few rosters, or were they trying to get me to quit my activity? I was no ring leader; I was just drifting along with the other members of the League For Love to see what would happen. But why think about it? Why think about anything? Ride with the tide, look and listen, speak when spoken to, and listen to the voice as it talked. My voice was saying some very interesting things. But when all was said and done, nothing would make any difference anyway. My act of violence in the garage office had disturbed me, caused my heart to beat faster. I had hit Eddie without thinking, and I had done it easily and well. Just like that. I hadn't been in a fight of any kind since the age of twelve when I had fought a boy in school who had stolen a peanut butter sandwich out of my locker. And as I recalled that fight, I remembered that I had lost it. . .

"Here we are, sir," the driver said.

I paid him off and entered the telegraph office. I had to send my wife some money. Not that I really felt responsible for Virginia. She was an adult. But she was dumb. I was afraid it wouldn't occur to Virginia to write or wire her mother for money to get back to Columbus. And I didn't want Virginia to notify the police that I was missing.

I put a hundred dollars down on the marble counter and told the girl I wanted to send a money order to Virginia Springer in Ocean Pine Terraces, Miami.

"Yes, sir." The girl consulted a small table. "That will cost you two dollars and fifty-two cents."

"That's a little high isn't it, for a money order?"

"I don't know, sir. That's what the table says. You can see right here—"

"Never mind." I took another five out of my wallet. "How about a message with it? That's free isn't it?"

"No, sir. A message with a postal money order costs six and five-tenths cents a word."

"You've got quite a little racket going here. I don't suppose you have special rates for ministers, either?"

"I really don't know, sir. I'll have to ask Mr.—"

"Never mind. The hell with it."

The girl's eyes widened and her eyebrows raised.

"What I mean is, I'll pay the regular rates."

I wrote Virginia's address on the form and a brief message: *Go back to Columbus and mother.* I pushed money and message across the counter to the girl and accepted my change.

"You didn't include your name and address, sir," the girl reminded me.

"That's right. I don't want the woman to know who sent her the money."

"Yes, but we need it for record purposes."

"Well, you won't get it. Do you want to send the money order or not?"

"Yes, sir. I'll send it. I know who you are anyway. I've seen your picture in the paper."

"You're a bright young lady. Your mother must be proud of you."

"She is," the girl said defiantly, shaking her pony tail.

I left the office, stood at the curb cracking my knuckles. I had come off badly, I decided. Getting sarcastic with an employee who was merely doing her job was no way for a minister to act. I went back inside, beckoned to the girl.

"I'm very sorry," I said. "I'm overwrought today. Please accept my apology."

"That's quite all right, sir."

"God bless you child." That was better. I left the office.

Outside I picked up an empty taxicab at the corner and told the driver to take me to the Southern Baptists of Saint John Church.

When I entered the basement GHQ, there was a lot of activity going on, but none of the ministers of the League For Love were in the room.

I tapped a young typist on the shoulder, and she leaped quickly to her feet.

"That's all right, young lady," I said. "Keep your seat. Where are Dr. Heartwell and the other League members?"

"He's upstairs in his regular office," the girl answered quickly. "Reverend McCroy and Dr. David are with him and," she looked around the room, "I believe Reverend Hutto is up there, too."

"What is it? A meeting?"

"Yes, sir. An investigator from the International Colored Advancement Society flew in from Atlanta, and he's talking to them now."

"Thank you."

So, the professionals had arrived. The I.C.A.S. had recently been outlawed in four southern states and, in a widely publicized move, this organization had shifted its main headquarters to Ghana, Africa. Devoted to advancing the cause of colored men throughout the world, this widespread organization had hired the best Negro brains available. Our little operation could get into some real trouble if the I.C.A.S. became involved. The smell of Communism hung over this dark organization, and although none of the rumors concerning Communism had ever been proved, the mere taint of the name—International Colored Advancement Society—could put the kibosh on our boycott in short order. Besides, this organization would demand a strict accounting of funds, and in all probability, would thoroughly investigate me and my phony religious background. The valid ordainment in my wallet would be a great joke if publicized in the newspapers, and my usefulness to the League For Love would be all over.

At the end of the basement hallway, I climbed the steps leading up to Dr. Heartwell's office three at a time. Without knocking I entered Dr. Heartwell's office and closed the door behind me. The Right Reverend Jason McCroy, Dr. David and Dr. Heartwell sat in chairs facing Dr. Heartwell's desk. The swivel chair in the place behind the desk was occupied by the investigator from Atlanta. He was a sharp-looking character, decked out in a Brooks Brothers suit with thin narrow lapels, and a gay Countess Mara necktie was tied around his powerful neck. His hair was black and straight and was combed back over his round skull in well-trained elegance, aided by a shiny, sweet-smelling pomade.

Reverend Hutto sat apart from the others behind his own small desk in the corner. There was a yellow scratch pad before him, and he was taking notes.

As the door clicked behind me I could feel a certain tenseness in the atmosphere, and I knew that I had been the subject under discussion.

"Gentlemen," I said cheerfully. "Please excuse my tardiness, but I was unavoidably detained."

Solemn faces greeted me, and then Reverend McCroy cleared his throat. "This is Mr. Fred Grant, Chief Investigator from the Atlanta I.C.A.S. branch office. Mr. Grant, this is Reverend Springer, our treasurer."

"How do you do," I said.

"Mr. Grant says that the I.C.A.S. is prepared to throw the weight of its entire organization behind our bus boycott," Dr. Heartwell said seriously, "both money and trained personnel. However," Dr. Heartwell lowered his eyes to the desk, "Mr. Grant wants to ask you a few questions first. I don't want you to feel that this is an imposition or a reflection on your motives, Reverend Springer," Dr. Heartwell said apologetically, "and well, if you don't want to answer any of his questions, it is up to you, sir." Dr. Heartwell finished lamely.

"I'm delighted," I said. "When the I.C.A.S. sends a representative to help us, it shows that our boycott is getting the serious recognition it deserves."

Mr. Grant pushed an expensive pigskin briefcase to one side and clasped his fingers together. His spatulate fingernails were manicured and highly polished.

"I didn't state that your boycott would receive any backing from the I.C.A.S., Reverend Springer. I was merely sent down to Jax to investigate for our organization. Any help you receive from us will be based, at least in part, on my report when I return to Atlanta."

"Wonderful," I said. "We are delighted by your interest, aren't we, gentlemen." My eyes slowly scanned by the faces of the assembled ministers, and my direct stare caused all of the eyes to lower or look elsewhere. I took a seat upon the edge of Reverend Hutto's desk and said, "Proceed, please."

"What exactly, Reverend Springer," Mr. Grant probed with a deep, well-trained voice, "are your personal motives in this bus boycott, and what is your interest in the individual Negro? You're a white man, and the I.C.A.S. is interested in the professed motives of any white man when he shows a sudden interest in the problems of our race."

"I'm glad you asked that question, Mr. Grant, and it's not a question I shall answer lightly." I closed my eyes and steepled my fingers, dropped my voice to almost a whisper. "I do not look upon myself as a white man, per se, Mr. Grant. All of us are God's creatures, God's lambs, members of His flock. I am first, second and always, a man of God, and I try at all times to listen and to heed His word. Each night I get down on my knees and humbly pray to the Lord. I ask God for the answer to our problems, not only racial problems as you imply, Mr. Grant, but how we can live better. How I can teach my flock the virtues of righteousness and charity and hope and love. Especially love. God's love is about mortal man who trods the stage for his brief scene upon the earth. And if I have found the way, it is because God has revealed it to me in answer to my prayers," I opened my eyes and raised my voice, "to all of our prayers!"

"Amen!" Reverends McCroy and Hutto said softly.

"Okay, okay!" Mr. Grant said impatiently. "This isn't a Bible class; don't get carried away. Just exactly what were your reasons in accepting a Negro church, Reverend Springer? Couldn't you find a white church?"

"When I asked the Lord for His guidance at the holy monastery of the Church of God's Flock, He answered thusly: 'Go and find thee the church which needs thee most—the poorest, the neediest—and preach My word there. Lift the darkness and the oppression from the poor and the humble. Because,' God concluded, 'The meek shall inherit the earth!'"

"Amen!" All of the ministers said in unison.

"Now look here, Mr. Springer," Mr. Grant began.

"The Right Reverend Springer," I corrected.

"All right! Reverend Springer. I'm getting fed up to here," and he crossed his throat with a forefinger, "with all this religious mumbo-jumbo in reply to a direct question."

"Mumbo-jumbo?" I asked. "Do you call the word of the Lord, mumbo-jumbo?"

"Of course not," Mr. Grant retreated. "I meant—"

"Are you a God-fearing church member, Mr. Grant? Do you regularly attend church on Sunday and pray to your Lord?"

"I'm a busy man, Reverend Springer."

"I can see you are," I said sternly. "Too busy to heed God's word, too busy toiling in the marketplace to put your faith and trust in the Lord. Without His help, we shall not lead our children out of the wilderness. Without faith we shall lose our bus boycott. Now you, sir, you have been questioning me at great length, and I would like to ask you a question. My life is a flyleaf out of God's Book, but I feel I should ask you one pertinent question."

"Okay, okay," Mr. Grant said wearily.

"What is your annual salary?"

Mr. Grant straightened in the swivel chair and narrowed his eyes. We all looked at him expectantly. The question was a good one.

"What has my salary got to do with the matter at hand?"

"A great deal," I said quietly. "Do you want to tell us, or do you have a reason for withholding this information?"

"I don't have anything to hide," Mr. Grant said defensively.

"Of course not." I smiled. "If you don't want to tell us, we can easily obtain the information from Atlanta." I turned and spoke over my shoulder to Reverend Hutto. "Perhaps you had better call Atlanta, Reverend Hutto."

"Are you trying to threaten me?" Mr. Grant said angrily.

"Threaten? That's an unusual word, Mr. Grant. Our interest here is in the sum of your annual salary. Will you tell us?"

"It's no big secret," Mr. Grant said sullenly. "I make eight thousand a year, that's all."

The investigator's admission of this sum was similar to dropping a bomb on the desk. With the exception of myself, the ministers were stunned by this announcement. In amazed silence, they stared at Mr. Grant with bewildered expressions. Under the direct gaze of these innocent eyes, Mr. Grant squirmed slightly in his swivel chair.

"And are you not paid per diem, traveling expenses, and other allowances besides," I pressed. "On field trips to Jax, for instance?"

"Naturally," Mr. Grant said impatiently. There was a faint glow of red beneath the surface of his bronze face.

"You may be interested to know, Mr. Grant," I said quietly, "that your annual salary is almost double the amount that the rest of us are paid in a single year altogether."

"Amen!" Dr. David said ominously, tapping the desk with his forefinger.

"And so, I question your motives, Mr. Grant! How many small contributions does it take to pay you and your colleagues such magnificent yearly sums? How many pennies do you put aside from these well-meant donations? Donations that are needed for food and shelter by your oppressed race! Are you for Mammon or your people, Mr. Grant? You do not attend church, and yet you question the motives of men of God. You question me, a humble preacher who needs God's help, when I am only attempting to lift the yoke of inequality from the downtrodden! I question your motives, sir! I challenge your right to investigate any member of the League For Love!"

"I quit!" Mr. Grant got out of his chair and picked up his briefcase. "If you listen to this man, you're crazy, all of you! I can't talk to an idiot!"

"God can talk to an idiot," I said calmly. "And I shall pray for you tonight, Mr. Grant, in the hope you will receive the spiritual guidance you so badly need."

Mr. Grant slammed out of the office, and we could hear his leather heels pounding on the wooden floor leading to the side exit.

"Eight thousand smackers a year!" Reverend Hutto marveled. "Whooee!" The tension broke, and all of the ministers except myself laughed gleefully at Reverend Hutto's exuberant outburst.

"We're in the wrong business!" Dr. Heartwell joked.

"I think not," I said. "Suppose we start with a brief prayer and then get down to the business of tonight's meeting."

The League For Love was once more on an even keel.

I left the planning of the evening meeting up to Dr. Heart-well and Dr. David. They were both experts in this line compared to me, and I left them alone. Reverend McCroy left the church as a missionary to the two colored taxicab companies who had refused to lower their rates like the others. He had worked out some rough figures to prove to them that they could make more money with lower rates. Reverend Hutto was busy with dispatching and the telephone, and he had procured a public address system so that the overflow crowd for the evening meeting could listen out in the street. I wrote a five-minute talk for Bessie Langdale to read over the Negro radio station that night, sent her to a corner of the office with a kindergarten teacher from the primary school as her coach. I didn't expect Bessie to memorize the speech, but I did expect her to learn how to read it. I also wrote some spot announcements indirectly encouraging the bus boycott, and the Negro station manager promised to have them read at least once an hour and without charge.

And so, the rest of the long afternoon passed away.

Volunteer workers and several of Dr. Heartwell's female church members had gone to a great deal of trouble to prepare a long buffet supper in the basement corridor. But I passed it by and walked home to eat the steak prepared by Ralphine.

Ralphine was gone when I reached home, but she had cooked a swiss steak, and it was bubbling in gravy on the warm burner of the electric stove. She had prepared candied yams and some fluffy biscuits to go with the steak, and I considered it an excellent meal. Perhaps I had misjudged the old crone.

After dinner I read the Bible for about half an hour to pick up some phrases to use in my prayers at the meeting. I then walked back to Dr. Heartwell's church. On my walk back I paused at a corner to wait for a red light, and one of the Intertransit Company's big green-and-white busses whizzed by. I was pleased to note that the bus was completely empty.

Our second mass meeting closely followed the pattern of the first meeting with some important exceptions: There was more of everything; more people, more music, longer speeches by Dr. Heartwell and Dr. David, longer prayers by me, more enthusiasm from the crowd, and more money collected.

After the meeting broke up at about nine-thirty, Reverend Hutto and I counted the money in the basement. There was a total collection of $1,272.37 for the meeting. Added to the donations received during the day and the night before, the sum was impressive. After I locked the safe and prepared to leave, Reverend Hutto returned to his desk to work on transportation schedules. I stopped by his desk on my way out.

"Don't work all night now," I said kindly. "Remember, tomorrow is another day."

"Don't I know it!" Reverend Hutto exclaimed. "But there are people who got to get to work at four-thirty in the morning. And if I don't get something worked out, a lot of white folks are going to miss their breakfast."

"Better break in three volunteers to work three shifts around the clock. You can't do it all, and we need you very much, Reverend Hutto."

"Once I get it all worked out, it won't be so bad."

"You get some sleep now before morning," I said. "I mean it."

"Don't worry, I will. You going home now?"

"Yes."

"You wait a minute, and I'll get somebody to walk home with you."

"I know the way," I laughed.

"So do a lot of other people," Reverend Hutto said darkly. "You best take along some protection."

"I'll be all right."

"Dr. Heartwell told me about that cross in your front yard last night."

"Teenagers." I shrugged indifferently. "Don't worry about me. You just take good care of yourself. Hear?"

"Yes, sir. Good night." He bent over his papers.

I had completely forgotten about the cross burning until Reverend Hutto reminded me. My cloth was a protective covering, but it wasn't armor; and in a dark street, a great many things can happen to a man alone. But somehow I couldn't really worry about myself and about what might happen to me. A persistent feeling of unreality cloaked my every action and every word. Only once in a while—like the conversation with the girl in the telegraph office—did I feel that I was the real me. The rest of the time I seemed to be outside myself, an observer, an anonymous member of a great movie audience watching some new kind of comedy on a life-sized screen, wondering how the plot would turn out in the end.

The walk home was uneventful, and I rather enjoyed it. There was a slight breeze for a change, and I was either getting used to the heat or getting used to my heavy, dark clothing. The temperature hadn't changed, and the humidity was just as heavy. I burned the tape in the kitchen sink, and it smelled pretty bad. But I had no real use for it.

After a shower, I sat listlessly in my shorts at the desk in the study. There were pencils, plenty of paper, but I didn't feel like writing anything. I didn't feel like doing anything except sitting, and I would have preferred sitting outside on the porch. But I knew that the mosquitoes would drive me inside in no time at all. With an effort I got out of my chair and switched off the light. The absence of light seemed to cool the room by an abrupt and magical ten or fifteen percent. I moved the swivel chair on its rollers over to the window, sat down, and looked into the night.

The streetlight on the corner put a pool of light on the sidewalk, and a larger circle of light on the street itself. The slow-moving pedestrians, walking in the darkness, appeared to come from nowhere as they stepped into the light. One, two, three and, on the fourth step, they were through the circle and in darkness again. I smoked cigarettes and watched this phenomenon with absorbed interested for a long time. My eyes gradually got used to the darkness, and the game lost interest for me as soon as I could pick out the pedestrians before they entered the circle of light. And then I saw a darker shadow against the blackness of the empty lot.

This shadow didn't belong there. Staring through the window, I concentrated on the shape and inventoried the contents of the vacant lot in my mind. The lot was not an empty lot except in the sense that it didn't have a building on it. The lot contained piles of tin cans, weeds, a large patch of mother-in-law tongue cacti, gama grass, cardboard boxes and other debris, but unlike a Florida vacant lot, there were no patches of jungly growth because traces of burning remained. Within the past year or two, the lot had been cleared and burned over. The shadow I stared at was not a part of the regular inventory I saw every day.

And then the shadow stretched.

Fixing the spot in my mind, I slipped into my trousers and entered the kitchen. I fumbled through the kitchen drawers to the left of the sink until I found a butcher knife. I tested the sharpness of the knife with my thumb. Not too sharp, but then a knife didn't have to be exceptionally sharp to cut somebody's throat. I giggled foolishly with excitement and then caught the hiccups. I breathed deeply with my mouth open and then drank a glass of water. The hiccups stopped as suddenly as they had started, and I was sobered and steadied by the deep breathing.

Barefooted, I eased open the back door and, bending low to the ground, I tiptoed silently around the house. At the corner of the building, I paused and stared across the lot until my eyes found the dark figure. I couldn't tell whether he was facing toward the house or toward the street, but I crept forward, knowing that if I got close enough to use the knife, the way he was facing wouldn't make any great difference.

The closer I got the louder my heart pounded. There seemed to be an audible drumming coming out of my chest, and although I knew there actually wasn't, I slowed my pace until I only took one short step at a time, waited, and then took another. When I reached a spot less than ten feet away from the figure, a match flared, startling me, and I blinked my eyes. I jumped forward, bringing the knife up as I jumped, but the fraction of delay had been too much.

My wrist was seized, a chopping blow on my elbow numbed my arm clear to the shoulder, and I was flat on my back in loose sand with two heavy knees on my chest. A match was lighted above my head and my burning eyes swimmingly recognized the face of Tommy Heartwell.

"You're just a cocky banty rooster, ain't you?" Tommy chuckled, helped me to my feet. "I believe you was going to tick me with that knife!"

"Yes I was, Tommy," I said, rubbing my numb and aching arm. "But I didn't know it was you. In fact, I didn't know who it was."

"And you didn't care!" Tommy laughed again. "Come on, I'd better take you up to the house."

The front door was closed inside by the bolt, so we had to enter by the back door. I turned on the light and washed my hands and arms at the kitchen sink.

"I better keep watch a little better than I been doing," Tommy said. "I didn't even see you till you was about twenty feet away."

"Why didn't you say something, Tommy? I would certainly have killed you. You know that, don't you?"

"I know it now. I'm sorry, Reverend. But I was glad it was me out there instead of somebody else. Daddy told us to set up a guard on account of them burning that cross, and another man takes over at midnight."

"I don't need any guard on me," I said angrily.

"That's what Daddy said you'd say. And that's why we didn't tell you anything about it."

"I can take care of myself, Tommy. Go on home and go to bed."

"I reckon we'll just watch a couple of more nights, Reverend," Tommy said pleasantly. "It won't hurt nothin'."

"All right! Good night." Why argue with him?

After another shower and when I was flaked out on my bed, the knowledge that a friendly giant like Tommy was guarding my sleep was rather comforting, and within a very few minutes I was fast asleep.

AT FIRST I couldn't understand what it was that aroused me from my slumbers. I am a sound sleeper, and a glance at my watch showed me that it was only six a.m. Much too early to get out of bed. I then heard an angry and hoarse-voiced whisper, followed by the mad cackling of Ralphine's voice. I was awake, so I got out of bed, left my bedroom and padded to the kitchen.

Ralphine and a young Negro were separated by the kitchen table, and the man was quite angry. His lips were poked out in a petulant pout, and he was scowling at Ralphine. She cackled as I entered, but it was a restrained and automatic utterance compared to her usual ear-shattering laughter. The kitchen table was littered with objects not usually associated with a kitchen. There was a small pile of chicken feathers dyed in primary colors, a neat pile of pig bristles, several tiny bleached bones, a fruit jar containing red dirt, (the jar was labeled RED DIRT) and a dozen or so dried and withered leathery objects that I couldn't identify. My appearance in the doorway had evidently halted a very interesting argument.

"Good morning, Ralphine," I said, "what's all this?"

"Nothin', Captain," Ralphine said. "I was just goin' to fix your breakfast."

The young buck looked at me sullenly. He was still angry with Ralphine, but he was also embarrassed by my presence and undecided as to what course he should follow. He glared at Ralphine for a second and then turned to me.

"I'm sorry, Reverend Springer, if I woke you up," he said, "but your cook owes me four dollars!"

"I don't any such thing, Captain," Ralphine denied. "He asked me for a juju, and he done got a juju. 'Cause a juju don't work ain't no fault of mine. It was a good juju."

"Juju?" I inquired.

The young Negro was now sorry he had said anything, and he edged toward the back door. "Never you mind, old woman!"

He said bravely at the door. "I'll get my four dollars back! You just wait and see!" The screen door slammed behind him and he was gone.

Ralphine gathered up the objects from the table and dropped them into an empty flour sack. She cackled twice, but her heart wasn't in it.

"Crazy boy!" she exclaimed. "Crazy boy! You want your breakfast now, Captain?"

"What was the argument about?"

"I made a good juju," she said. "Man, he wear around his neck, he never get VD! This crazy boy say he wear juju, get VD anyway. I say to the boy he never wear juju. He say he did wear juju, get VD anyway."

"You mean venereal disease?"

"That's what I say. You wear juju, you don't get VD."

"I don't think my church members would approve of my having a witch making jujus in my kitchen," I said, laughing, "especially if they don't work."

"Always work before," Ralphine replied. She filled a pot with water, poured a liberal amount of grits into the pot, clicked the burner on the electric stove.

"How do you make such a juju?"

"My daddy not from Jax. He learn how to make juju in Nassau, and he teach me before he died. That's why I always work for minister like you. Make juju in minister's house, juju powerful." She said simply.

"How many of my church members come to you for jujus?"

"They all come to Ralphine," the old witch said proudly. "I make all kinds of juju. Make babies, no make babies, win money, no win money, stop VD, get VD. I make all kinds of juju. Dr. Jensen buy juju from me all the time. He keep me on this job."

"Dr. Fred Jensen, the trustee?"

"Yes, sir. He buys juju all the time! He old, but he want to be young again!" Ralphine was now in good spirits again, and she let out a cackle that blasted my ears. "Dr. Jensen, he think juju help him make baby."

"That's fine, Ralphine," I said happily. "You make all the jujus you want."

I shaved in the bathroom, a new and daring plan forming in my mind. If Dr. Jensen was buying jujus from Ralphine, he was in desperate straits. I was surprised. It was difficult to believe that an educated man could believe in such things, but then, Dr. Jensen was a Negro. And what did I know about Negroes? They were emotional, I knew that much, and even if they didn't believe in magic, perhaps they played it safe, just in case. Dr. Jensen had struck me as a God-fearing Christian and a sincere believer! I suddenly began to laugh and nicked my chin rather painfully.

After breakfast I mixed a pinch of salt and a pinch of sugar together, crumbled an aspirin tablet into the mixture and scooped the tiny, glittering pile of white powder into an empty match box. I had made a juju. Only a test could prove its effectiveness. But what could I lose?

Dick Ames, the *Advertiser* reporter-photographer, was waiting for me when I reached the basement GHQ of the League For Love, a wide grin on his inquisitive face.

"This is turning into a terrific story, Reverend," Ames said, taking his camera off my desk, "and I've got some good pictures this morning. After I get a statement from you, I'd like to have a few poses of you and the other preachers out in the motor pool. You know, directing things, shots like that."

"I liked the story you did in dialect, Mr. Ames," I told him. "It helped us more than a straight story would have done. But I don't want any more pictures of me in the paper. Dr. Heartwell is the president, and you'd better concentrate your stories and photos on him."

"I see," Ames winked at me. "He's the real head, but you and I know different, don't we?"

"No," I said seriously. "Dr. Heartwell is in complete command of the boycott. I'm just another member of his league."

"Okay," Ames shrugged, "you have your way till you die, and then I'll have mine. How about a statement?"

"We will be glad to give you a statement, Mr. Ames. Any kind of publicity will help us win in the long run. But you'll have to get your statement from Dr. Heartwell. Keep your seat, and I'll get him."

I found Dr. Heartwell in his upstairs office, head down on his desk. A half-eaten ham sandwich and an empty milk bottle were on top of a stack of papers. He raised his head wearily as I sat down, a weak smile curling the corners of his lips.

"I think I'm getting old, Reverend Springer," he said hoarsely. "A night or two without sleep didn't use to bother me so much."

"Everybody has to sleep, Doctor. I'm sorry I bothered you. That reporter from the *Advertiser* wants a statement. Play ball with him. We need all the publicity we can get."

"Is it the same reporter who—"

"That's right. Dick Ames. He isn't for us, but he's a reporter, and he'll print something. Just express confidence."

"All right." Dr. Heartwell pushed his chair back and got up.

"Before you go, Doctor," I stopped him, "I want to discuss an important matter. We are getting a sizable fund on hand. We need a certain amount in cash for immediate expenses, but I'm going to bank the rest of the money in Atlanta."

"Why? I know the money should be in a bank, but why Atlanta?"

"I think I know a little more about law than you do," I smiled, "and I want to beat the Intertransit Company to their first and obvious move. In essence, we are operating a transportation system with our car pool and trucks. This is strictly illegal. We don't have a license, and we can't get one. If the bus company moves in with a court order, they can impound our funds and records. Then where would we be?"

"Can they do that?"

"They certainly can. I'm surprised they haven't done so already. But if our money is banked in another state, they can't touch it!"

"Good! Good!" Dr. Heartwell said approvingly. "You'd better get on that right away!"

"Leave it to me," I said. "I'll take care of the money."

After getting Dr. Heartwell and Ames together and accompanying them outside to the motor pool, I returned to the safe and wrapped the money in a newspaper. I left a hundred dollars in the safe, which would be plenty to operate on for the day. There would be a lot more money coming in, I figured, both by mail and from the evening collection, in case the hundred wasn't enough.

First things first. I caught a taxicab to Dr. Fred Jensen's office.

To achieve success in the United States, a man must be able to do two things well: First, he must be able to think and speak on his feet with conviction; and secondly, he must be able to write a good letter. This was the thought that came to me in the cab as I rode to Dr. Jensen's office. Somewhere along the line I had gotten sidetracked into being an accountant, when all of the time I had the gift for speech inside me. I would soon know whether I had a true gift or not.

Dr. Jensen was sitting in his dental chair when I pushed open the door to his office. He jumped out of the chair at the sound, and there was a trace of surprise in his voice when he discovered it was me.

"Reverend Springer," he said cordially. "I'm expecting a nine o'clock patient. It's a little too early, but I didn't expect you."

"I didn't expect to be here, Doctor," I said seriously, "but it was God's will that I talk to you." I felt my forehead with my right hand and closed my eyes.

"Are you ill? Please sit down."

"No," I shook my head and dropped my arm to my side. "You sit down, please. I'll sit on your stool."

"The dental chair is more comfortable."

"I insist, Dr. Jensen. Please take your seat. I am overwrought, and I believe I have a touch of fever, but I am far from ill. My heart is light, and my body has gained new strength." I looked Dr. Jensen directly in the eyes and then said deliberately. "I have been privileged to have a visitation from the Lord. In answer to my prayers, the good Lord sent an angel to see me!"

Dr. Jensen dropped his jaw. "You saw an angel?"

"Yes," I nodded, dropped my eyes. "It isn't the first time such a visitation has happened to me. Several times in my lonely monk's cell at Orangeville, I was privileged to converse with an angel. But I never told anyone about it—not even the saintly Abbot—but this time the angel spoke to me about your problems."

"My problems?"

"Yes. Have you been praying a great deal lately, Dr. Jensen?"

"Yes, sir, I have," he replied piously.

"I thought as much. I, too, have prayed for you, Doctor. But I haven't prayed for you alone. There are many others I have prayed for, men and women who have sorely needed my prayers. But the combination of both of our prayers must have touched the Lord's heart, because he sent an angel to see me, an angel who told me the course that we must follow."

"You have been working hard on the boycott, perhaps—"

"You're a good man, Dr. Jensen," I smiled gently, "and you have faith, but your faith is not as great as mine. I thought you might think something like that, and it is not easy for me to go on. But I must do as I have been ordered to do. If you are skeptical, we shall fail. But if you believe, and you must believe in me as I believe in you, we shall succeed." I turned on the stool and looked out of the window for a long moment. "My time has come," I said softly, "but if it is God's will that I must perish, I thank him fervently for singling me out of the multitude."

"Did the angel say that you were going to die?"

"Yes," I nodded. "I am going to die, but another will live in my place." I turned back to Dr. Jensen, who sat mutely in the dental chair. I fixed my eyes on his and began my tale. "Last night as I prepared to retire, I got down on my knees to pray, Dr. Jensen. There were a great many people on my list who needed these prayers. I was on my knees for more than an hour, beseeching the Lord to help us in our fight for equality, and begging him for guidance and knowledge that would let us win the boycott. But I did not forget you, Dr. Jensen, not by any means."

My voice was under perfect control. I spoke slowly enough for each and every word to sink into Dr. Jensen's receptive mind, and with great conviction. An unbeatable combination was working for me. I was able to speak with *mezzo forte* conviction, and Dr. Jensen wanted to believe! As I warmed, I almost believed what I was saying myself!

"Yes, I got to you, Dr. Jensen, and to your wife, Merita. I told the Lord of your desire to have a child and of the good Christian life you now lead. But I also told him of the sins of your youth. I know that you have not always been a good and faithful servant, and I told Him so. You were a great sinner in your youth, and your mind contained evil thoughts, and your body conceived and accomplished evil deeds. But I asked Him to forgive you. You have confessed your sins, and you are doing everything in your power to lead a decent life and to follow in His steps. I told God these things and begged him to grant you your one desire, your single desire to have a son to bear your name. And I prayed for Merita, too. I told God of her shiftless ways, and about her denial of Him, and of her love and taste for alcohol. But I beseeched Him on her behalf. A child can change this woman, I told Him. And on and on I went. I did not keep track of the time I spent on my knees because prayer is timeless, and God listens to all of our prayers with His infinite patience and wisdom."

I paused for dramatic effect.

"Lo and behold!" My voice rang out. "A clap of thunder sounded, and I knew fear and trembling!" I dropped the tone of my voice to *piano*. "And there, standing gloriously upon my dresser, was an angel! A beautiful angel, all in shining white, with long silvery hair and a white, pure face! Tiny motes of diamond dust dropped from the massive wings, which were the shiny whiteness of an egret's wings. I was afraid, Dr. Jensen, and I trembled. And then the angel smiled—such a sweet and gentle smile—that my fear vanished. I spoke to the angel then, and I have since wondered why I did so speak, but I knew that the angel had visited me to speak of you. 'Why have you come?' I asked. 'Is it because of Dr. Fred Jensen?' and the angel nodded. I waited for the angel to reply and, after a long moment, the angel said to me: 'Dr. Jensen will not conceive a child.' His voice was gentle and sweet and musical, but I knew that his words were true. 'But why?' I asked. 'Dr. Jensen is a good man.' And again the angel nodded. 'Yes, Dr. Jensen is good now,' the angel replied, 'but he must pay for his youthful sins!'

"I started to say something—I don't remember what it was—but the angel held up his arm for silence, and I did not speak. 'Stay!' the angel said. 'Listen!' And the angel said to me: 'But Merita shall have a child, and it shall be as Dr. Jensen's own. But he shall conceive it not. The child shall be conceived by a pure man, a man who has sinned hardly at all, a man who has been purged of his sins. This man shall plant his seed in Merita Jensen, and the child shall grow. And as the child swells in her belly, this man shall wither away. And when the child is born, this man will die, and the child will take his place. This is the will of the Lord!' That is what the angel said to me. And I said, 'But who shall this man be? Where shall I find this good and pure man who will plant his seed in Merita Jensen?' Again the angel smiled and said, 'Look unto thyself!'

"With another clap of thunder, the angel disappeared. I stood up in the small bedroom, and my heart was heavy because I knew that I must die. And for a moment, I'll admit, I thought of several ways to get out of the situation. You think that I'm a brave man, Dr. Jensen, but I am not. I am merely a mortal, and I was sorely distraught that I had been chosen to die. And for another moment,

I wanted to dismiss the angel as a figment of my imagination, but I was prevented from doing such a thing by a sign!"

I held my newspaper-wrapped package out to Dr. Jensen. "Here," I said, "hold this money for a second."

Dr. Jensen reached out with both hands, but they were trembling so violently I didn't hand him the package. "Never mind," I said, "I'll just put the money on your work table."

I dug into my trousers pocket, pulled out the match box containing my improvised juju. I opened the box and showed the mixture of salt, sugar and aspirin tablet to Dr. Jensen.

"You see," I said, "here is the sign. After I dropped into a fitful sleep last night, I awoke this morning with a clear head. And this powder, which dropped from the angel's wings last night as he disappeared, is what I found on top of my dresser." I closed the match box, replaced it in my pocket.

Dr. Jensen sat staring into space, but I had said enough. The conclusion of the conversation, if any, would have to come from him. I picked up the package of bills and waited.

"I am very moved," Dr. Jensen said thickly, "very moved. And you will die, is that right?"

"As the child grows inside Merita, I shall wither. That's what the angel said."

"What must I do?" Dr. Jensen said with a trace of anguish in his voice. "Merita doesn't believe! She will never consent to a union of this kind, Reverend! Not with you or anybody else."

"You must make her believe," I said simply. "Tell her to come to my house at two-thirty sharp this afternoon. It is up to you."

"I'd better cancel my nine o'clock patient."

I looked at his trembling hands and nodded. "Yes, I think you better at that."

From Dr. Jensen's office, I took a taxicab into downtown Jax and had the package of money wrapped for shipping in brown, heavy paper at a department store. I addressed the package to myself, care of General Delivery, Atlanta, Georgia, and printed on the outside in large, black letters HOLD FOR TEN DAYS. I mailed the package first class, special delivery, at the Post Office, and then took another cab back to GHQ.

There was little for me to do. I entered the money received by mail in my ledger, entered a bank deposit for the money I had mailed to Atlanta, and I was through.

The car pool was a smoothly running operation. Reverend Hutto had made large charts and hung them on the wall, and his volunteer dispatchers could check them and, thereby, send out the correct number of vehicles at the right time and to the right place without asking him any questions. After he explained his system to me, I congratulated him.

The bus boycott was not entirely effective, and it probably never would be. Jax was too large, and bus transportation was the principal means for the colored population to get to work. The cars we were using were beginning to have trouble with the city police. The police would stop a car and tell the driver he was overloaded. Then the driver would have to let two or three passengers out. After being stranded, the passengers were more or less forced to take a bus in order to get to work on time. But a great many people who were unable to get a ride, or who were stranded, walked to their destination. Few Negroes who rode the busses did so in ignorance. Every Negro in Jax knew there was a bus boycott, and everyone in the basement office was cheered by the progress we were making.

As yet, the bus company hadn't visited us, and the City Council hadn't met to talk about the situation. This was a lull before the storm, with both sides attempting to wait the other side out.

When I left GHQ to go home for lunch, I informed Reverend Hutto that I wouldn't be back that afternoon, and that I would see him and the rest of the ministers at the evening meeting.

After a lunch of black-eyed peas, cornbread and a tomato-and-lettuce salad smothered with mayonnaise, I stretched out to take a nap in the bedroom. Ralphine was washing my laundry in the kitchen, and I had decided to let her work on until Merita arrived—if she came. And I wasn't too sure she would come. I thought about the wild story I had told Dr. Jensen and wondered how much of it he swallowed. He had given the appearance of believing everything I had said, but how much of it had been vanity on his part or, if not vanity, desire to have a child by anybody? I believe he knew in his secret heart that he couldn't hold on to a woman like Merita very long. He only hoped that if she had children, she would be forced to settle down whether she wanted to or not. I really didn't know, and I couldn't understand why I had felt that his official sanction was needed for me to feel right about seducing his wife. The fabrication I had made up and delivered with such convincing earnestness hadn't really been necessary. I had just wanted to try to see if I could get away with it. That was all. I quit thinking and smoked cigarettes instead, staring at the ceiling. If Merita didn't arrive by two-thirty, I would sleep the rest of the afternoon. I certainly was tired.

Merita knocked softly at the door at two o'clock, a half-hour ahead of time.

Ralphine let her in, and I recognized Merita's voice from the bedroom.

"I'll be with you in a minute, Mrs. Jensen!" I shouted. I slipped into my trousers and shoes and put on a clean sport shirt instead of my clerical shirt. I smiled at Merita when I opened the bedroom door. She was wearing a white silk dress with a low-cut bodice and a pair of white high-heeled slippers. Her long black hair had been piled high on her head and was secured with a rhinestone-studded Spanish comb. I stepped to the kitchen door.

"Ralphine," I said, "you can go for the day."

"I ain't fixed your supper yet."

"That's all right. I'll get a sandwich at the church tonight."

Ralphine cackled wildly. "The wet laundry's on the line."

"I'll bring it in. Go on home." Ralphine picked up her loaded shopping bag and left by the back door, muttering and cackling to herself. I could have fed a family of five on the food she carted out the back door every day. The grocery bill must have been enormous by this time. . .

"Aren't you going to offer me a drink?" Merita asked me, after Ralphine had slammed the back screen door.

"I don't have anything." I handed her a cigarette. "Have a smoke instead." I lit her cigarette, then mine, and there were a few moments of embarrassed silence. Merita broke the tension.

"Is it up to me or to you?" she asked softly, a faint and derisive smile on her lips.

"What did your husband tell you?"

She laughed. "What did you tell him?"

"I told him if he wasn't man enough to get you pregnant, he'd better give somebody else a chance."

"When he came home this morning," Merita said with a bubbling laugh, "I almost had a heart attack! I made him repeat the story three times. I couldn't believe he was serious. All he said was that you and he had discussed the situation, and that he had agreed for you to have relations with me."

"You didn't agree, did you?"

"Of course not! I thought he was trying to trap me. But when he wrote out a check for a hundred dollars and gave it to me, I did say I'd come over and talk to you." Merita opened her white patent-leather purse and showed me the check. I admired her aplomb and her frank and easy manner.

"Okay," I said, "we'll talk. I'm the phoniest minister that ever muttered a homily. And you're a phony, too. You aren't an old dentist's respectable wife. You're vicious, mean, and too God damned beautiful! The moment I saw you, I wanted you and decided that I would get you on either your terms or mine. Am I going too fast for you?"

"Not at all, Deut! Lay it on the line."

"Sooner or later you're going to kick over the traces, Merita and, when you do, your beloved husband is going to throw you out. I know it, and you know it. It would hurt him to do it, but I know the type of man he is, and so do you. But on the other hand, you aren't going to knuckle under and be the sort of woman he wants you to be. Ever been to New York?"

"No, Deut, I haven't been anywhere." Merita shook her head. I sat down beside her and took her hand in mine. Her hand was soft and cool to the touch, but mine was slightly damp.

"I was raised in Macon, Deut, married to Fred there, and then he brought me to Jax. I've never had a chance," she said bitterly. "I don't have a cent of money, and prying a nickel out of Fred is like—it's impossible! I've got charge accounts, sure. I can charge anything I want, but cash—uh uh!" She shook her head comically.

"How old are you?"

"Twenty-three. Why? Do I look older?"

"No. You just don't know the angles. Did you ever consider charging a fifty dollar dress, selling it back to the saleslady for twenty-five bucks in cash, and then pocketing the money? Or does Dr. Jensen inventory your clothes and compare the charge tickets with the garments you buy?"

Merita's eyes widened in surprise, and she smiled. "That's some advice for a minister to be giving out!"

"But you never thought of it, did you?"

"No."

"Dr. Jensen said you were a dental assistant for your father. How come you won't help your husband in his office?"

"And have him pawing at me all day? No thanks!"

"Who could blame him?" I held out my hands. "Look at them shake. It's all I can do to keep my hands off you myself."

"Who asked you to keep them off me?" she whispered boldly.

"I'm getting out of Jax, Merita, very soon. And when I go, I want you to go with me. I'm coming into some money, not a little money, but a great deal of money, and I'm going to New York. It's your chance to get away, before you either get like these other church women or get kicked out by your husband for taking up with a passing field hand with a lusty virility. It's in the cards. What do you say?"

"I don't know, Deut, I just don't know!"

"Come here." I put my arms around her and kissed her hard, crushing my lips against her teeth. For a moment she resisted, and then her body relaxed, and she parted her lips. I took my lips away, and she gave me a sharp, little cry.

"I'm afraid of you, Deut! I never had anything like this— not like this—happen to me before!"

"You're smart to be afraid," I said grimly. "I'm dangerous. But that's the way it is. Better go into the bedroom and take off your clothes." I helped her to her feet. On impulse I jerked the Spanish comb out of her hair, and the long black tresses fell to her shoulders.

"I like you this way," I said. I dug both hands into the mass of loose hair and pulled her face against mine, kissing her gently on her bruised mouth. "Now get in there." I whacked her hard across her firm buttocks, and she had her dress over her head before she reached the bedroom door.

I followed her in, closed the door behind me and leaned against it, watching Merita as she undressed. She kicked off her pumps, leaned down and unfastened her brassiere and, as she straightened up again, her long, golden breasts smiled at me with their funny pink faces. Merita looked at me boldly with flashing black eyes and licked her lips.

"Like?"

"Like." I nodded.

Knuckles pounded on the front door. I had to laugh.

"Maybe they'll go away?" Merita said anxiously.

"Never." I shook my head. "Stay in here. I'll see who it is and get rid of him."

I was too optimistic. As soon as I unlatched the door, a large suitcase was tossed in, followed by a booming, almost idiotic laugh; and then a short, red-faced man wearing a hounds-tooth plaid jacket leaped on it to catch up with his laughter.

"The famous and Right Reverend Deuteronomy Springer himself!" the little man exclaimed. "And in the flesh, in the flesh. Yes, sir! Allow me to introduce myself, Reverend. I'm the unknown, but well-traveled, Raz Irby! Texas is my home, and I stay away from it, sir, by traveling for the Del Rio Religious Art Company; and in just a second, I'm going to show you something you've never seen before and you'll never see again unless you see me again!" He knelt on the floor and began to unfasten the buckles on the suitcase.

"Look, whoever you are," I said angrily, "I don't want any. Don't unpack anything, just take off!"

"You don't have to tell me how busy you are, Reverend! I know! Yes, sir! And that's why I won't take up any of your valuable time. Now look at this, Reverend! Isn't it a beauty?" The suitcase was open, and the salesman had a tablecloth in his hands and was unfolding it with impatient movements of his short arms. "Just look!" He said admiringly. "Ever see anything like it?"

The table cloth was enormous, and there was a life-sized painting in three colors of Jesus Christ on the cross in the middle of the tablecloth. In spite of myself, I was interested. I'd never seen anything like it before.

"Do you think that's all, Reverend? Not on your tintype, sir! Six napkins to match! All in color, all hand-painted, and all half Texas cotton and pure Irish linen! Raz Irby, that's me, is the only man in Florida you can buy such religious napery from, and I won't sell it! No, that's right. I refuse to sell this table cloth. Take it. Yours, sir. No strings attached. Absolutely none." Raz Irby threw his head back and laughed idiotically, ran stubby fingers through his blond crewcut.

"Now look, Irby—"

"They said it couldn't be done!" Irby continued with his booming voice. "But the Del Rio Religious Art Company did it just the same! And these paper tablecloths and paper napkins were stamped by hand, all in three primary colors, in exact replica of the pure linen and half Texas cotton table cloth. Beautiful?" Irby gingerly unfolded a flimsy paper tablecloth with a crude reproduction of the original painting block-printed in garish shades of red, yellow and blue ink.

"We can't make enough paper tablecloths and napkins to meet the demand," Irby said sadly, "not nearly enough! The craftsmanship is too good, and we refuse to lower our standards. That's why we refuse to sell to white churches. The Del Rio Religious Art Company will only sell these beautifully designed tablecloths and napkins to bona fide all-Negro congregations. They have a million uses, these napkins. They can be easily framed and hung on every wall; wonderful for children's lunches, too. Reminds the children to say grace but, best of all, they add enjoyment and reverence to a meal. As you wipe your lips, you kiss Jesus, you see. And the paper tablecloths have countless uses, too, as you can readily see. A fine covering for a cheap coffin, a table cover, of course, a bedspread; and you can use them in church—"

"Hold on, Irby! I don't want any."

"Of course you don't, Reverend; you don't need anything to remind you of your Lord and Savior, but your congregation does need such reminders! And if you will just tell them so at your mass meeting tonight, I will—"

"You've got the wrong man," I practically shouted, afraid that he would get started again. "Dr. Heartwell is in charge of the mass meeting."

"I thought you were."

"No, Mr. Irby, I'm just a cog in the machine."

"Good!" he exclaimed. "I'm glad to hear that. Last year I was through Jax, and Dr. Heartwell and I didn't quite see eye-to-eye on a couple of matters, if you see what I mean; and if you'll soften him up for me, well, I'll handle the rest. Now what about it, Reverend, and of course you can keep this beautiful pure linen, half Texas cotton tablecloth for your own table."

"Okay," I said. "I'll talk to him tomorrow."

"What about tonight? I don't like to miss an evening without making a few sales. My time in Jax is limited, and I have all of Florida to—"

"I'll talk to him tonight. Please leave!"

"I'm glad to leave, Reverend, I know how busy you are." Raz Irby packed his suitcase, buckled the straps quickly and shook my hand with a firm grip. "God bless you, Reverend, and maybe there'll be a little of the pecuniary measure in it for you on top of everything else! Goodbye, sir, and don't let me bother you any longer!" Irby opened the door, laughed idiotically, and started across the empty lot at a fast trot.

Merita opened the bedroom door with a loud bang. She was fully dressed again. Her lips were sullen, and her eyes met mine defiantly. "That's the kind of talk I hear at home all the time," she said scornfully. "Religious talk—silly, meaningless, religious double-talk! I'm out of the mood, Deut. I couldn't do anything now if I tried."

I nodded. "We'll have plenty of time. Go on home. Pack a bag and wait for me to call you. I may call tonight, tomorrow morning, but it will be soon. Be ready to go."

"When you're talking, everything seems to be all right, but I know how I am. I'm a coward really. At least with Fred I've got security, but with you—what can you give me, Deut?"

"Nothing," I said. "Adventure. Excitement. New York City. Love. That's all I can offer you, and the offer is open. When I leave, Merita, the door will close."

"I'll be ready." Merita tightened her lips grimly. "I'm afraid of you, Deut, but I kind of like being afraid." She lifted her chin defiantly. I brushed her lips with mine.

"Go home," I ordered. "Pack a bag and cash that check."

Merita opened the door to leave, and I stopped her. "Wait." I folded the hand-painted, pure linen, half Texas cotton tablecloth into a tight square and shoved it under her elbow.

"A present for Dr. Jensen," I grinned. "Something to remember me by."

Merita laughed musically and picked her way down the steps. I watched her dainty walk and free-swinging hips until she reached the sidewalk, and then I closed the door.

After Merita left I made a glass of iced coffee, using plenty of ice, and carried it into my study. I sat at my desk, poured a generous amount of canned milk into the murky liquid and watched the fascinating swirls of milk filter down through the coffee. The designs were beautiful to watch. I wouldn't stir the milk into the coffee; I would wait until the two liquids mixed by themselves before I drank it. Then I would do some thinking.

Sooner or later I would have to make a decision.

I wanted to take Merita with me and leave Jax forever. The knowledge that I had money in the Atlanta Post Office with my name on it was a powerful incentive to leave. But I liked it here. Something new and exciting seemed to be going on every minute. And I didn't have to run away with Merita to have her—I could have her right here. Dr. Jensen was completely snowed under, and I could keep him that way. But I couldn't make up my mind one way or another. And every time I tried to think anything out, I got a headache.

Luckily, I didn't have to do any thinking.

"Hey! Anybody home in there?" The unmistakable, booming voice of the Right Reverend Jack Dover, Abbot of Orangeville, came through the door with a familiar roar. I was delighted, and I could hardly open the door fast enough.

"Come in, Abbot! Come in!" I greeted him and grabbed his big right hand with both of mine. The Abbot's black, ground-length cassock had been discarded, and he wore a pair of eggshell linen trousers and a green silk shirt with short sleeves. His thick muscular arms were covered with damply matted red hair, and his head and eyebrows were freshly shaved.

"Well, Springer," the Abbot boomed, "what have you got to say for yourself?"

"Sit down," I replied. "Over here on the couch. It's more comfortable."

"Looks like you're raising all kinds of hell up here, Springer. How'd you get mixed up in all this mess?"

"I don't know, sir. Everything just seemed to happen, and there I was right in the middle. How about some iced coffee?"

"No, thanks." Abbot Dover shook his bald head. "I can't stay long. I just dropped in to say hello and goodbye. I sold the monastery, at my figure, to a real estate combine out of Miami. They're going to subdivide the acreage and sell lots for project houses, eight thousand on up. They'll lose their shirts.

"But the hell with that, I came to talk to you. You fooled me, Springer, you certainly did. I've only made one mistake in my life, but I think that you're my second mistake. When I was a boy in Lincoln, Nebraska, I went into a movie one afternoon and sat in the balcony—"

"You told me about that mistake, Abbot," I broke in. "About the colored girl and you under the projector?"

"That's right, I did. The moral of that story was never look at the projection booth. Well, I can carry the moral a little further now. Never look at the movie on the screen, either. Instead, just watch the people in the audience who are watching the movie!"

"What do you mean by that?"

Abbot Dover took a fresh plug of Brown Mule chewing tobacco out of his shirt pocket, looked at the plug with affection, and then returned it to his pocket. "I'm trying to give up chewing," he growled, "but it ain't easy. Here's what I mean. I read your novel, *No Bed Too High*."

"Really?" I was pleased. "What did you think of it?"

"It was worth two-bits all right. I picked it up at the Orangeville Drugstore, off the rack. After you left that morning to come up here, I got leery, wondered if I'd done the right thing. I was anxious to close the books on the monastery, and a minister for the Jax church was a loose, dangling end. Besides, I liked you. This church could be a good setup for a writer who really wanted to write. A couple of sermons on Sunday and the rest of the week to himself—"

I laughed. "Are you kidding? I've never worked so hard in my life."

"That's what I mean. You don't want to write, Springer. Not really. I read your novel. You don't have anything to say. You don't know anything about people, and you don't want to learn. A successful minister is the minister who does as little as possible. He listens, but he seldom speaks. A man in trouble who is allowed to talk will automatically feel better just for the opportunity to get it off his chest. A troubled man doesn't want any advice; he wants a sympathetic ear. You talk too much, and you talked when you should have been listening, and now you're in a lot of trouble."

"I wouldn't say that, Abbot. The boycott is going along fairly well and, in the long run, the Negro race will probably benefit."

"But do you care? Does it make any difference to you, Springer, one way or the other?"

"No. Not really." I didn't lie to Dover. His flat blue eyes with their frank and piercing stare demanded the truth and nothing else.

"I found that out when I read your novel. A clever little book. Why not? You're a well-read man, and the characters said brittle and clever things, the surface brilliance of a thousand books you've read and not an original idea of your own on a single page. Cute situations, complications in the right places, and the inevitable straight romantic plot with the obvious ending. You don't know a damned thing about people and even less about yourself."

"I think you're being a little hard on my book, Abbot. It's only a first novel, and I had to start somewhere."

"Right. It was your escape novel, and it provides escape reading. Fifty paperbacks a week are published just like it and probably for the same reason. But I'm not concerned with the novel's literary merits. Reading the book was an insight into your character. You had me fooled on the surface, and I made a mistake when I ordained you as a minister."

Again, Abbot Dover took the Brown Mule plug out of his pocket. "I think I'll have a small chew, and then afterwards I can rinse my mouth out with a little water, and nobody'll know the difference." He bit off a good third of the plug and chewed reflectively before he continued.

"I'm the efficient type, Springer. But in your case I was in too much of a hurry. I should have waited and ordained one of the church members here instead of you. I'll tell you why. Religion is a funny thing. You can be too religious and make your life miserable. A man who follows the Bible too closely begins to look on everything he does as a sin, and he's soon in a miserable state. At the other end, an atheist is too damned happy. In either case, the person gets along all right. But you're in that category which is the worst of all. You are groping, and so you pretend indifference. An indifferent minister is a sorry son-of-a-bitch. Not only is he unhappy, he makes everybody else unhappy."

"Did your twenty years in the Army as an enlisted man qualify you as a cheap psychoanalyst?" I asked scornfully.

"I apologize, Springer," Dover said sincerely. "I came here to thank you, and I start out by raking your personality over the coals."

"Thank me? For what?"

"For providing me with something I've never known. Love!" The Abbot's red face beamed, and he smiled broadly.

"Love? Perhaps I'm clever, as you say, but—"

"Never mind," Dover said, "just sit there and drink your iced coffee. I'll explain. I like to talk. Perhaps you haven't noticed it, but I really like to talk."

"I've noticed," I said.

"What a man hasn't had he doesn't miss, and that goes for love, too. Not that my years of professional soldiering were continent years. Continence is for the very very young and the very very old. But I never knew love, and I didn't allow myself to associate with the type of women I could fall in love with. I was afraid of love and didn't know it, both with my mind and body. My body grew this paunch of mine." Dover patted his round hard stomach fondly. "For more than ten years I've kept my head and eyebrows shaved. In order to love a man who looks like me, a woman would have to work two shifts. My nose is too large, and my personality is overbearing. I know myself, Springer.

"I ought to boot myself in the ass for not seeing it sooner!" He shook his shiny head and pursed his lips. "A man is nothing but a complex defense mechanism. As a substitute for love—I realize now that I had substitutes—I collected things. Things that couldn't love me in return. I started out with a rock collection. I could love the rocks, but they couldn't love me. I've got a foot-locker in storage in Washington containing more than one hundred three-act plays with the first act ripped out and destroyed. Did you ever hear of a play collection like that?"

"No, sir. Not like that."

"Nobody else ever did either. A psychiatrist would love to get ahold of that one. He could write a paper on it. What I was doing, you see, was reading the plays by starting at the second act.

If I refused to read the first act, I'd never know how a love affair started! A brilliant defense I devised in my subconscious. I've never seen the start of a movie either. I've always entered in the middle and left before it began again. Once, I kept a rattlesnake in a cardboard box as a pet. Kept the snake for over a year in my wall locker right in the barracks. I loved that snake, Springer, and I called him Mary Lou. But Mary Lou didn't love me."

"This is all very interesting, Abbot, but what has it got to do with me?"

"Because I met you, and because I sent you to Jax," Dover laughed, "I got your wife. Virginia and I have been shacked up for two days now in my little cell in Orangeville!"

This was a startling bit of information, and I couldn't think of a reply. Abbot Dover left the couch, went into the kitchen and got rid of his chew at the garbage can. He rinsed his mouth out with a glass of water at the sink before he returned to his seat.

"I don't believe you," I said at last.

"Take a look out the window." Dover shrugged indifferently.

I slowly got out of the swivel chair and walked the three steps to the window, pulled the sleazy curtain to one side. Parked at the curb was the Abbot's black-and-white convertible Ford. The top was down, and my wife sat placidly in the right-hand seat, the sun glistening in her blonde hair. As I stared across the lot, I thought I saw a muscle move in her cheek. She was chewing gum, I suppose, and she stared straight ahead, patiently waiting. She could sit still for hours on her broad pedestal, and with the patience of Job. She had waited for me like that in Columbus, sitting in our car while I was on errands or shopping, for hours at a time.

"You have a very voluptuous wife," Abbot Dover said pleasantly.

"She's fat, if that's what you mean," I replied, returning to my seat in the swivel chair.

"No, that isn't what I mean. You treated that fine girl mighty shabbily, Springer, but now that things have worked out the way they have, I'm mighty grateful to you. I'll never forget the sight of that chubby, pathetic figure when she climbed out of a truck at the monastery. She didn't have a penny to her name, and she had hitch-hiked all the way to Orangeville carrying a heavy suitcase looking for you. That's how love begins, I discovered, with pity. As soon as you can feel sorry for someone other than yourself, you discover love."

"I wired her a hundred dollars," I said.

"When?"

"Yesterday."

"Too late, thank God!" Abbot Dover crossed himself, and smiled. "She's mine now, unless you want to fight me for her!" He got to his feet and flexed his arms. "And I hope you do. I'll break you in half, you raw-boned, no-good bastard!"

"Take her," I said, "I don't give a damn! At your age pity may be your notion of love, but I'm only thirty-two, and my idea of love is still sex."

"Again you prove to me how little you know about people," the Abbot said grimly. "I've been in bed with a lot of women, Springer, but your wife is the only woman who truly gave herself to me. She has changed my entire life. I'd do anything to make her happy. I've got more than twenty-five thousand dollars saved and a pension coming in at one hundred fifty-six bucks a month for life. I told her this and gave her a choice of where she wanted to live. She wants to live in Columbus, Ohio, and that's where we're going. If Columbus is only half as good as Virginia says it is, we'll be damned happy there."

"It's the deadliest, dullest provincial city in the world," I said sincerely.

"I feel sorry for you, Springer."

"And I feel sorry for you, Dover."

"Don't!" He shook his head and glared at me. "Before I met Virginia, you should have been sorry for me. I was all set to enter the Soldier's Home in Washington and rot away. I'm only forty-four, Springer, not an old man by any means. My entire life lies ahead, and now I've got a loving woman to share it with me. Thanks to you, you sorry bastard." Abbot Dover opened the front door, turned to make a final crack. "Look inside thyself."

"Keep your cheap enlisted man philosophy to yourself!"

I followed Abbot Dover onto the porch. He started briskly across the lot and, when he was halfway to his car, I shouted after him: "Go with God!"

My farewell shout halted Dover in his tracks. He turned completely around and hesitated for a couple of seconds. "Thanks, Reverend. I've got that coming!" He boomed cryptically.

The Abbot climbed into the driver's seat, patted Virginia fondly on top of her blonde head, and drove away. Not once, and I watched closely, did Virginia look in my direction. I know she heard me shout at Dover, but she kept her eyes straight ahead, and she didn't even look back over her shoulder. . .I watched the convertible until it was out of sight.

How did I feel? I had known my wife since high school days, and if I knew any person in the world, I knew Virginia. How could Virginia willingly engage in an illicit relationship with a clown like Abbot Dover? A man who resembled a parody of a television wrestler; a man with a nose like a potato, a shaved and shiny head, a big red face, and a round hard paunch . . . it didn't figure. I felt no poignant sense of loss, no pangs of regret to see her leave with the retired first sergeant. If she thought she would be happy with Dover in Columbus, more power to the old girl. My vanity wasn't hurt; I didn't have any vanity. Whatever had been between Virginia and me had fallen apart years ago, and maybe there had never been anything between us in the first place . . . I just didn't know. But I did think she could have taken a last look at me, a farewell look, out of curiosity if nothing else. A wave of the hand maybe.

I felt nothing. Absolutely nothing.

And here I was, standing idly on my front porch with the afternoon sun going down, when there were a million things I could be doing at the GHQ of the League For Love! I could draw up a list of demands to present to the Intertransit Omnibus Company. I could write an article on Bessie Langdale, about how she had inspired our boycott, and send it to all of the northern newspapers. I could get on the telephone and contact all of the white ministers in Jax, win them over, talk them into preaching sermons in favor of equality and justice. Certainly I should ask Dr. Heartwell to put me on the evening program; as yet, I hadn't delivered any great and inspiring speech. I would make notes at GHQ and give a crackerjack pep talk tonight! To gain sympathy among the white people of Jax, I could write a proclamation, dig references out of the Bible to prove how God was in favor of the bus boycott, have the proclamation mimeographed, organize teams of volunteers into leg men and stuff a copy of the proclamation into every mailbox in Jax!

I went into my bedroom, ripped off the sportshirt and slipped into my dirty shirt with the backward collar. I donned my heavy, covert cloth coat. There was a great deal of power in this black uniform, and I could make my name ring throughout the United States. Maybe I could make a speech over one of the local television stations? As I marched down the sidewalk toward the Southern Baptists of Saint John Church, I made a mental note to check with Reverend Hutto on the cost of television time.

At the motor pool I paused for a moment to watch the vehicles as they pulled out into the street and headed for downtown Jax. Most of them were empty except for the drivers. They were leaving to pick up loads of working people who were through for the day. At the exit a harried dispatcher handed each driver a handwritten list of stops with the names of the passengers he was to pick up. Some of the volunteer drivers were unable to read and write, and the dispatcher was practically foaming at the mouth. His voice was hoarse from repeating a thousand impatient instructions. Something else I could do. Work out a better dispatching system.

As I entered the basement office, Dr. Heartwell called to me excitedly, and I joined him at his desk.

"I think now," he said, "that we are getting someplace! I had a call a few minutes ago from the Intertransit Company representative. They want to talk." He glanced at a name on a piece of paper. "A Mr. Corwin. I was just about to send for you when you came in."

"Did he sound serious or belligerent?"

"Aloof." Dr. Heartwell mused. "Arrogant would describe him better. They won't talk to me or to all of us at once, but he said they'd be willing to discuss terms with you."

"Have you or any of the other ministers drawn up a list of demands? I've been thinking about it, but that's as far as I got."

"No. We should get on it right away. Things have been so hectic—"

"All right, Dr. Heartwell. Is that the phone number there, on that slip of paper?"

"Yes. He said for you to call him immediately."

"While I call, round up the other members, and we'll meet in your office as soon as I've finished."

Dr. Heartwell left his desk, beckoned to Reverend Hutto, and the two ministers left the office. I sat down at Heartwell's desk, picked up the telephone and dialed a familiar number.

"Hello?" a voice answered. It was Eddie Price.

"Mr. Price, this is Reverend Springer."

"Oh. Just a minute, Reverend."

I waited, and Mr. Corwin spoke into the telephone. His voice was smoothly apologetic. "I'm glad you called, Reverend Springer," he said. "And believe me, sir, I wouldn't blame you if you hadn't. That was a damned fool stunt we tried to pull on you, and we're both sorry. Hold the line a second."

I held the line, and the next voice I heard was the fawning whine of Eddie Price.

"I want to apologize, Reverend," Eddie said. "I got a lump on the back of my head the size of a turnip, but I had it coming to me, and I don't blame you a bit. You accepted our offer in good faith, and then we tried to pull a stinker on you. Please let bygones be bygones. I'm pretty sure we can work something out. Here's Mr. Corwin."

"Eddie was sincere, Reverend. Both of us are," Mr. Corwin took over again. "I explained the situation to the Company, and they gave me the twelve hundred dollars. All we want to do is avoid trouble and, with the Citizen's Council behind us volunteering to call on the niggers involved in the boycott, I believe we can end this thing amicably."

"What do you want me to do, Mr. Corwin?" I asked.

"Just give us the rosters as we discussed originally and, as soon as I get them, you'll be given twelve hundred dollars in cash; and I guarantee you that your name will never be mentioned or connected with it."

"Let me think about it," I hesitated.

"Time is running out on this business," Mr. Corwin said seriously. "And really, there isn't too much to think about anyway, is there? You don't want to see anybody hurt, and as we see it, this is about the only way to stop the boycott peacefully."

"I need a minute or two," I said. "Hold the phone till I light a cigarette." Before he could reply I put the telephone down on the desk.

I lit a cigarette. The office was almost empty except for a half-dozen men and women. Most of the volunteers were out eating supper. The place was a mess. No real organization. What did I owe these people, anyway? Nothing. Negative. I could stay and work my head off, and if we won, what would be in it for me? Nothing. There was money in the Atlanta Post Office, and it was waiting for me. All I had to do was pick it up. Twelve hundred more would round out the sum very nicely. And there was Merita. She was willing to go anywhere with me. All in all, I had an easy decision to make. I picked up the telephone.

"Okay, Mr. Corwin," I said. "It's a deal. Where do you want me to meet you?"

"Price's Garage. Same place. Can you get the rosters by, say, eight o'clock?"

"Easily."

"We'll be waiting. Goodbye, Reverend." The telephone was racked at the other end. I replaced my receiver and walked down the corridor and up the stairs to Dr. Heartwell's little office.

With the exception of the Right Reverend McCroy, who was still at home eating supper, the rest of the ministers of the League For Love were present in the office, all of them talking at once. Reverend Hutto had a tablet and pencil and repeatedly interrupted the other two ministers, asking them to slow down. I listened silently for a moment and then said: "Let me talk."

Dr. Heartwell shushed Dr. David and looked in my direction. "We will all talk, Reverend Springer," he said calmly, "but I certainly think that the issue of allowing our race to enter the bus by the front door is an important point. Many times a Negro has paid his fare at the front door, stepped out to enter by the rear door, and then watched sadly as the driver pulled away leaving him standing there—"

"Of course it's important, Dr. Heartwell. But everything about this bus riding business is important. I say no concessions at all! Complete equality as far as the bus is concerned. Enter by the front entrance and take seats on a first in, first seated basis. The Negro population of Jax makes up to sixty percent of the business for the bus company. Let's not make any concessions at all. Complete equality, or we continue the boycott indefinitely."

"You mean an unconditional surrender, then?" Dr. David asked in a dry, clipped voice.

"Exactly."

"I don't agree," Dr. Heartwell said solemnly. "If these representatives are willing to make bona fide concessions that will improve the service, I think we should consider them."

"Are you an advocate of gradualism, Dr. Heartwell?" I sneered.

"I don't favor gradualism, no, but we should bargain, because we aren't going to get everything we want. Even if the bus company is willing to concede to everything, there's a state law, and they can't do anything about that!"

"They'd better!" I snapped. "In the long run we can win. I say we concede nothing. We have the upper hand. Let's keep it!"

"He's right, of course, Heartwell," Dr. David said. "Why not try it? If things go badly against us later, then we can talk about concessions."

"All right," Dr. Heartwell said wearily. "What time do you meet with the bus company representatives?"

"Eight p.m."

"It's in your hands then. We can at least find out what they're willing to offer and tomorrow, after a night's sleep, we'll all be able to consider the matter reasonably. We should have had our demands on paper already. But there's too much, too much. And we have the mass meeting tonight—"

"I won't commit us to a thing," I said. "I'll just listen and tell them our demand is complete equality. Agreed?"

The ministers all agreed.

"I have you down for the program tonight," Reverend Hutto said, as the meeting broke up. "Should I take you off?"

"I don't see how I can be at two places at once," I replied. "And between now and eight o'clock, I want to get our decision on paper so I can give it to the newspaper following my meeting with the representatives."

"I just asked," Revered Hutto apologized.

I returned to my desk in the basement and sat down. An elderly woman brought me a barbecued pork sandwich and a cardboard container of coffee.

"I don't know if you has had your supper or not," the woman said, smiling, "but I never saw the time a man couldn't eat him a barbecue."

"Thank you," I said kindly. "I certainly can eat a barbecued sandwich."

I bit into the hot, greasy sandwich and swallowed some coffee. My eyes picked up the dark green cover of the Jax telephone book on Dr. Heartwell's desk across the room. I crossed the room, snatched the telephone book and brought it back to my desk.

I began to scribble rapidly on a ruled yellow tablet, writing down names and addresses picked at random as I riffled through the pages. I didn't owe these Negroes a damned thing, but I didn't owe Corwin & Company anything either. He'd get a roster, all right, for his twelve hundred bucks, but wait until he tried to use it! I giggled delightedly and quickly scribbled Eddie Price's name and address onto the third page of my hastily improvised roster.

My finger had inadvertently stabbed into his name as I had flipped a page.

THE MEETING UPSTAIRS IN the auditorium was going strong at seven-thirty. Time to go. A few minutes before the meeting began, Dr. Heartwell had offered me his Buick and Tommy as my chauffeur, but I had declined. Tommy was too belligerent, I told him, and I would be better off with a taxicab.

Except for a dispatcher seated at Reverend Hutto's desk, the basement office was empty. I bent down, unlocked the safe, took the three stacks of folding money out of the corner and stuffed them under my shirt. There were three canvas bags of coins inside the safe, but I could hardly carry them around with me.

"Good night," I told the dispatcher as I started out the door. "Tell Dr. Heartwell that I'll see him in the morning."

"Yes, sir," the man said.

"Is everything going all right?"

"Pretty good, Reverend Springer. Folks is stayin' pretty much to home in the evenin's, except for the meetin's."

"That's good."

Approximately one hundred men and a few women were outside in the street listening to the loud speakers. Dr. David was speaking, and his barbed syllables, magnified by the speakers, demanded privation and fortitude from the listeners. Many men liked to stand outside and listen instead of crowding into seats inside. Outside they could smoke. Inside the church they couldn't. Across the street from the church, I climbed into the first taxi in line. There were more than a dozen cabs parked along the curb waiting for the meeting to end.

I gave the driver the address of Price's Garage, and he drove away. The driver was a thick-bellied Negro, and a sausage roll of fat hung loosely over the back of his collar.

"Do you know where it is?" I asked him.

"I sure do, Reverend, over by Flagler Park."

"That's right."

I lit a cigarette and rode the rest of the way in silence. We passed the entrance to Flagler Park, and the driver continued right past the garage without stopping.

"You passed it," I said. He slowed down and stopped.

"I thought Price's Garage was in the next block."

"No, it's back where that light—" I looked over my shoulder through the window. There were no lights on inside the garage, but there had been when we had zipped past. The driver put the gear in reverse.

"I can back up," he said. "I don't see no policemen around."

"No. Wait," I said. "Keep your motor going." I snapped the door locks on both doors. "Let me look a minute."

Across the street there were three cars, new ones, parked along the curb bordering the park. Why? This was not a residential area, and if the owners were in the park, why hadn't they parked in the parking area at the entrance? I had noticed the parking lot when we had passed it, and it was practically empty. The black, gaping door to the garage was only three buildings away, and I strained my eyes through the back window looking for a sign of a light or movement. A small door near the gas pump and to the left of the garage itself suddenly flew open, and the beam of a flashlight hit the back window, blinding me for a second.

"There he is!" The high unnatural voice belonged to Eddie Price. "The son-of-a-bitch is in that cab!"

"Move it out, man!" I screamed at the driver.

Across the street, four men flew out of the parked cars and began to run toward my cab. Inside the darkened garage, I could hear the pounding of running feet. Eddie Price kept the beam of the powerful flashlight trained on the back window and called the men to hurry. But my driver sat stupefied, paralyzed.

"Move out!" I screamed again. I leaned forward and dug my fingers and thumbs into the roll of fat around his neck. "I said move out!" As quickly as possible, I rolled up the window on the street side, which was down, and the driver let out his clutch. Still in reverse, the cab jumped backwards. The driver then shifted into second, and the cab bucked and jigged forward for ten yards or so before the engine caught and roared. If he stalls now, I thought—a man was running alongside, trying to jerk open the door handle on the street side—but we were off and running!

The driver shifted into high, and the cab gained speed until he was doing sixty-five, and we were in a twenty-five mile zone. "Slow down," I told him. "Do you want to kill us?" He didn't pay any attention to me and sailed through a red light as though it wasn't there, narrowly avoiding a panel truck. I opened my hand, leaned forward and slapped the driver viciously across the ear. "Slow down, you goddamned rabbit!" I yelled.

He eased up on the gas, dropped down to a crawl, pulled into a lighted gas station and stopped beneath an overhead sign of blazing neon tubing. Tears were rolling down his cheeks, and he whimpered and blubbered, his big fat body shaking convulsively. The station attendant came over to the cab, and I rolled down the window.

"We don't need gas," I smiled at the attendant. "The cab driver's a little sick." I handed the attendant a dime. "Maybe if he drinks a Coca Cola. . .?

"Sure, Reverend," the attendant went over to the Coke machine.

"Pull yourself together, Boy," I told the driver. "You aren't going to get hurt, and we aren't being followed either."

"I'll be all right, I'll be all right." He wiped his face and gradually caught his breath. I accepted the Coke from the attendant, gave it to the driver.

"Now, drink this."

He downed the Coca Cola in one long gurgling pull without taking the bottle away from his lips. I lighted a cigarette and handed it to him. "All right now, Boy?"

"I reckon. Whooeee!" He laughed, and his fear had vanished. "Who-all was after us, Reverend?"

"Members of the Citizen's Committee," I said. "They don't like Negroes or anybody who does."

"Way they acted, they don't like nobody!" He laughed again, got out of the cab to put the Coke bottle in the rack and slid under the wheel again, puffing away on the cigarette I had given him.

"Do you think you can drive now?"

"Yes, sir! Where to this time?"

I gave him Dr. Fred Jensen's home address. As we crossed the bridge over the St. John's River, I apologized. "I didn't mean to smack your head so hard, but at the time it seemed like a good idea."

"That's all right, Reverend."

"I was supposed to attend a peaceful meeting concerning the bus boycott, and if I hadn't thought it would be, I wouldn't have risked your neck or mine otherwise."

"I just goes to where they tells me to go." He replied simply. I considered this a wise philosophy for a cab driver.

When we pulled up in front of the duplex where Dr. Jensen lived, I saw that a light was on in his living room, and I kept my seat.

"How much do you make in a night?" I asked.

"Six dollars, about. Sometimes eight, and maybe ten. It all depends. Since the bus boycott, I been doing better. I work the six-to-six shift at night, and daytime's better. Next week I go on days."

I gave the driver a ten-dollar bill. "Take the rest of the night off. Go on home and get some sleep. I don't want you driving around any more tonight. Will you do that?"

"If you say so, Reverend." He tucked the bill into his watch pocket.

"I say so, and I mean it, too."

"All right."

"Good." I got out of the cab and shook hands with the driver. "And if you don't go home, I've got ways of finding out."

"I'm glad to go home, Reverend!" he protested.

Before I climbed the steps to Dr. Jensen's front porch, I waited until the cab was out of sight. I peered through the window. Dr. Jensen, wearing a white flannel nightshirt, was seated on the long couch, bending over an open Bible on the coffee table. He wore a pair of horn-rimmed glasses, and there was a glass of milk on the table beside the Bible. Merita wasn't in the room. I rapped softly on the door with one knuckle, waited, and Dr. Jensen opened the door.

"Good evening, Dr. Jensen," I said, brushing past him and entering the living room without waiting for an invitation. He closed the door and followed me in, his bare feet silent on the worn, rose-colored carpet. I leaned over the Bible, tapped the open pages with the tips of my fingers, straightened up and smiled. "An admirable trait," I said. "No man can ever do wrong who reads the Holy Bible before he retires."

"The Bible is a source of great comfort to a troubled man." His voice quavered. The lines leading down from the wings of his broad nose to the corners of his thick lips were deeper than I had ever noticed. His eyelids drooped wearily over yellow, pink-rimmed eyes; but as he returned my frank, inquisitive stare, I could detect a firmness to the set of his jaw that had never been there before.

"Where is Mrs. Jensen?" I inquired.

"Locked in her bedroom." He wet his lips. "And that's where she's going to stay," he added, again licking his lips.

"I see. I came to take her with me. I've been praying for guidance, and the Lord told me that now was the time. I talked with Merita this afternoon, but somehow—"

"I, too, have been praying for guidance, Reverend Springer!" Dr. Jensen cut me off in mid-sentence. "And I've been reading the Good Book for wisdom as well! All day long I've been sorely troubled, and I haven't been able to keep anything in my stomach. I've been torn by doubts and fears, but the Lord has shown me the way."

"And what has He shown you?" I asked reasonably.

"Genesis, thirty-two, twenty-four!" 'And Jacob was left alone; and there wrestled a man with him until the breaking of the day!' "That is the passage God revealed to me in the Good Book, and I have found comfort and decision in these words!"

"I see. And your decision was to lock Merita in her bedroom to await my coming?"

"Not at all," Dr. Jensen shook his head vigorously. "Not by any means, Reverend Springer! I do not doubt that an angel appeared to you, Reverend, for you are a good and holy man and sincere in your faith. But you were visited by a false angel! An evil angel who would lead you into sin! An angel who was clever enough to deceive you, Reverend, and I, too, was taken in by this angel's words. But you should have been like Jacob; you should have wrestled with this angel! You should have thrown him to the ground and wrung the truth from him, as I have done!" He sank wearily onto the couch and covered his face with his hands.

"You mean I should have wrestled with an angel of the Lord?"

"It was not an angel of the Lord!" Dr. Jensen dropped his hands to the couch and wet his lips again. He rolled his eyes apprehensively and dropped his voice to a whisper. "It was a dark angel from the devil! A devil who would have had you sin with my wife! And I cannot let you do this, for it would lead you away from the path of Heaven and down the road to Hell!"

"You're overwrought," I said soothingly. "Do you think I'd believe the words of a false angel?"

"It's in the Good Book!" Dr. Jensen said excitedly. "I have pored through the pages of my Holy Bible all day, and God has revealed the answer in Genesis!"

"You're a vain man, Dr. Jensen," I said, "and you have looked through the Bible to find a way to keep Merita for yourself. I can show you many contradictory verses in the Bible. But as your minister and spiritual adviser, I know what is best. And although I will perish as a result, as the good angel told me, I'm taking Merita away with me right now!"

"No!" he screamed. "It's a sin, a sin!" With these anguished words the old dentist launched a surprise attack, jumping up from the couch and coming for me with outstretched hands, great veins standing out like ropes in his throat. He was a heavy man, and I easily dodged his rush, circled the couch, retreated into the dining room and put the dinner table between us. He stumbled after me, anxious to get his hands around my throat. I pushed open the swinging door to the kitchen and hurriedly shoved the kitchen table in front of the door. Dr. Jensen pounded on the door with both fists and shouted crazily.

"I will wrestle with the dark angel, and I will cast him down! All night I shall wrestle with him until the light of day shines upon his face!"

If he stopped to think a moment, all he had to do was to pull the door inward toward the dining room, and he could get through, table or no table. The door swung both ways. In the dark kitchen I searched rapidly through the drawers bordering the sink, looking for a suitable weapon. Had Jensen been calm, I would have taken the time to talk him around to my way of thinking but, in his present state, he was hardly reasonable. My fingers found a heavy wooden potato masher. I hefted it in my hand, and it weighed approximately three pounds. Edging along the sink, I braced my back, put a foot on the edge of the kitchen table and shoved hard. It cleared the door with a squealing scrape. Dr. Jensen stumbled in blindly, and I brought the potato masher down hard on the top of his head. He fell to his knees, shaking his head and mumbling, and tried to get up again, but his feet had gotten entangled in the skirts of his long nightshirt. I stepped behind him and with a short, sidearm blow, I hit him again at the base of the skull. He dived forward, face downward upon the floor.

I watched, the masher poised above my head, but he didn't move a muscle. There was a pounding on a door down the hallway, and then the door rattled as someone shook the handle. Merita. I stepped over Dr. Jensen's unconscious body and rushed down the hall to the rattling door.

"Merita," I said. "It's all right. It's me—Deut. Where are the keys?"

"I don't know," she cried excitedly. "What's going on?"

"Hold on," I replied, "I'll be back in a minute."

I switched on lights as I searched, first in the bathroom in a linen closet, and then in Dr. Jensen's bedroom at the far end of the hall. His clothing was neatly arranged on a black walnut valet beneath the window and, in a shallow tray on top of the rack, I found his wallet, penknife, cufflinks, change and the ring of keys I wanted.

I unlocked Merita's door, and she flew into my arms, hugging me tightly around the neck. She was fully dressed in a tight black skirt and an even tighter white sweater.

"No time for that," I pulled her arms away. "We'd better get going."

Her eyes were round with excitement. "Where? To your house, or—?"

"New York!" I said.

Merita squealed happily in reply, picked up a battered but serviceable suitcase and handed it to me. "I've been waiting," she said triumphantly. "I knew you'd come for me."

I handed Merita the ring of keys. "Where's the old man's Buick?"

"In the garage. We can get to the garage from the kitchen."

"Better not," I said. "We'll go around from the front door, and you'd better drive."

A few minutes later we were riding down the street, Merita at the wheel and me beside her. I had calmed down considerably, and I inhaled deeply on a fresh cigarette.

"You'd better go by my house," I told her. "I don't have much, but there are a few notes I want to keep and an essay on D. H. Lawrence's *Plumed Serpent* I don't want to leave behind."

Obediently, Merita turned left when we reached my block, but we didn't stop. There were more than a dozen cars parked around my church, and the empty lot contained a milling mass of men, all white men!

"Keep going!" I said quickly, but unnecessarily, because Merita had already floorboarded the gas pedal. "One more stop," I said, "and then we'll take the highway. But first pull up at the entrance to Dr. Heartwell's church."

We covered the familiar six blocks before I could fathom my reasons. The crowd outside was an overflow that blocked the entire sidewalk and most of the street. Merita had to stop in the center of the road. I leaned out the window and shouted above the blare of the loud speakers.

"They're burning my church!" I called shrilly.

"It's Reverend Springer," a voice yelled in reply. "Listen to him!"

"They're burning down my church," I shouted again. "The Church of God's Flock!" As if to punctuate my sentence there was a muffled explosion, and a bright red glow lit the night six blocks away. "Now they're dynamiting the church," I yelled. "Stop them! Stop them! Don't let them destroy the house of God!"

There had been a surge toward the car as I had yelled. But the press of bodies now broke into tight knots of running and shouting men as the crowd dispersed down the block in small, wedge-shaped groups. Another group of excited men and women poured through the wide doors of the church and down the steps. I shouted again, but another explosion cancelled my words. The black mass flowing out of the meeting followed the running figures who were already leading the way to my church.

"Drive on, Merita," I said. "There's nothing else to do."

At White Springs we ditched the Buick in a thick grove of pepper trees. We waited for the midnight bus to Atlanta at an independent filling station, which had been closed for the night but displayed the Greyhound sign. The bus was crowded when it pulled in, and Merita was forced to stand in the aisle. Fortunately, I found a seat right behind the driver and managed to get a few fitful hours of off-and-on sleep before we reached Atlanta. The long Georgia night seemed to be filled with black, lonely pines and isolated patches of light as the bus stopped intermittently to load and unload passengers in places I had never heard of before.

But Atlanta was a city, and I was right at home as soon as my feet felt the pavement. I took Merita to one side, gave her two hundred dollars, plus instructions to take a taxicab to the airport and obtain two one-way tickets to New York.

"Maybe I better go with you," she pleaded. "They may not sell me any tickets to New York."

"Don't worry. Atlanta has an international airport and, if you've got the money, they'll sell you a ticket to anywhere. Get the tickets and wait at the entrance for me. I don't want to be looking all over hell for you at the airport."

She nodded. "I'll wait at the main door."

"Outside at the main door," I corrected. I looked at my watch. Nine a.m. "Get tickets for any plane leaving at eleven or after, and we'll be okay."

"Deut?"

"Yes."

"I want you to kiss me."

"Let's be practical, Merita. It looks funny enough to be seen here talking to you. You know I can't kiss you now!"

"I know," she pouted prettily. "But that don't stop me from wanting to kiss you."

"Get going," I grinned. "By five this evening we'll be in another world."

I left Merita at the bus station and caught a taxicab to the post office. My package was waiting for me at the General Delivery window, and I signed for it after the clerk checked my mimeographed ordainment certificate to verify my identity. A black suit and a backward collar was not enough identification for the Post Office Department. As I started out a bold headline caught my eye at the blind man's newsstand.

RACE RIOT IN JAX—4 KILLED

Without thinking, I dropped a nickel on the counter and reached for the newspaper. An inch away from the paper I stayed my hand, and a film of perspiration broke out on my forehead. No, I thought, I don't want to read about it. That is a chapter in my life that is over and done with, and I must only look ahead. I reached for my nickel, but the blind man had already scooped it off the marble counter and pocketed it. I shrugged and left the post office.

My stomach was practically knotted with pain from being empty, and I ate breakfast in a nearby cafe—ham steak, four eggs, a separate plate of grits—and washed it all down with three cups of hot coffee. Following breakfast most of my fatigue seemed to lift, and my step was lighter on the sidewalk. I bought a canvas money belt in a pawn shop, much to the amusement of the broker.

"You're the first priest I ever sold a money belt to," the broker laughed, displaying a set of well-decayed teeth.

"I'm not a Roman Catholic priest," I replied. "I'm an Episcopal Catholic priest."

"That explains it." He laughed again and cut the price down from three dollars to one-fifty.

I continued down the street until I found a gas station, obtained the key from the attendant and entered the men's room. There wasn't time to count all of the money, but the loose bills looked like a fortune as I transferred them into the money belt. I kept one hundred dollars in my wallet for expenses and strapped the thick canvas belt around my waist under my shirt.

A taxicab took me to the International Airport, and I climbed out at the main entrance at exactly ten-thirty. Merita's face broke into a radiant smile at my appearance, and I made an impatient signal with my hand to prevent her from leaping all over me.

"Did you get the tickets?"

"Eleven-fifteen," she smiled. "Aren't I smart?"

"Give them to me." I put both tickets in my inside coat pocket.

"The airplane lands in New Jersey, but the man said it wasn't far from New York."

"It's right across the river. You look tired."

"I'm dead, but I'm so excited I won't sleep for a week."

"Maybe you can catch some sleep on the plane?"

"Not me!" she exclaimed excitedly. "I'm going to watch every minute!"

We walked through the building and down the covered corridor to Gate Six. When they called our plane, we boarded first in line and obtained seats together. I showed Merita how to fasten the seat belt. As I bent over the aluminum buckle, she whispered in my ear.

"Are you sure it's all right to sit together?"

"Of course," I said. "But we'd better not talk till we reach New York."

At the far end of the field where the pilot tested the engines, Merita began to get frightened. She gripped the arms of the seat until her knuckles paled, and her face dripped with perspiration. The flight was smooth and even, but she spent the first hour up-chucking into a paper sack provided by the stewardess. There was nothing I could do for her. A person who is air sick is air sick, and that is all there is to it. But she got used to the idea of being in an airplane and, despite her resolution to stay awake, she slept the rest of the way to the International Airport in New Jersey.

We had dinner at the airport cafe, preceded by two martinis apiece and, after eating a sirloin steak, Merita was happy and excited again. The realization that she was being waited on by a white waitress did more for her morale and well-being than anything else. And when the waitress addressed Merita as "Madame," she knew that Florida was a million miles behind.

Instead of taking the limousine into Manhattan, we took a taxicab for just the two of us because I wanted to go directly to a hotel. I was no stranger to New York, but I didn't know the city any too well. I had spent a ten-day leave in the city when I had been in the Army, and I had made four or five visits from Columbus with my wife. However, my knowledge of the borough was confined mostly to the Times Square district. Two different hotels on Forty-fourth Street claimed to be filled, but the second desk clerk called the Anderson Hotel, and they held a room for us. On the drive to the Anderson we stopped at a liquor store, and I bought a fifth of gin and a six-pack of Seven-Up.

Finally installed in the third-rate hotel room containing a creaking double-bed and a set of beat-up furniture, I got under a shower. I let the hot water sluice over me for fifteen minutes, gradually decreasing the cold water until the hot water almost scalded my skin. I couldn't get enough of the shower, and when I did turn off the water, I still didn't feel completely clean. After toweling my boiled and glowing body, I slipped into my shorts and rejoined Merita in the room. She handed me a squat glass of gin and Seven-Up.

"We made it, Deut!" she said happily.

The drink was a strong one, and it raced through my blood. I refilled our glasses with two more fingers of gin and without adding mix. We finished the second drink, and I sent Merita into the bathroom.

On my back, I stretched out on the bed, my mind a perfect blank. I was tired, but it was a delicious weariness, a feeling of deep well-being, of self-satisfaction. . .I closed my eyes.

A voice above my head whispered: "Are you my evil man?"

"You know it," I replied.

The tips of Merita's breasts brushed slowly across my chest. She laughed—a low, musical sound that promised dark, unknown secrets.

"Make me know it!" she said.

I dug my fingers into her loose, long hair and pulled her face down against mine and lost myself in the softness of her lips.

MERITA TURNED OVER in bed, and the springs creaked. But she didn't waken. The girl was exhausted. The past thirty-six hours had been frantic, tiring hours for Merita and, like a child, she would sleep soundly until all of her energy was restored.

Then what?

In the airplane to New York I had toyed with shadowy half-formed plans, wondering what to do with Merita when we got to the city. This was the edge of Harlem—not the center, but the edge—the creeping curve that was inching its way, building by building, across the island of Manhattan. Merita was a Negro. But then there were plenty of places in New York where all hues lived together indiscriminately—thanks to years of Puerto Rican immigration—as vari-colored as the rainbow. I figured we shouldn't have too much trouble finding a cozy enough place in which to settle down.

But now I had her, I didn't really want her anymore. Right now I was surfeited and, although I knew that desire for her body would return within a few hours, this desire was the only thing we had in common. Sex alone was hardly enough for a sustained and happy relationship. In many ways Merita was actually stupid. And worst of all, every time I looked at her, I would be reminded of the sight of Dr. Fred Jensen stretched out on the floor in his kitchen, the blood pouring from his head. I didn't want to be reminded of my week in Jax; I wanted to completely forget this dark chapter in my life and start all over again, from scratch and alone. I wanted a new life, a small two-room apartment somewhere, a place where I could write. I had the money to keep going for a long time if I kept the money all for myself. Merita would want excitement, night clubs, jazz, jewelry—all of the things she had been denied as the wife of the old dentist. She wasn't worth it, and yet I didn't want to desert her, leave her all alone in a crummy hotel room in a foreign city. The best thing for Merita to do was to go home, back to Jax, back to the dentist.

She could lie to him—tell him anything, tell him she got frightened in all the excitement and went home to Macon for a few days. He would be so happy to get her back, he would believe anything she said.

I took my ballpoint pen out of my coat pocket and, leaning over the dresser, I wrote a note on a sheet of the hotel stationery. (*Anderson Hotel—In New York, your home away from home*).

> *Dearest—*
> *It will never work out for us. I'm leaving and I won't be back. I have left some money for you. Take a bus and go back to your husband. If he's in the hospital, he may not have missed you. I'm sorry.*
>
> Love,
Deut

The note was cruel—mean—and it would hurt Merita. I knew this, but I wanted to make it strong enough so she would go back. I dropped fifty dollars in small bills on top of the note. She had more money in her purse: a hundred dollars from her husband in addition to the change left over from the two hundred dollars I had given her to buy the airplane tickets. Plenty of money to get back to Florida.

Making as little noise as possible, I strapped the money belt around my waist and began to dress. The white, backward collar of my shirt was filthy. My socks were stiff at the toes, but I put them on anyway. I laced and tied my scuffed and dusty shoes. My black covert cloth suit was wrinkled and heavy. There were foxtails and sandburs on the cuffs, picked up from many crossings of the lot between my church and my little house. I settled the straw skimmer on my head and grinned at my reflection in the mottled dresser mirror. The straw was cracked on the left side, and the stiff brim drooped at a sharp angle. I was a seedy-looking minister, all right.

Dressed, I unlocked the door and eased it open, closed it softly behind me. I almost tiptoed to the elevator, but I didn't look back at the door. Whatever it was that passed for a heart inside my chest ached like a tooth.

Outside the sun was out, and it was a bright beautiful day. The sky overhead was a royal blue filled with skittering tufts of small white clouds. At the corner I paused at an obelisk, debating as to whether I should take a taxicab or ride the subway. I hailed a taxi.

"Madison Avenue," I told the driver.

"Any particular address, Reverend?" he asked as he bluffed his way into the slow-moving stream of traffic.

"I want to buy some clothes. Good clothes."

"You can get a good black suit almost anyplace on Madison."

"I'm aware of that. Let me off on Madison near Radio City."

I knew that area of Manhattan fairly well. Virginia and I had once made the rubberneck tour of Radio City. We moved along slowly, and I watched the people scurrying along the sidewalk. The city never changes, I thought. There were more people maybe—more automobiles, more taxis, newer and higher buildings—but city people were the same. The men and women who walked alone wore serious, downcast expressions. Only when two or more people walked together did smiles and laughter appear on their faces. But I knew the laughter was false. What did they have to laugh about? They had to work all day at dull and deadly tasks, the way I had done for ten long years in Columbus. . .

The driver pulled into the curb on Madison near 52nd Street and stopped. I counted out the fare indicated by the meter into the driver's outstretched hand.

"I'm not used to cabs," I lied. "How much of a tip should I give you?"

"You don't have to give me a tip, Father," the driver said piously. "I didn't do nothing for you. Just give me what you want."

I gave him an extra quarter.

"Thanks a lot, Father!" He smiled, exposing a row of gold teeth, and dropped the coin into a cigar box at his side. How easy it was to make people happy! The driver had expected nothing, and the surprise of obtaining a quarter from the minister had made his day. Perhaps the driver would drop the same coin into the collection basket when he attended the Sunday mass and, in turn, his priest would be happy. . .

I sauntered down the broad crowded sidewalk looking into windows. A tan cashmere sport-coat caught my eye. The coat was soft and lustrous-looking. A bronze cut-out numeral beneath the model gave the price as $85.00. If I wanted it, I could buy it. But maybe a suit of some kind would be more appropriate than sports clothes now that I was in the city again. Anything would be better than the black, dreary uniform I was wearing. I entered the store, and a middle-aged salesman approached me with a smile on his lips and a cheery greeting.

"I want a suit," I told him, "something—"

"Something in black? Yes, sir."

"No." I was nettled by his patronizing manner. "Nothing in black. Something in red or yellow, perhaps in blue, but nothing in black!"

"Yes, sir. We'll take care of you, Reverend." He put a forefinger to his nose, looked me over appraisingly with a deep frown furrowing his forehead and then nodded. "You're a forty-two."

"Most of the time," I agreed.

We looked through racks until I found a suit that I wanted. The material was thin, a mixture of Dacron, nylon and polished Egyptian cotton. The color was a glistening tint of powder blue matching my eyes exactly. The jacket, without shoulder padding, hugged my round shoulders perfectly.

"I'll take this one," I told the salesman. "Put the cuffs in, and I'll wear it."

"This suit costs one hundred and a quarter, Reverend," the salesman said softly.

"That's cheap for a suit like this. Now get the cuffs in, please."

He squatted and marked the cuffs with a piece of tailor's chalk.

"I don't think we'll have to do anything to the jacket."

"Neither do I," I replied.

"The cuffs will take about an hour."

"Rush it up," I said. "And while I wait, I'll get a few more things. I need a shirt, socks, belt, shoes, a new hat, handkerchiefs—"

"Yes, sir!"

In less than an hour I was a new man, if clothes do make the man. To go with my blue suit I had purchased a Hathaway button-down shirt with tiny blue-and-red checks. A knitted maroon tie looked well with the shirt and, to match the tie, I had chosen a pair of all-wool maroon socks. Broad-winged cordovan shoes and a chestnut Tyrolean hat with a gay yellow feather in the band completed my outfit. My clerical garb and battered straw hat were packed for me in a long red-and-white striped clothing box. The box was tied securely with red string.

In the center of the block I shoved the box into a large round barrel that had a stenciled sign—KEEP YOUR CITY CLEAN— on its side. I entered a new and glittering bank after first admiring the shiny, massive steel door to the vault through the windows.

"I want to rent a lock box," I told a guard. The guard wore a dark red uniform with yellow piping on the jacket, a black patent-leather Sam Browne belt and pistol holster. He directed me politely to a girl behind a cage with bronze bars.

I filled in a form signing my name as S. D. Springer, received a key and the girl unlocked the barred door. She accompanied me into the vault and, with her key and mine, we unlocked a tiny door in the wall, and I withdrew the long narrow black metal box.

"That room is empty, sir," she said, pointing.

"Thank you." I entered the small room, not much larger than a telephone booth, latched the door and switched on a small fan above the shelf. I kept five hundred dollars out for my wallet and folded the canvas belt containing the remainder of the money into the long black box. As an afterthought, I added my ordainment paper to the contents. A souvenir. After replacing the box in the wall and locking the tiny door, I pocketed my key and buzzed the exit door.

The girl apologized as she let me out. "I'm sorry, Mr. Springer," she lisped prettily, "but you only signed your initials on the form for the lock box. The bank requires your full first name. You can sign your signature anyway you want to, but for record purposes—"

"Of course," I waved my hand. "Judas is my first name." I giggled at the startled expression on the girl's face. "Judas D. Springer—sometimes known as Sam."

After leaving the bank I set off briskly down the street. And then I suddenly stopped. Where was I going? What was I running away from? Myself? That was impossible. As long as I was alive, I would always be there, wherever I happened to be. The business, the activity—shopping for a suit and accessories, the business at the bank—had shoved all thoughts of Merita out of my mind. I must have been crazy to leave such a cruel note for the girl, to send her away. She was all I had. One man alone without someone to love him hasn't got a chance! If she hadn't loved me, she would never have fled friends, family and husband across half a continent. I hurried to the curb and waved violently at a cruising cab. The return trip to the Hotel Anderson was agonizingly slow. If Merita was still asleep, I could tear up the note and waken her with a fervent kiss. But if she had read the note there would be arguments, denials, crying on her part and clever lies on mine. Either way we would end up in bed; I had that much confidence in myself.

A long line of cars blocked off the side street leading down to the hotel. To save time I paid off the driver at the corner; I could make better time on foot. Keeping to the less-crowded far right side of the sidewalk, I hurried toward the hotel; but before I reached the marquee, I stopped and pressed myself back against a wall.

Merita had emerged from the revolving door followed by a male Negro carrying her suitcase. He was a prime specimen of American man: wide shoulders, with a thick powerful neck and an erect athletic posture. There was a broad, self-assured smile on his shiny handsome face, and he was obviously amused by the steady stream of chatter Merita was babbling so cheerfully. As I watched her animated face and dark flirting eyes as she looked admiringly at the big Negro's face, I knew that I had lost her forever.

Not that I was too late. There was still some time, and I knew I could have rushed up and talked her into coming back to me. But the pattern of suspicion had already been established. She would never have really trusted me again, and it would only have been a matter of time before she left me for another handsome specimen like the one she had in tow. Merita knew she had met a kindred soul. He seemed to relax her, ease her. She finished whatever she was saying and laughed, throwing her head back with joy. The man laughed with her and put his arm around her shoulders, pulled her into his chest and hugged her friendlily. A taxi stopped in the yellow loading zone—the same cab I had vacated—and both of them got inside. I turned abruptly and walked slowly up the street in the opposite direction.

I was no longer a man in a hurry. First I must find and rent an apartment. Obtain writing materials. Typewriter. No problem. Then? Eat, sleep, write. But what should I write? Notes from under the floorboards, like Fyodor Dostoyevsky? Or should I write another brittle and superficial novel like my first book, *No Bed Too High*? Escape writing for escape readers, like Abbot Dover had said. But I had already escaped! I had the money. I was no longer responsible for my wife or for Merita.

I was walking aimlessly, without purpose, so I stopped and leaned against the glass store front of a drugstore. I shivered. Despite the sun, I was cold. I was used to much heavier apparel, the protective covering of a man of God. Should I buy a sweater to wear beneath my light blue jacket? The pedestrians rushed back and forth. Not one of them looked in my direction. I was another nothing in the street. In my black uniform I had been something. The backward collar had allowed me to speak to others without permission, and it gave others the right to speak to me, to smile at me, to love me. But the church was not my way; I didn't have a way.

I didn't know whether I should turn left and walk up the street or turn right and walk down the street. What difference did it make? All of the city noises seemed to drop away. I looked up. Ten stories high a pigeon flew across the street. That was the only way to travel. Fly. Of course, when he landed on a window ledge, a bored office boy might slam the window down on his claws. . .

"God save him," I muttered automatically.

And then I laughed, a wild uncontrolled sound welling out of my throat. Only last Sunday I had saved an entire church full of sinners. All except one. I had failed to save myself. And now it was too late. My power to save was gone, shoved into a rubbish can. What an ironic twist of fate!

Again I laughed wildly.

Two teenage Puerto Rican girls linked arm and arm swung by.

"*Mira*! Look at the screwball, Marie," one said. Both of the girls giggled and continued down the sidewalk, swinging their hips as they walked.

She was right, of course. I was a screwball. What did I believe in? Anything at all? Nothing. I shook my head. Nothing. But just the same, I had better play God safe, just like everybody else. I lifted my eyes above the people—above the pigeons, above the buildings—and looked at the clean blue skies.

"Thanks, God," I whispered, "for nothing."

THE ORDAINMENT OF BROTHER SPRINGER

A PLAY BY CHARLES WILLEFORD

DRAMATIS PERSONAE
Abbot John Dover
Brother Springer

SCENE
All of the action takes place in the one-room office
"cell," belonging to Abbot Dover, at Church of
God's Flock Monastery, Orangeville, Florida.

TIME
Six A.M. A working day.

Abbot Dover's cell, The Church of God's Flock monastery, Orangeville, Florida. The "cell" is sparsely furnished with a card table, two straight-backed chairs, a practical hotplate on a sideboard, a small desk—littered with papers—, a wardrobe, a sagging couch covered with rumpled sheets, an enormous six-candled candelabra, and assorted utensils, cups and dishes. On various surfaces there are several old containers (pitchers, glass jars, vases, etc. filled to the brim with goat milk; and there are a dozen or so jars of honey on the card table and lined up against the back wall. The screen upon which slides are flooded as indicated, is on the wall, S.C.

At curtain's rise, Abbot Dover is discovered, S.C., aiming a .22 single-shot, bolt-action rifle at a small regulation target on the wall. Dover, a man in his mid-forties, wears a black, ankle-length soutane and a pair of thong sandals. Pinned on the left breast is an army Expert Rifleman's Badge, with crossed rifles. Dover stops aiming, places the rifle on top of the table, heists his cassock in back, exposing red-and-blue plaid Bermuda shorts, takes a bandana handkerchief out of his hip pocket and wipes his tonsured head and then his face. Dover aims again and fires. He ejects the empty cartridge, reloads, puts the rifle on the table again, and crosses to check the target.

DOVER: *(Nodding with satisfaction)* Bull's-eye! *(He looks up.)* Thank you, Lord.

SPRINGER: *(There is a hesitated knock on the screen door, center.)* Abbot Dover?

DOVER: Come in, come in! Don't stand out there in the hot sun!

SPRINGER: *(Enters. John Springer is in his late twenties. He is wearing a multi-colored sport shirt, yellow linen slacks, and white tennis shoes. He has a small overnighter suitcase in his right hand. There is an air of uncertainty in his speech and in his actions.)*
Are you Abbot Dover, Sir? The Right Reverend Jack Dover?

DOVER: That's me, son. What can I do for you? Are you a pilgrim, boy? Or are you interested in buying a little Florida real estate—or are you just a mendicant looking for a handout?

SPRINGER: None of those, sir, I'm afraid—but as a writer, I might be a little of each. I'm tired though. I know that much. I rode up here from Miami on the bus to interview you, and the driver let me off in town, back there in Orangeville. It was my mistake, not his. All I knew, you see, was the Church of God's Flock monastery was in Orangeville. So he took me on into Orangeville. If I'd told him I was going to the monastery, he could've let me off here and saved me the five-mile walk back down the highway.

DOVER: Many pilgrims from Miami way make that mistake.

SPRINGER: *(Chagrined grimace)* No harm done, I suppose. Been a long time, though, since I walked five miles. As I came down the path, I thought I heard a rifle shot.

DOVER: *(Pointing to target on the wall)* You did. *(Simply)* I am a sharpshooter for the Lord. But then, you're here to interview me, you said. Sit down, sit down. Had your breakfast yet?

SPRINGER: No, sir. Just a Coca Cola down the road at the Save Gas Station.

DOVER: Then have breakfast with me. I've got plenty of grits, and some delicious orange-blossom honey, made by our own holy bees. Do you like grits, son?

SPRINGER: Yes, sir. I'm so hungry after riding that bus all night, I could eat almost anything.

DOVER: Good! And I made some fresh hoecake, too, before target practice period. *(He serves two plates at the hotplate, and pours two cups of coffee. Springer sits at the card table.)* Now just what did you want to interview me about, Brother—?

SPRINGER: Springer, sir. My name is John Springer. I'm a free-lance writer; not a reporter, or anything like that, from any magazine or newspaper. What I am, really, is a novelist. The trouble is, though, I haven't sold any novels lately. And the main reason I haven't sold anything lately is because I haven't written anything lately. I've had this awful writer's block, you see. That's what they call it—writer's block. But I think the real reason I haven't written anything lately, the last year and a half, is because I haven't been able to think of anything to write about.

DOVER: You don't sound like much of a writer to me. What gave you the idea that there's a story here, in the Church of God's Flock monastery?

SPRINGER: Well, I read about the monastery closing down in the *Miami News*. And as soon as I saw the news item, I got to thinking. In the first place, I didn't know there was any such thing as a Protestant monastery—I thought they were all Catholic monasteries. And then I figured if *I* didn't know that there were any Protestant monasteries, a lot of other people probably didn't know about them either. And then, the paper said the monastery was closing down, so there must be a good reason why—and I couldn't think of any good reason for a monastery to close. You know, a monastery has always seemed like a pretty good deal to me—for those who like that sort of thing, I mean. Sit around and pray, and stuff like that, no worries or responsibilities.

DOVER: *(Dryly)* So you've already written your interview; and now you want me to confirm it for you.

SPRINGER: No, sir! I didn't mean it that way at all. I was merely explaining how I got the idea to come up here from Miami. I didn't mean any offense, sir.

DOVER: I don't know what kind of a novelist you were, but you're certainly a lousy reporter. Let me see your credentials. *(Dover holds out his hand.)*

SPRINGER: *(Apologetically)* Like I said, sir, I'm not a real reporter, and this is the first time I've ever interviewed anybody. I'm really a novelist, sir, and novelists don't need any credentials, sir.

DOVER: Just a minute. Let's you and I stay on friendly terms. I don't like to be "sirred" by anybody. I was an enlisted man in the Army for twenty years before I became Abbot here, and I don't like to have people "sir" me.

SPRINGER: I'm sorry, sir—I mean, Abbot Dover. But how should I address you? I don't know anything about church titles, or things like that.

DOVER: Just call me `your holiness.' Or, if you prefer, you may call me `Abbot,' or `Papa'—that's the familiar for `Pope,' or just plain `Sergeant.' I'm a retired Master Sergeant, and still I'm entitled to my rank. All right?

SPRINGER: Yes, sir. Your holiness, I mean. What I was going to say is, if I could get an idea for another novel I'd go ahead and write that instead of writing a feature story—on speculation—about your monastery. But I can't seem to get any good ideas.

DOVER: How many novels have you written?

SPRINGER: One. *(Proudly)* It was called *No Bed Too High*.

DOVER: *No Bed Too High*. An interesting title. I like it. In fact, the connotations are intriguing. Was it published?

SPRINGER: Yes, it was, your holiness. It was published two years ago by the Barrabas Press in New York. I got a $250 advance in royalties on it. Enough to quit my job immediately. The book didn't sell very well, though—not the way I thought it would. But by the time I found out that the first advance royalty check would also be my last, I'd quit my job and moved from Cleveland down to Miami. But then I got a break. The Barrabas Press sold the reprint rights a few months later to a paperback publisher, and I got a check for $1,100—just as my savings were about to run out. But since then, since my first novel, I haven't written much of anything. I'm working on a sort of essay, however, about D. H. Lawrence; but just about everything's been said about Lawrence already. So I've been having trouble trying to think about something new to write about him, too, you see. *(Slide: 2 seconds, D. H. Lawrence.)*

DOVER: Yes, I see. What I *don't* see is how you even managed to write your first novel. Don't be afraid to put some of that good goat butter on your grits!

SPRINGER: *Goat* butter!

DOVER: That's right. There's plenty. It isn't rancid, son, it only smells that way.

SPRINGER: *(Uneasily)* I've never been much for goat butter, your holiness.

DOVER: Suit yourself. Tell me about your novel.

SPRINGER: There isn't much to tell. I was an accountant, and I worked seven years for the Tanfair Milk Company in Cleveland, Ohio. I kept their books. To be completely frank, Abbot Dover, I didn't like the job. I hated it. And all I could think about, day in and day out, was a way out. Escape. And then one evening I got the idea that if I could write a book in my spare time, at night, after work, well, I could make enough money to quit my job forever. In the beginning, writing was just a way out of a terrible job. But now I know that I was cut out to be a writer all along.

DOVER: Except that you now can't think of anything to write about?

SPRINGER: But I will! I got this idea, didn't I? To interview you for an article? All I need is a little time to get organized; that's all. I finally ran out of money in Miami, even though I lived pretty cheap. If I hadn't seen that item in the paper about your monastery closing, I really don't know what I'd have done for an idea. I still owe room rent in Miami, and my landlady's holding on to my typewriter until I pay up. So if you'll just give me some background information, your holiness, I'll be on my way and stop bothering you.

DOVER: How much do you know already?

SPRINGER: Just what's in this clipping. *(He takes a ragged clipping from his shirt pocket, and reads it.)* "Orangeville, Florida. The Church of God's Flock Monastery, established in 1936, is being sold, according to the Right Reverend Jack Dover, Abbot of the Protestant religious order. All of the monks have been reassigned, and only Abbot Dover has remained at the site to oversee the sale of the property. Long a colorful part of the Orangeville scene, monks of the Church of God's Flock order were self-supporting, raising goats and citrus and selling orange wine and honey for subsistence." And that's all it says.

DOVER: *(Takes the clipping, crumples it, and tosses it on the floor.)* I'm familiar with it; I sent this news release out myself, hoping to get a few bids on the property. But that's the whole story, Brother Springer. I doubt very much that the readers of any commercial magazine would be interested in this small religious order.

SPRINGER: Oh, I disagree, sir! Your holiness. *The Reader's Digest*, for example, is always printing articles about religious matters.

DOVER: All right, Brother Springer. I'll tell you a few things about the monastery. And then you'll know for yourself why it isn't worth writing about for a magazine. If you want sweetening for your coffee, use some of that good orange-blossom honey.

SPRINGER: You'll let me be the judge, then? *(He has some trouble getting a spoonful of honey out of the jar on the table.)*

DOVER: Of course, not! I won't okay anything you write, and if you do write and publish anything about this order, I'll issue a denial and then institute a civil action against you!

SPRINGER: That doesn't sound fair—!

DOVER: Of course it isn't fair. Who said it was?

(Dover crosses to the wall and taps the poster (24"x30") of Cosmo Bird. It is a poster of a Negro. He wears a high Herbert Hoover collar, and his hair is a snow white halo encircling his dark face.)

Take a look at this picture.

SPRINGER: *(Examining photo)* I don't believe I've ever seen such beautiful bone structure in a man's face before! And the cheekbones are high, too—for a Negro, I mean.

DOVER: That is a photo of the Right Reverend Cosmo Bird, of Birmingham, Alabama. He was part Indian, I believe; that probably accounts for his high cheekbones. But handsome is as handsome does; and Cosmo Bird was filled with great spiritual beauty as well as being handsome physically. He started our Church of God's Flock in Birmingham, after making his pile in Pratt City real estate. And the more money he made, the more churches he started. There are two Church of God's Flock churches in Birmingham, two in Mobile, one in Atlanta, one in Tuscaloosa, and one in Jacksonville. And every one of these churches is poor as hell. Their poor because their parishioners are poor.

SPRINGER: These churches are all in addition to the monastery?

DOVER: I'm getting to that. When Cosmo Bird died in 1936, he left all of his remaining money to a fund to establish this monastery in Orangeville. He owned the property already through a previous real estate deal. Back in 1936, this was truly an isolated location. And an ideal spot for a monastery. That was long before the state put the main highway through, and before anybody even dreamed of the Sunshine Parkway, seven miles away— *(He points.)*

SPRINGER: But why did Reverend Bird want to start the monastery?

DOVER: He was an idealist, that's why, a man of great vision. And he was way ahead of his time. Reverend Bird believed that white men and Negroes could learn to love one another. And that was the base on which this monastic order was founded. The monastery was supposed to balance out at a constant ratio of one white monk for every Negro monk—or vice versa, if you prefer. In 1936 this ratio was easily maintained. There was a Great Depression scourging the land, and a monastery was a good place to sit it out while waiting for prosperity—which was right around the corner—only waiting for a war to show itself again. *(Slide: 3 seconds, Herbert Hoover)*

In the beginning there were six monks, all from Birmingham; three white men and three Negroes. They pitched tents, cleared out the palmettos and the jungle and planted the orange grove. It was an inauspicious beginning but, for the first couple of years, everything worked fine. The first Abbot, a white man by the name of Terence Norton, kept a diary, and I found it inspiring indeed to read of the day by day progress; it was quite a struggle getting organized.

By 1939, however, the money began to run out. And along with the shortage of money, the trustees up in Birmingham gradually began to lose control. First there would be all Negro monks here, and then there would be all white monks. This kind of trouble flared up off and on until the war started. Then the monastery got some national publicity: All of the monks flatly refused to be drafted into the Army as Privates. Their complaint was legitimate enough. They were all perfectly willing to serve the country as officers, with reserve commissions as Chaplains—but not as Privates.

SPRINGER: What happened to them?

DOVER: *(Shrugs)* They went to jail. All of them—except for one white man and one Negro who were both too old to be drafted anyway. Do you begin to see the picture? How about some more coffee?

SPRINGER: *(Dubiously)* It doesn't sound like a religious order to me, not if the Army wouldn't recognize it as such, I mean. Let me get the coffee, Abbot Dover. *(Crosses to hotplate for the pot)*

DOVER: The Army was wrong. Religion is religion. The Church of God's Flock has never been recognized formally as an official religion by any of the big Protestant combines, but still, when the chips are counted at the end of the game, we're religious enough for anybody! We preach the good word from the good book, just like any other Protestant church, so what's the difference? And despite low funds and worse attendance by worshipers, every church founded by the late Cosmo Bird is still going—weaker, perhaps, but strong.

The big problem, Brother Springer, was this monastery. Orangeville, Florida, is too far away from Birmingham to be controlled efficiently by correspondence. And the trustees failed to set up regular inspection visits, either by themselves or by designated representatives. As a consequence, the Abbot-in-Charge, who is also the titular Daddy-O of all the churches and the administrative head as well, had complete fiscal control of the money on hand. *(Slide: Chart of Chain of Command)*

Some of the early Abbots absconded with funds; others kept the monks on short rations, pocketing the money they saved; and some were regular tyrants. A monk doesn't mind a little fasting from time to time as a spiritual exercise, you see, but if you try to starve one to death, he'll quit and get himself a job somewhere. A lot of hungry monks left during these tight administrations. But all the same, being the Abbot was like—did you ever read Frazer's *Golden Bough*?

SPRINGER: I've heard of it, but I haven't read it. It's about myths, isn't it?

DOVER: No. Reality! There's a legend in *The Golden Bough*, however, that fits this place. One of the ancient Greek islands had a king, and the only way a man could become king of this island was to kill the current monarch and take his sword of office. So no matter who was king, he had to sweat blood all the time because, at any moment, some son-of-a-bitch might be sneaking up behind him with a knife! Well, that's just about the size of things here.

SPRINGER: You seem to have avoided such a fate—

DOVER: That's because I got down to fundamentals. Here, have a cigar. (*He takes a cigar case from his cassock breast pocket and offers it to Springer.*)

SPRINGER: No, thanks. I don't smoke.

DOVER: (*Lighting his cigar*) Brother Springer, you're looking at a man who only made one mistake in his entire life. Perhaps you can learn something from my one mistake. I'm from Lincoln, Nebraska—originally. And one bright sunshiny day, many years ago, when I was a mere youth of eighteen, Mama gave me the rent money to take downtown to the man. Thirty-eight dollars. On the way to the landlord's house, I passed a pool room—only I didn't pass it—do you follow me?

SPRINGER: Yes, sir. I follow you.

DOVER: Well, to continue into the pool room. There was a poker game going on in the back room. I had these thirty-eight dollars, and I felt lucky. `Why not double this money, Jack?' I said to myself, and I sat in on the game. A few minutes later I found myself in possession of three fours, a jack, and an ace kicker. I bet accordingly. There was one fellow left in the game with me, and he said—mark these words—"I don't know what you're so proud of, Jack; I've got three queens myself." And then he asked me how much money I had left. I told him, and that's exactly how much he bet—the amount of money I had left. And that's where I made my mistake, Brother Springer. I didn't *believe* that man! He told me he had three queens, but I called his bet—and sure enough—he had three stinking queens!

SPRINGER: That's a lot of queens.

DOVER: You're telling me that's a lot of queens! It was a month of rent money worth of queens! Needless to say, I've never made a mistake like that again. One little mistake can change the course of a man's life. After losing the rent money, I couldn't very well go home and explain to Mama that I'd been playing poker.

So I left town, hitchhiked to Saint Louis, and joined the regular Army. And I haven't been back to Nebraska since.

SPRINGER: In a way, your experience was like mine—only mine was fiction.

DOVER: So was mine. Who would believe a story like that? Anyway, twenty years later I came out of the Army, a retired first sergeant, with a desire to live down here in Florida. And, I might add, with a tidy little bank account. This was three years ago. I was wheeling down the highway out there in my brand new Buick convertible, and I spotted this place. It was just about sundown, and the row of monk's cells, all painted a bright orange, made me think that the monastery was a motel. Of course there were a lot of goats around—out in the yard and standing on tops of the cottage roofs, the way goats like to do—but I didn't think anything about that. I figured the goats were merely a come-on advertisement or something for the motel. So I pulled on in. There were only three monks here at the time, two Negroes and a white Abbot. They put me up for the night at no charge, and the next morning, after I sized up the situation, I decided to take the monastery over for myself. The place was going to rack and ruin—

SPRINGER: Just like that? How'd you get control so easily?

DOVER: I simply told the three monks that I'd put the monastery on a paying basis. The orange grove was ready for picking, and the oranges were beginning to rot on the trees. The monks were too lazy to get out there and go to work; they were living on grits and goat milk. The original funds were long gone, and there were two years of back taxes due on the property. The Abbot, a long, lean ornery fruit tramp named Hank Childers, didn't have enough sense for himself to pound goat butter in a rat-hole. In fact, Hank Childers couldn't write his own name. To make a complicated story short, I ran Hank off the property for malfeasance, malpractice, misuse of monastery funds, and downright incompetence. The two Negro monks who were left were decent enough men, but they were truly monk types. *(Slide: Pop! Pow!)* They merely needed the right kind of leadership, and I provided it.

I hired some Puerto Rican fruit pickers and salvaged most of the orange crop—and I got rid of most of the goats. I sat here in my cell and read through all of the accumulated papers, appointed myself Abbot, paid the back taxes, and had the property rights searched over in Orlando. And then I bought myself a monastery for a one-dollar bill. So now I am the sole owner of the monastery and church, as well as being the administrative and spiritual head of the church. The Birmingham trustees were rather chagrined; but legally, there wasn't a damned thing they could do about it.

SPRINGER: What happened to the other monks, your holiness? The news clipping said they were reassigned. Reassigned where?

DOVER: *(Slide of chart on wall—Dover uses it to illustrate chain of command)* The late Cosmo Bird, Brother Springer, was a man of great vision. He worked out a method of perpetuating the Church of God's Flock forever. But forever is a long time, and the world changes. His basic plan was sound, however, and the church lives on, as I told you already. If the monastery had been built near Birmingham, instead of down here in Florida, the church would probably have been twice as large by now. The original idea was to have two types of monks here. One, the contemplative kind who sit around praying and meditating until they die. But the other type was to take seminary training; and when they finished training, they were supposed to go out as missionaries to start a new church somewhere. That, or they were assigned as replacement ministers, when needed, for one of the established churches. The monastery was not only to be self-supporting, it was supposed to make some money besides, to ensure its continued existence. Each church in the chain was to kick in so much money each month and, in fact, I still get a small trickle of money from my churches each month. The Abbot, as titular head, you see, is much like the Pope in Rome. Have you studied religious history, Brother Springer? *(He brings the rifle to "present arms" position.)*

SPRINGER: No, not very much. I saw the movie about Martin Luther, but—

DOVER: *(Places rifle on table in original position)* In other words, then, you don't know a damned thing about religious history. On the first go 'round, Brother Springer, all churches have got a tough row to hoe. Islam, Buddhism, and Christian Science. But the provisions were all spelled out here, all the rules, and I followed them, legally and by the book. I reassigned the two monks to churches needing ministers in Mobile and Atlanta, after training them, of course. *(Reflectively)* One of them, Reverend Luke Harrington, is doing so well in Mobile that I've been considering the idea of making him a saint before I close down here. *(Dover begins to clear the table, taking dishes and cups to the sideboard and putting them in a wash pan.)* It pays sometimes to beatify a good minister; it gives the coasters and backsliders a little incentive, don't you know. *(Pause. He looks at Springer sternly.)* Every church of the Church of God's Flock, except one, has a pastor. And the exception's the little all-Negro church up in Jacksonville. When I sell this place, and I've got several deals cooking, I plan to stop by Jax on my way to Washington, D.C., and ordain one of the lay members as the pastor. And then— *(Dover looks up. Piously.)* my work will be done; with the Lord's help, of course.

SPRINGER: *(Bewildered)* Do you actually have the power to ordain somebody as a minister, or to make a man a saint, just like that? *(He snaps his fingers.)*

DOVER: Of course! I'm the had of the church and, in spiritual matters, I'm infallible. Who else could ordain ministers, if I didn't do it?

SPRINGER: *(Shaking his head)* I don't know, you holiness.

You've told me so much, so fast, I guess it all hasn't had time to sink in yet. I do wonder, though, how you picked up so much religious knowledge as a sergeant in the Army.

DOVER: *(Laughing softly)* Listen, Brother Springer, don't ever get the idea that just because a man spends twenty years in the Army that he's a stupid son-of-a-bitch. In the Army, I was what you might call a fair-weather first sergeant. In peace time, being a first sergeant is a very pleasant life. But when the bugles blow for war, and they blew them twice on me, I looked around for a safer assignment. *(Sound: Off-stage: Stable call, Bugle. Dover & Springer do not hear it.)* When there's a war going on, a man certainly doesn't want to spend it standing around on some battlefield—not if he's got any sense at all.

Now, where's the safest place to be in the Army during a war? The Chaplain's Office, of course; and every Army Chaplain has a sergeant as his administrative assistant. Altogether, I spent eight years overseas, but during World War II and the Korean War, I preferred to stay on an Army post here in the States. The work isn't hard in an Army Chapel. You assist two or three Chaplains sometimes, writing their sermons, writing letters home to the mamas, telling them that their boys are attending church regularly, and so on. I kept up the card files on religious preferences, answered the telephone and, on Saturday afternoon, I used to get a detail of men and have them sweep and mop the chapel. Chaplains, as a rule, are weak, ineffectual men, like ex-presidents from Ohio—

SPRINGER: *(Resentfully)* I'm from Ohio—and—no weak, ineffectual man can write a novel! Let's take D. H. Lawrence, for example—

DOVER: But you aren't an ex-president, or a chaplain, Brother Springer. Or Lawrence either. In the Army, these chaplains are all rather bewildered by their good fortune. They never had it so good. As a commissioned officer, captain or major, they make from three to five times as much money as they ever made as ministers in outside churches. As a consequence, they get interested in things like promotion, Army politics, social life, and so on—and sergeants like me did most of their work during the week. What are you frowning about?

SPRINGER: Nothing. You never let a man say anything, that's all. How can I interview you if you won't let me ask questions?

DOVER: I've anticipated your questions, haven't I? I've been watching you as I talked, and your mouth has been hanging open most of the time. Tell me, Brother Springer, did you ever meet a man of the cloth like me before?

SPRINGER: No, Sir! I certainly haven't!

DOVER: Well, so, I am one of the few honest ministers that you'll ever meet. I've got the Bible down pat; I've read the good book many, many times; but one thing I've never done and one I'll never do is to put on a mealy-mouthed act about saving your soul. That is something each man must do for himself, and in his own way. You're an educated man, and a writer, so you should know a few things about people. Do you honestly believe that there's such a place as Heaven, with milk and honey on California redwood tables; and that there's a golden throne waiting some place for you to put your lazy ass on?

SPRINGER: I don't know. I don't even think about such things. But I'm positive that other ministers believe strongly in such things.

DOVER: You're wrong, son. They believe as you do: They *don't know*! But the difference is that they're playing it safe. I am a minister of the gospel, and I have the papers to prove it. And you, too, can become a minister, Brother Springer. Being a man of the cloth is no different from any other good job. Most ministers are a little wiser than the average run of people, that's all. The real difference is that they're a lot lazier. They tell the people what they want to hear on Sunday, and let it go at that. If they are truly good as public speakers, they get into the high income brackets on the revival circuits. In fact, the less a minister believes, the more effective he is when he talks to people about spiritual matters.

SPRINGER: I don't know what to believe, Abbot Dover, when I hear you talking this way. Why should any man become a minister, if he didn't believe in what he was preaching? Why— with so many other roads open—would any man deliberately choose to lead an inauthentic life?

DOVER: That's easy *(Shrugs)* Why did you decide to become a writer? Isn't that inauthentic?

SPRINGER: I'm different. I wanted to escape from a miserable job. I was an accountant; and there isn't a worse job in the world than working with figures all day. And *cost* accounting! That part used to drive me almost crazy.

DOVER: Nevertheless, you've answered your own question. It's that simple. A man becomes a minister to escape honest, but tedious, employment. And two, he wants to make a little money. Not a lot of money, mind you, but a little money. Most ministers are in that category; they desire simple security with minimum effort. Some of them, of course, want power. If I wanted power, I'd become a priest in the Roman Catholic Church, but I'm not interested in power; I'm only interested in money. The strange thing about this world, however, is that when a man goes after money through the church, he usually gets a good deal of power along with it.

SPRINGER: What you say may be true, Abbot Dover. But being a minister doesn't seem like an easy life to me. Even the pastor of a small church has got weddings to perform, baptizing, christenings, sermons to prepare, sick people to visit, committee meetings, fund-raising—

DOVER: *(Scornfully)* Do you call that work?

SPRINGER: Well, his time isn't his own. A minister's on call twenty-four hours a day.

DOVER: Good God, Brother Springer! A man has to do something to justify his salary. The things you mention are only minor annoyances. The hard part—although it's simple enough when you get the hang of it—is preparing a twenty-minute sermon to preach on Sundays. *(Dover gets a Bible from his desk, plunks it down in front of Springer, and riffles through the pages.)*

Everything you need for a sermon is right here. Every chapter and verse can be turned into a sermon by a man who can talk on his feet. You can preach an entire lifetime and never get through this book. Right?

SPRINGER: *(Wearily)* I suppose so.

DOVER: Of course you can!

> *(He opens Bible, glances at it, and then points a finger at the audience. His voice is merely frightening at first, but he builds to a terrifying climax.)*

Woe unto thee, O people! Woe to the traitors of Judah and the drunkards of Ephraim, to those who dwell in the fat valley and stagger with fumes of wine!

Let them pass away as water that floweth, as the slug which melteth in its going, as the dead child in the womb that doth not see the sun.

Then must thou flee into the cypresses like the sparrows, and like jerboas into the caves. The gates of the fortresses shall be broken faster than nutshells, the walls shall crumble, the town shall burn; and the flail of the Everlasting shall not halt. It shall turn your limbs over in your own blood, like wool in a dyer's vat; it shall tear you like a new harrow; it shall scatter all the morsels of your flesh upon the hills!

The little children shall crawl on ashes by the corpses of their mothers. A man shall go by night to seek his bread among the ruins, in the peril of the sword. The jackals shall snatch bones from one another in the public places. Thy virgins, swallowing their tears, shall play the lute at the stranger's banquets, and the backs of thy most valiant sons shall stoop and be flayed with burdens that are too heavy! *(Turning to Springer, quietly)* See what I mean, son?

SPRINGER: Is all that in the Bible?

DOVER: *(Quickly closing the book)* Of course. And much, much more. After they drop the bomb, boy, this world'll be a lousy place to live in all right. *(Kindly—sotto voce)* You're broke, aren't you, Brother Springer?

SPRINGER: *(Nodding and swallowing)* I'm almost flat...I can't deny it.

DOVER: I suspected as much. And you aren't much of a writer either, are you?

SPRINGER: *(Half-defiantly)* I've got a published novel to my credit!

DOVER: But you haven't written anything else, you said. And how long ago was it that you wrote your novel?

SPRINGER: Two years now, thereabouts. But I'll write another novel one of these days—if I can only get another idea.

DOVER: Brother Springer, why don't you give up the idea of being a writer and get a job? I can get you an accounting job over in Clewiston. Quite a few people over there owe me some favors, and—

SPRINGER: *(Adamantly)* No, sir! *(Shaking his head)* I'm a writer, and even if I starve to death, I'll never go back to accounting again! If I have to, I'll wash dishes to get a meal maybe, but I'll never enter the trap again!

DOVER: Good! You're a gambler, and I had you sized up right from the very first! Now listen to me for a moment. When I sell the monastery, I'm going to enter the Soldier's Home up in Washington, D.C. I'll get free room, free board, laundry, and I also get to keep every cent of my retired pay. It's a good life up there. I can take the train to New York on weekends to see the new Broadway shows, and I can spend many profitable months in the National Gallery and the Smithsonian. I intend to fritter away my time for the rest of my life. You many not have noticed it, Brother Springer, but I like to talk. And I like best of all to talk to old soldiers. We speak the same language, you see. There's too much responsibility here for me, and it's a lonely life.

Now, at the moment, I'm in a position to do you a favor; at no expense to myself, but a favor all the same. I am going to give you the opportunity to write full time, without any financial worries. Whether you ever write another line or not doesn't make any difference to me, but you should have the opportunity. I like you, and I want to help you. How much money have you got?

SPRINGER: Not quite sixty bucks.

DOVER: Give me twenty dollars.

SPRINGER: I guess you didn't understand me, your holiness. I've only got sixty bucks between me and nothing.

DOVER: I heard you the first time. Give me twenty dollars, and I'll ordain you as the minister of the First Church of God's Flock in Jacksonville. I'll send you up there, and you can have the church.

SPRINGER: *(With a dismayed little laugh)* Why, I can't do that—!

DOVER: You can also have this Bible. Free. It's all in there, Brother Springer, everything you need to know about preaching. The church trustees in Jacksonville will pay you a few dollars every month, and you'll have a free house to live in, right next to the church. You can write six days a week, and then preach a sermon on Sunday. If you're too lazy to do that much, you're too lazy to live!

SPRINGER: Oh, I wouldn't mind that! But, I simply don't know how to do it!

DOVER: *(Suspiciously)* Maybe I've got you wrong: Are you prejudiced against Negroes?

SPRINGER: *(Indignantly)* Of course not! I'm from Cleveland.

DOVER: The way you keep trying to back out, you sound like you're prejudiced. The church in Jax is an all-Negro congregation, and if you really aren't prejudiced, you should *like* the idea of preaching to them...

SPRINGER: *(Picking up his bag and backing toward the door)* You must think I'm ungrateful and all, after giving me breakfast and— I just don't think I'd be capable of it, your holiness...

DOVER: *(Shaking his head)* Prejudice is a terrible thing, son, in this troubled world. Although we are equally distant from the sun, we all share in its warmth. There's a thought to live by, Brother Springer.

SPRINGER: I'm not prejudiced, really I'm not. But I can't make up my mind on something like this just like that! I'd need a little time, to think it over.

DOVER: Brother Springer, the time is always *now.* No important decision of any kind should ever be delayed. When the enemy out there is shooting at you, you'd better duck right now—and without waiting to think about it.

SPRINGER: But if I don't think things out, how'll I know whether I made the right decision or not?

DOVER: Every decision is right because you made it—and it will still be *now* after you've made it.

SPRINGER: That's a little involved for me—

DOVER: We're talking about religion, son, and religion is based on faith, not on logic. So by that simple reasoning alone, your decision to become a minister of the gospel is the most logical decision you could possibly make.

SPRINGER: But I don't *have* any faith! I'm—I'm just a writer, a novelist, and deep down inside me, I—I guess I'm not a very good writer, either— *(Suddenly)* But I *can* be a good writer! I know I can! All I need is time, just a little time, some time to think—just a little freedom from money worries. A desk, a chair, a pencil, and time to think, and—

DOVER: Now you're talking some sense, boy! One man's reason is another man's rationalization.

SPRINGER: All right, then, Abbot Dover. Ordain me!

DOVER: *(Holds out his right hand)* Give me the twenty dollars.
> *(Dover puts the bill in his cassock pocket, opens the wardrobe and takes out a black suit, a shirt with a white, backward collar, and a large black cross on a chain.)*

I'll throw in this ministerial garb, Brother Springer. Go ahead and shuck out of those Dade County duds. I want you to try on the suit for size.

SPRINGER: *(Removes his pants and shirt, and pushes his arms into the black shirt with white backward collar the Abbot holds for him. Springer buttons the cuffs, and the Abbot buttons the collar in the back.)* The shirt's a little large, your holiness—

DOVER: And so are the pants, but that doesn't make any difference. Try them on.
> *(As Springer puts on the black pants, Dover takes the belt from Springer's yellow slacks and helps thread it through the belt loops on the new trousers.)*

I'll tell you what, Brother Springer. If you just bunch up all that extra material in the back, it won't hardly show at all after you put your coat on.

SPRINGER: *(He puts on the coat. The suit is four times too large for him.)* How do I look? *(He looks anxiously at Dover.)*

DOVER: Hmmm. Maybe you'd better roll the trousers up one or two turns, but the sleeves are just right.
> *(Dover folds the sleeves under to make them come out even. As Springer bends down to roll up the trousers, Dover backs away for a long, critical examination.)*

To tell you the truth, Brother Springer, you look fine! I don't think the trustees in Jax will say anything, but if anybody asks you why the pants are so loose, you just tell 'em you've been fasting.

SPRINGER: *(Shaking his head)* It's—it's comfortable enough.

DOVER: It's just a matter of getting used to it. Now wait a minute till I fix the altar.
> *(Dover puts a chair center, takes a dish towel from the rack above the hotplate, and drapes it over the chair. He*

places the Bible, the candelabra, and the cross and chain
on this improvised altar. Dover then takes a voluminous
floor-length white robe from the wardrobe and puts it on.
The robe is covered with Zodiac signs, all painted in gold.
Dover secures the robe around his waist with a red sash.
He takes a red fez with a gold tassel out of a hatbox in the
wardrobe and places it carefully on his head.)

Ordinarily, Brother Springer, we'd use the chapel out in back for the official ordination, but nowadays I'm using the chapel as a garage for my Buick convertible. *(He lights the six candles with his cigar lighter.)* This Florida sun'll fade a paint job on a new car in no time at all—

SPRINGER: I understand. You don't have to apologize.

DOVER: I'm not apologizing, I'm explaining. I just wanted you to know that everything here is done legal and aboveboard, whether we use the chapel or not.

SPRINGER: *(Nodding apprehensively, licking his lips)* Yes, sir—your holiness, I mean.

DOVER: *(He takes his place behind the altar, beckons*
Springer forward, and says solemnly,) Kneel, son. *(Springer*
kneels. Dover bows his head, crosses himself, and then
raises his arms, shoulder high. Dover looks up.)

God, I've got us a writer here, and he needs a place to be. He's a good man and a gambler. In Your name, take him into Your heart and blood and give him Your love. He'll make a good man for us, and he'll spread Your teachings to Your flock up in Jacksonville. And they need a man like Brother Springer in Jax. And please, Lord, give him something besides a cotton string for a backbone. Amen.

(Dover drops his arms, places the chain with cross over the
younger man's neck. He puts his right hand on Springer's
shoulder.)

I ordain, John—what's your middle name, boy?

SPRINGER: *(Whispering)* I don't have one. I dropped my middle name when I became a writer.

DOVER: I'll give you one, then. I ordain you as the Right Reverend John Deuteronomy Springer Pastor of the First Church of God's Flock Church, Jacksonville, Florida, in the United States of America. And may God have mercy on your soul. *(Bends down to Springer)* Do you want to say a prayer, Reverend?

SPRINGER: *(Whispering)* I can't think of one!

DOVER: That's okay, it isn't a requirement. *(Dover helps Springer to his feet, warmly shakes his hand.)* There, now, that wasn't so tough, was it, Reverend Springer?

SPRINGER: *(Wiping his wet forehead)* Well, it was pretty tough for a moment—that part about the prayer. I almost panicked. If you'd only told me about the prayer before the ceremony, I could've written one and then read it off.

DOVER: Dismiss the thought. A mere technicality. *(Dover crosses to desk, sits down and fills in a mimeographed form. He beckons to Springer.)* Just sign here, on the dotted line. This is your official ordination certificate as a minister, so be sure you don't lose it. *(Springer signs the paper, folds it, and puts it into his wallet.)*

Now, Reverend, be sure you use that middle name up in Jax. Deuteronomy is a mighty fine name for a minister, and it's officially yours, just like my middle name is Cardinal. The first thing you do when you get to Jax is report to Dr. Fred Jensen.

SPRINGER: Doctor who?

DOVER: Fred Jensen. He's in the telephone book, and he's the head of the board of trustees for our Jax church. You'll get a warm welcome, I assure you. Dr. Jensen's written me several times lately asking for a new pastor—and you'll fit in fine.

SPRINGER: All right. *(Springer packs his bag with his sport shirt and slacks.)* Right now, I'm still a little nervous about everything, Abbot Dover, but I'm a writer; and I ought to be able to write as good a sermon as anybody else. I've got the Bible here, and I can throw in some quotations from D. H. Lawrence and Kafka from time to time—

DOVER: Stick to the Bible at first, and add Kafka later.

(Springer puts the Bible into the bag and locks it.)

Just put your trust in the Lord, and you'll be all right.

SPRINGER: Thanks. *(The two men shake hands.)* Thanks for everything, your holiness.

DOVER: Go with God.

(Exit Springer. Dover turns to the altar and blows out the

candles. He removes his fez, his red sash, and his white ceremonial robe, throwing the apparel carelessly on his bunk. Suddenly, Springer reenters, bursting angrily through the screen door.)

SPRINGER: *(Loudly)* How many men have you ordained and sent to the church in Jax? For all I know, you've sent a dozen different men up there! How do I *know*?

DOVER: You don't! But *good* for you, Reverend Springer! Healthy skepticism makes for good preaching. Don't worry, boy, everything's on the up and up. Go with God.

SPRINGER: *(Sullenly)* All right. I *don't* know. And I have to trust you. But I'm telling you right now—if this is some kind of a con game, I'm going to come back down here and kick the hell out of you!

DOVER: Why, you were a godsend, Reverend. Thanks to you, I'm able now to close out the books on my last church. Go on up to your church, and put your faith where it belongs—with the Lord.

SPRINGER: *(Grinning)* Thanks, Abbot. I'll drop you a line one of these days, and let you know how I'm making out.

DOVER: You do that. Soldier's Home, Washington 25, D.C. I'll be glad to hear from you. Any time.

(The two men shake hands again. Springer turns toward the door, and Dover picks up his .22 rifle from the card table. Dover shoots from the hip, and Springer falls forward and is still.)

Well, Lord— *(Dover looks up)* I've saved and integrated another one for you. Don't forget the old Sarge now, when the roll is called up yonder.

(Dover takes a large roll of bills form his pocket beneath his cassock, takes the twenty-dollar bill out of his cassock pocket and adds it to the roll. He turns to the card table and slowly counts the money, twenty at a time, just under his breath, as the curtain falls.)

About the Author

Charles Willeford worked as a professional horse trainer, boxer and radio announcer. He wrote over a dozen novels, including *Miami Blues*, *The Burnt Orange Heresy*, *Cockfighter* and *Kiss Your Ass Goodbye*, numerous short stories, essays, poetry and two autobiographies. He was a tank commander with the Third Army in World War II. For his courage he received the Silver Star, the Bronze Star, the Purple Heart, and the Luxembourg Croix de Guerre. He also taught English and philosophy in Miami. He died in *1988*.

"If you kneebones achin'
and your body cold...
You just gettin' ready, honey,
for the cypress grove."
Skip James

CYPRESS GROVE

james sallis

Sallis...pulls off the story with panache...fast and stylish.
Entertainment Weekly

Sallis combines an intensely introspective hero with a
detail-rich plot... A strong series debut from one of the
genre's most original voices.
Booklist

Brilliant, disturbing... Sallis seems completely
comfortable in this solid, lyrical and very human-scale
mystery. Fans who appreciate his more quirky touches
won't be disappointed... This one may well draw a larger
readership to his work.
Publishers Weekly

Sallis shines again...appealingly complex characters, and
a prose style to savor.
Kirkus Reviews

USA: Walker Books ISBN: 0-8027-3380-8 $24 walkerbooks.com
UK: No Exit Press ISBN: 1-84243-094-7 £7.99 www.noexit.co.uk

www.jamessallis.com

"Willeford, writing with quiet authority, has the ability to make his situations, scenes, dialogue, sound absolutely real . . . No one writes a better crime novel." **Elmore Leonard**

The SECOND HALF of the DOUBLE FEATURE
CHARLES WILLEFORD

THE SECOND HALF OF THE DOUBLE FEATURE is available in two different editions; the trade paperback and the deluxe hardcover. The trade edition contains 25 stories, and the hardcover adds Willeford's complete published poetry and nearly 50 previously unpublished poems.

"Willeford's experience of his life led him to a certain attitude toward the world and his place in it, and this attitude, ironic without meanness, comic but deeply caring, informed every book he ever wrote, from his two volumes of autobiography through all the unnoticed novels. " **Donald Westlake**

". . . a remarkable piece of writing . . . the stories in this volume are absolutely delicious." **Paul Kopasz, LEO Weekly**

wit's end
publishing
www.sendwit.com

Trade Paperback ISBN: 1-930997-29-9 $17.95 240 pages
Hardcover ISBN: 1-930997-30-2 $35.95 332 pages

STREET 8

DOUGLAS FAIRBAIRN

"The cornerstone of modern South Florida fiction."
James W. Hall

STREET 8 is the quintessential Miami thriller, the progenitor of the many books that have come to constitute South Florida noir in its many forms.

The book tells the story of Bobby Mead, an Anglo car dealer on SW 8th Street, ("Calle Ocho") who hires a Cuban salesman in an attempt to keep up with the changing demographics of his customer base in 70's Miami. Bobby is just a little guy trying to make a living, but before he knows it, a man by the name of Oscar Perez has embroiled him in an international terrorist plot that will change his life forever.

Controversial, shocking, and even more relevant today than at the time of its original publication in 1977. A neglected masterpiece of damaged people, domestic trauma, violence and the root causes of terrorism. *This new edition is introduced by Les Standiford.*

"taut...tight...a gripping piece of work!"
The NY Times Book Review

Available Winter 2003/2004

wit's end
publishing
www.sendwit.com

DOUGLAS FAIRBAIRN

"brilliant" **Stephen King**

"This is what happened. Myself and four friends were hunting along the Sturrup River one weekend in the deer season . . . When we got there we noticed that there was another party of hunters standing over on the opposite bank . . . Then, all of a sudden, without any warning, and I swear to God without the slightest provocation from us, one of them raised his rifle and fired at us, hitting Pete Rinaldi in the head."

Ranked by Stephen King along with Robert Louis Stevenson's *Dr. Jekyll & Mr. Hyde*, Stephen Crane's *The Red Badge of Courage*, Henry James' *The Turn of the Screw* and James M. Cain's *The Postman Always Rings Twice* as a "masterpiece of concision," this shocking tale of violence escalates furiously from this spare beginning into a full scale war. . .

"unusual, gripping, menacing"
The New York Times

"A fast, tough tale. . ." **John Updike**

Available Winter 2003/2004

wit's end
publishing
www.sendwit.com

Lightning Source UK Ltd.
Milton Keynes UK
UKHW011557060421
381526UK00003B/773

9 781930 997356